Acclaim for
GHOST WALK

"Wonderfully intriguing adventures."

—*Poisoned Pen*

and the previous Dido Hoare Mystery
DEATH'S AUTOGRAPH

"A solid, satisfying mix of amateur and police investigation. . . . Highly recommended."

—*Library Journal*

"[A] deftly plotted, cleverly resolved debut. . . . Dido proves to be engagingly resilient and resourceful. . . . Readers will eagerly anticipate the return of both Dido and her dad."

—*Publishers Weekly*

"Macdonald is dandy at creating a sense of menace from the daily routine gone askew, and Dido and her father are an extremely appealing and affectionate duo. Fine writing done with style and energy."

—*Booklist*

"Dido is fun and Barnabas surprisingly quickwitted. . . . [A] clever hot-potato plot."

—*Alfred Hitchcock Mystery Magazine*

"A satisfactorily complex plot, appealing characters and authentic atmosphere."

—*Manhasset* (NY) *Press*

Books by Marianne Macdonald

Death's Autograph

GHOST WALK

A DIDO HOARE MYSTERY

Marianne Macdonald

HarperPaperbacks
A Division of HarperCollinsPublishers

HarperPaperbacks
A Division of HarperCollins*Publishers*
10 East 53rd Street, New York, NY 10022-5299

This is a work of fiction. The characters, incidents, and
dialogues are products of the author's imagination and are not to
be construed as real. Any resemblance to actual events or
persons, living or dead, is entirely coincidental.

ISBN 0-06-101426-5

HarperCollins®, 📖®, and HarperPaperbacks™
are trademarks of HarperCollins Publishers Inc.

Cover illustration © 1999 by Joe Burleson

A hardcover edition of this book was published in 1998 by Thomas
Dunne Books, an imprint of St. Martin's Press, and was first
published in Great Britain by Hodder and Stoughton.

First HarperPaperbacks printing: February 2000

Printed in the United States of America

Visit HarperPaperbacks on the World Wide Web at
http://www.harpercollins.com

❖ 10 9 8 7 6 5 4 3 2 1

Acknowledgments

The Nag Hammadi Codices, or papyrus books, are less well known than the slightly older Dead Sea Scrolls. They were discovered in 1945 by two local farmers at a site on the Nile north of Luxor, where they had been hidden in about AD 400. The collection may have consisted of about twelve leather-bound volumes.

One volume is supposed to have been burned by the widow of one of the finders—though given the long history of tomb-robbing in Egypt, it seems strange that even a simple farmer's wife did not realize the find was valuable. The history of the other volumes is obscure. It was a time of unrest in Egypt. Some were sold to a Cairo antiques dealer. One, the "Jung Codex," was smuggled out of the country and offered for sale in the USA and Europe in 1949, before being returned to Egypt years later. All of them are supposed eventually to have been acquired by the Egyptian Department of Antiquities. There are several popular accounts of the Nag Hammadi story. Elaine Pagels's *The Gnostic Gospels* (London,

1980) and John Dart's *The Laughing Savior* (New York, etc., 1976) are both fairly easy to find in libraries.

In the course of writing this book I have received information and helpful suggestions from a variety of people and organizations, ranging from the offices of Ampleforth Abbey to the Metropolitan Police to Mike Quinn and Maurice Whitby. My thanks to them all for their kindness.

Thanks are also due, as always, to Eric Korn (M. E. Korn Books) for help with various antiquarian matters, and especially for telling me about an eighteenth-nineteenth–century con artist called Thomas Ashe who, although he died two centuries before my Tom Ashe was born, nevertheless started me on this book. Special thanks are also due to my Gnostic son, Andrew, who first told me about Nag Hammadi.

GHOST WALK

PART 1

Ashe

1

Looking back on it, I blame the weather. By mid-July something had gone badly wrong. As though London had slid southwards in some earthquake and lodged against the equator. I think of myself as a careful person nowadays, thoughtful, even responsible. Maybe if it hadn't been so hot I would have kept a cool enough head to mind my own business. Because whatever else you can say, one thing is certain: Tom Ashe's problems were nothing to do with me.

It was nearly eleven-thirty at night and still so hot that all I could think about was getting home. My old Volvo estate was stuck near Highbury Corner in traffic that shouldn't have been there at that hour, and I could feel sweat trickling down my spine and sticking my new dress to my back. No amount of dry cleaning was going to leave the fine flowered silk the way it had been when we'd set out four hours earlier to celebrate Barnabas's birthday. My father. His seventy-fourth.

The pubs were closing, their customers spilling out across the pavements on the Holloway Road.

They must have been sweating and drinking iced beer all evening, to a man. Or woman. A figure wavered on the kerb and my headlights shone for a moment on a blind, sweating face: I executed an instinctive swerve to avoid catastrophe. Beyond the pedestrian crossing at the station I rolled my window down, hoping the movement of the car would bring in a stir of air. But the heat had hammered down a lid of ozone and exhaust fumes over the city. When it stung my nose, I cranked the handle again.

A red light stopped me in front of the public library, and I caught myself on the point of opening the window again. All very well for me—thirty-three years old and tough enough—but I wasn't alone. In the baby seat beside me, Ben sprawled half-naked, drugged by the heat. Before the traffic had moved on I'd made up my mind absolutely positively for the twentieth time in a month that I was going to replace my beloved twenty-year-old car. I wanted dust filters, air-conditioning, all the gadgets that London's most astonishing infant could possibly need in this long summer.

He should have been at home, of course. I'd considered leaving him with his sitter. Except that Barnabas would have been so understanding about his absence that it would have spoiled dinner for all of us. If anything, Barnabas is even more daft about Benjamin David Hoare than I am. Which is saying quite a lot.

The sky ahead had taken on a muddy darkness in which light flickered briefly. There'd been no rain in weeks, but as I was signalling a turn out of the main road a few oily drops hit the windscreen, oozing through its film of dust. By George Street they had already hesitated and stopped. When I bought the new car I'd drive north. For sure. Possibly to Lapland.

Heat-sodden, I squeezed into a space at the kerb and dragged myself onto the pavement.

The ground floor of my early nineteenth-century terraced house is the converted shop where I earn a living for Ben and myself. The gilt letters of the sign gleamed dully in light from the street lamp opposite: *Dido Hoare ~ Antiquarian Books and Prints.* Two doorways flank the display window. The one on the left was my immediate destination.

Ninety seconds to get upstairs to the flat. A minute to settle Ben in his cot under the open window in my bedroom—say two minutes if he woke up. In about four and a half minutes I intended to be naked and supine with a glass—no, a *bottle*—of ice-cold mineral water in my hand. Ben's sleeping face was tranquil in the light from the street lamp. I unstrapped the seat, slid it out of the car, and sweated across the road. How could he possibly have gained so much weight in one evening?

The street light was throwing a deep shadow into the doorway, so I was only a few feet away when I saw the shape there. For one second I assumed that somebody had dumped a sack of rubbish on my doorstep. Then I saw a foot. I had been presented with a body: probably a drunk. Maybe lying in wait— my heart lurched. Maybe dead. I backed off. The obvious thing to do was retreat into the shop and phone the police from the back room. Getting myself to bed departed into the middle distance. *Damn it!* My key was actually in the lock before my pathetic conscience took over: so—some poor homeless kid has dared to creep into your sacred doorway for a night's shelter? And you're so *ladylike* that you're going to have him *arrested*?

London streets are full of the homeless nowadays. A lot of them are only children. If you really look at them you can't bear it. I dithered. The sweat trickling down my chin persuaded me that I only wanted to get the baby up the stairs to where there were damp towels, cool drinks, and bed.

As far as I could see, the heap wasn't stirring. I crept back to the foot, braced for the stink of alcohol and then surprised by its absence, edged past the legs and reached gingerly to the door. The light switch was just inside it.

And I knew him, even though he was lying with his head under his bent arm and his face turned away from me. With a sinking feeling I reached down and touched his shoulder. For one heart-stopping moment there was no response. Then it seemed that he sagged and I heard the rasp of a difficult breath. *Damn it all!*

I deposited the sleeping baby just inside the street door. "Mr. Ashe?"

Nothing. I touched his cheek and felt its warmth under my palm and tried to think what to do.

2

His name was Tom Ashe. He had wandered into the shop one morning last December. At first I'd been dubious. The layers of shabby clothing seemed to mark him out as one of the local homeless, perhaps one of the group I had often seen around the corner in St. Mary's churchyard, sitting on the benches with their consoling bottles of cider or cans of export lager. Apparently the vicar exercised Christian charity towards them, and the local police tolerated the gathering as long as they kept to themselves. Anyway, there wasn't much point in moving them on: they had nowhere to go.

As I watched that first day from the desk just inside my little office, he drifted towards my tiny Classics section and stopped. The best thing would be to let him get bored and go away. Unless I found him trying to fill his inside pockets, of course. You get used to dealing with thieves when you run a bookshop. What is it about old books that makes people think stealing them isn't really a crime?

So I watched him: a stocky, clean-shaven old man with white hair and economical movements. I would have put him down as seventy or older, but it's hard to tell with the homeless: they don't wear well. He was sidling along the cases looking at the titles on the spines of the books. I watched him run an index finger along the shelf he had finally chosen. The volume that he selected eventually was only a cheap student edition of Thucydides. He began leafing slowly through the pages, holding the book at arm's length like someone who needs reading glasses.

I can't say that I get a lot of customers who are not only interested in the Peloponnesian Wars but prepared to read about them in classical Greek, so I smiled at how I'd been judging by appearances.

He'd spoken. I said, "I'm sorry . . . ?"

"I said, I once taught this."

I answered stupidly, "Oh, I see," and adjusted my ideas: classics master at some vanished grammar school, teacher's pension that either hadn't kept up with inflation or had been drunk away . . .

He spoke again while I was working it out. "I imagine that you're Dido Hoare?" His voice seemed to shift from the careless London accent that swallows its consonants to the more middle-class tones of those old schoolmaster days—his voice was caressing Latin words, placing them like glassy jewels, and it was a moment before I grasped what he was saying:

> . . . *in freta dum fluvii current, dum montibus umbrae lustrabunt convexa, polus dum sidera pascet, semper honos nomenque tuum laudesque manebunt* . . .

I must have been gawping at him, because he grimaced and declaimed, "Some time I was a Trojan, mighty Queen. But Troy is not, what shall I say I am?" His pale blue eyes stared at me.

As it happened, I'd recognized both the passages. Oxford High School for Girls had taken us along the first steps of an old-fashioned classical education, and I'd had to put up with some teasing during the autumn term that we started Virgil's *Aeneid*. The Marlowe had at least come a few years later, when I was more prepared: or more resigned to my mother and father having christened me "Dido" after the Queen of Carthage whom Aeneas had abandoned on his way to more important masculine pursuits like founding the city of Rome.

And Ashe even bought the book.

Of course I didn't know his name then, but he came back from time to time. Often he ignored me, wandering along the shelves like a ghost. At other times it was as though a switch had been thrown that returned him to the real world, and on those days we talked about books—if I wasn't busy with other customers—and eventually he told me his name, watching me out of the corner of his eye.

Other information came bit by bit. Tom Ashe could read not only classical Greek and Latin, but Arabic; and he once even translated the title of a Persian art book that had turned up in a mixed auction lot and needed some kind of identification before I could attempt to price it.

If anybody else came in he fell silent and slid away. It struck me, one morning, that he was covertly examining another customer from behind the central row of bookcases as though trying to remember whether he had seen him before. If my father was there— Barnabas was coming to the shop more and more often after Ben's birth, his excuse being that I had become too fragile (or maybe too preoccupied) to be left all on my own to run a business—then I noticed that Ashe vanished. I assumed he was a little mad.

But he always seemed to have some money. He bought a few more books over the months: mostly Latin poetry or cheap travel books, classic reprints of Thesiger, Burton, and Robert Byron—nothing costing more than a couple of pounds. And I'd wound up accepting him for what he appeared to be: an impoverished retired schoolmaster, only one step above the men in the churchyard and not entirely in the real world. One of life's casualties.

Bending over the silent heap, I recalled something else. Last New Year's Eve I'd had a couple of bottles of sherry in the office so as to offer a drink to regular customers. Ashe had sidled in at about four-thirty, just as I was deciding to close, and I'd offered him a glass; but he'd refused. My face probably showed surprise, because he'd looked at me quickly, hunching his shoulders under the layers of old cardigan, threadbare jacket, and patchy greatcoat. "I am an alcoholic," he announced with a kind of toneless formality. "I never drink." And I had said I was sorry for offering, although there was no reason why I should have known. Instead of the sherry I gave him a nearly new paperback—Thubron's Chinese journey—which he accepted with an unreadable expression that might have been either anticipation or amusement. Anyway, whatever had happened to the silent bundle on my doorstep, it seemed unlikely that he had drunk himself into unconsciousness.

Which left me at a loss.

My hesitation was ended by a noise which was half-groan, half-snore, and I leaned over looking for a pulse in the bony wrist. I thought I felt a shudder under the layers of clothing. When I put my hand on his forehead I realized that he was shockingly hot.

If only I'd joined the Girl Guides all those years ago instead of learning Latin, I would now be more prepared to deal with unconscious men on my doorstep. What I wanted was to step over the recumbent form, close the door on him, and put myself and Ben to bed. But what I was going to have to do instead was get my prostrate customer to a hospital.

I squatted beside the bundle.

"Mr. Ashe—can you hear me? It's Dido Hoare. Don't move. I'm calling an ambulance. You'll be all right."

"No!"

I thought that he hadn't heard me properly. "Don't worry, I'm just going to phone . . ."

A hand shot out and grabbed the hem of my dress. "Get me home."

Home? I made an effort to remain polite and heard my voice say very distinctly, "You're ill. You're in the street in front of the shop. You may have had a heart attack." I'd been thinking about heart attacks ever since my father's had nearly killed him. "I'm going to phone for an ambulance."

There was a heave, and the old man pulled himself into a sitting position against the wall. His watery eyes looked past my ear and then flickered and focused on my face. "I'll be all right. I don't go to hospitals. Help me stand up."

His other hand shifted to my arm, and the two of us straightened up together, me hauling and Ashe leaning and struggling. When he seemed to be balanced, I could pay more attention to minor details like the smell of the unwashed body so close to me. I disentangled myself and said faintly, "I think you've had some kind of attack. You must see a doctor."

The hand that shot out again and grabbed my elbow showed no weakness. "I said no! I know what's wrong. I have medicine at home. I'll get a bus."

I knew that I was going to say "I'll drive you" a second before I had spoken, but I was too tired to stop myself.

"Yes? Good," he replied and was silent. The grip on my arm grew more desperate; I thought he was trying not to fall down.

I sighed. "I'll get you to the car, and then I'll come back for Ben."

Ashe pulled away, and I knew he'd forgotten.

"The baby," I said between gritted teeth.

It was lucky that he was a small man because I'm only five foot three myself—though hauling cartons of old books to and from book fairs and auctions keeps me fit. But he was too weak to walk far. I pushed a shoulder under his arm and manoeuvred him across the road and into the backseat, where he slumped silently. I wasn't sure that he was conscious. Then I returned for the baby seat. Ben was still sleeping gently. At least somebody was cooperating.

I'd started the engine before I remembered I had no idea where I was going. The man behind me was so still that I thought he was unconscious until I heard a whisper.

"Where?" I made my voice sharp, trying to penetrate his illness.

"Horsell Road . . ."

Somehow I'd let myself in for this nonsense months ago when he called me Queen of Carthage. I almost snapped, "Hospital," but I thought I'd just give it a try, because I happened to know the road. It wasn't far: an easier journey than driving to the nearest hospital that still has an emergency department. But when I'd turned off the Holloway Road and brought the car to a halt in a narrow street lined with tall Victorian terraces, Ashe was silent and motionless. It was nearly midnight, and there were a few lights on in scattered windows, but nothing that shouted, *This is it.* . . .

When I turned around, he was unconscious again. For a moment I listened to the air rasping in his throat. When I whispered his name and got no reply, I let in the clutch and headed for the emergency department at the Whittington.

3

In daylight, sitting in the kitchen with the window wide open and Ben solemnly finishing his breakfast bottle, I found it hard to think about last night.

Mr. Spock posed in a favorite spot on top of the fridge, regarding us benignly in the intervals of washing behind his ears. For some reason the sight of him reminded me this morning of the man who had given my ginger cat his name. I didn't think of Davey very often any more—my former husband, Ben's father, poor Davey.

Things had changed since Davey. First, most obviously, there was Ben, the last thing that Davey had done for me before he'd been killed. Having a child is an absorbing, intimate thing that fills the world and leaves you not only permanently exhausted but strangely forgetful of everything else. One year ago I'd been the independent, impoverished and unexpectedly pregnant owner of a fairly promising, undercapitalized antiquarian book business. Barnabas, newly recovered from his heart attack, had been my main worry. He and Davey between them had changed all that, though Davey certainly hadn't

planned his contribution to my welfare. They were,
jointly, the reason why I was able to sit comfortably
drinking coffee in the redecorated kitchen of my flat
on a late July morning and waiting for Phyllis, Ben's
sitter, to arrive so that I could saunter downstairs to do
a little work. Davey had left me an uncomfortable
legacy, but I'd long ago decided to accept the facts and
believe all's well that ends well.

My mind skittered away from that old uneasiness
to the more immediate one—the unfinished business
of the night. I'd have to contact the hospital and
enquire. Now.

When the phone rang in the sitting room I hoisted
Ben's sticky, comatose form over my shoulder and
went to answer it. As on most mornings first thing, it
was Barnabas. We exchanged greetings and then I
had to assure him that the baby hadn't suffered at all
from the party.

"And you?" I could hear suspicion in his voice.
"You sound odd. You got home safely? You didn't
overdo it, I hope?"

I hesitated long enough to appreciate the comedy
of having a seventy-three—now seventy-four-year-
old parent worrying about whether his all-too-
grown-up daughter was getting to bed early enough;
and decided that my story was too good to keep to
myself.

"You should have called for an ambulance, of
course. What if the old boy had died on you?"

I said, "He didn't, and I managed perfectly well!"

"What was wrong with him?"

"I don't know. A fever."

Barnabas snorted down the line into my ear,

implying that the cause must lie in drink or some other vice and that this went without saying only because we had urgent arrangements to make. He was taking over from me for the afternoon while I went to a book auction.

Barnabas retired nine years ago from an Oxford Chair in English. He misses the university life, the arguments and enmities, and so it pleases him to look on the shop as a hobby, a place where he can indulge his passion for books. For telling people about books. It is just that his audience now consists of my luckless customers rather than his students. Today he also had the privilege of supervising Ben after his early evening feed, if I wasn't back before Phyllis had to go home.

That essential matter organized, I lowered Ben and his bottle onto the settee and made my own phone call. It took the hospital switchboard a few minutes to trace Ashe to a ward. I identified myself to a second voice as the friend who had brought him in last night.

The hesitation should have warned me. "I'll call Sister," the voice said eventually, and I twiddled my thumbs for another minute or two before I heard the receiver being picked up.

"I'm Nurse Fletcher," this voice said after another of those hesitations. It was a deep Jamaican voice, and I pictured the owner of it as a big, motherly, comforting black nurse, and relaxed. "We're real anxious to find the next of kin. Are you related to Mr. Ashe?"

I assured her that for all I knew Mr. Ashe had no relatives: he had certainly never spoken of anyone. "Is he dead?"

She sounded startled. "Goodness, no! Much better this morning. But restless. He doesn't like us very much, and he says he's goin' to discharge himself. We want somebody to make him stay until he's well—that's all."

I promised I'd have a go, or at least try to persuade the invalid to give them the name of somebody with more authority than I had. Then I found a sleeveless pink cotton sundress and white leather sandals, and was tiptoeing around the bedroom looking for my hairbrush when I heard the street door close and footsteps marching up my stairs.

"Dido? You awake?"

I ignored the evidence that the speaker knew my habits all too well. "Phyllis? Shhh . . . he's almost asleep."

Phyllis Digby said, "Excellent," and appeared like an angel in the doorway.

Which is just about the right description.

Phyllis was a tallish, scrawny, sandy, freckled, toughminded, fiftyish Australian who had appeared four months ago in response to my advertisements when I'd finally admitted that I had a problem looking after a business, a baby, and an over-anxious father all at the same time. Of course I knew it was impossible that anyone else could really be trusted to take care of my excellent son. But Phyllis and Ben had come to an instant understanding at the interview, and we'd struck a deal. It turned out that she had taken us both on. It was a bit like being bullied by an Australian school mistress. Or to put it another way, we'd discovered that we trusted one another.

I explained in whispers about Tom Ashe and was

shooed off on my journey. But what on earth was I supposed to accomplish once I got there?

The doctor's rounds had finished by the time that I skirted the little queue of patients at the public phone in the hall and pushed through the doors of the ward. In here, they were mostly old men who lay propped motionless in the white beds, staring at a shrunken world. A television set high on the wall was broadcasting a morning chat show, but the sound had been turned to an inaudible rumble, so that the faces on the screen mouthed and smiled meaninglessly. I felt a moment of panic, wondering whether I was going to recognize Ashe in this gathering of old bones.

A voice behind me asked, "Can I help?"

I recognized it from the phone. Its owner was indeed black, though younger than me and as skinny as a broom; but her name badge said that this was Sister Fletcher.

I explained myself. She threw me a look that seemed worryingly relieved. "Second from the end," she said, and then I recognized the face on the pillow. His eyes were closed.

"Is he asleep?" I asked. Maybe I could leave.

I thought that I detected a flicker of amusement. "He ought to be tired out," she said, "but he was awake and fussin' a minute ago. Don't worry—you go on. He'll be glad to see a friend."

I edged past a dozen pairs of eyes that slid over me hopefully before they gave up, and inserted myself onto a chair at the bedside. The old man was looking strangely brushed and clean, like (the thought intruded and I had to make an effort to push it away) a corpse laid out for burial. I located the faint rhythmical rise and fall of the sheet-covered chest and a fluttering of eyelids and waited, conscious that I was sweating and that the air in the ward was barely breathable for the heat, the tang of antiseptic, and the faint sweet smells of old bodies and sickness.

"You're here." The voice was louder than I'd expected; it made me jump.

I tried to cover my surprise by babbling that he looked a lot better.

Still with his eyes closed, Ashe allowed the shadow of a lopsided grimace to appear and vanish. "Of course I am. I told you—a mild attack. You shouldn't have brought me here. I'm all right."

There's a limit to what I will take. I said, "Good! I'm glad you feel all right now. You certainly didn't when I found you! You were lying on the ground in front of my door. I couldn't know what was wrong with you." Don't bother to thank me.

"I have a good constitution," he said in a slightly more conciliatory tone. "Very good for my age. I was unconscious? That's bad." He hesitated. "Did I have anything with me?" When he looked at me, I saw once again his habit of looking beyond my head before he focused on my face. It struck me that he might have an eye problem. Either that, or he was expecting to see somebody hiding behind my back.

"I said, did you find a parcel?"

I told him that he hadn't been carrying anything when I found him, and got back to the point. "I'll look for your parcel this afternoon, and I'll take you home again when you're well enough."

"Well?" he repeated, coughing. "I'm ready now. Get my clothes."

I stood up. "Not now. You're still weak." I could hear my voice bullying him in the way that I bullied my father when he was being stubborn. *Dido . . .* Then I saw that he was surreptitiously moving his legs under the covers, trying to decide whether I was telling the truth. At that point I remembered the ward sister's plea and added, "I'm on my way to an auction anyway. Look, I'll come back at the same time tomorrow. If you're well enough by then I'll get you out. Just rest: you aren't invited to die in the front seat of my car, you know."

"I'm not dying anywhere now," he said grumpily; "maybe next time, maybe. All right, I can last twenty-four hours." He closed his eyes again and lay silently while I made one or two inane remarks that were supposed to be cheerful. When I'd done my duty, I gathered myself together and left. Why was I so sure he was pretending to be asleep to avoid having to speak to me?

I found Sister Fletcher shuffling forms in a little office by the lifts and tapped on the glass of her door.

"You get any sense out of him?" she asked, hands hovering over the files.

I told her I wasn't sure. "He wants me to take him home. I told him I'll come tomorrow." I hesitated, not quite sure how much I could expect when I wasn't even a relative. "Was it a heart attack?"

She looked up, surprised. "What? No, not at all. His heart is just fine, no problem there. He just had a mild recurrence of malaria."

I gawped at her. *Malaria?*

"He says he got it in the Middle East just after the war. That's the Second World War? We got his temperature down fast, and he'll be over the worst of it in a couple of days. He's safe now. He's pretty strong."

I shrugged and realized that I was smiling stupidly. When I'd got my face under control I told her I hoped he'd behave himself for the time being, and promised I'd be back in twenty-four hours.

And then I pushed the whole thing out of my mind and fled to the car because I had just fifty minutes to get to the sale rooms in Mayfair. I was in fact only just in time to hurtle inside and bid on the first lot of French Revolutionary pamphlets, which included the one I'd arranged to sell on to a New York dealer. In the rush I paid twenty pounds more than I'd meant to and nearly wiped out my profit. Then I spent the rest of the afternoon and evening getting on with my business. When it came down to it Tom Ashe was not my business.

Perhaps I should have phoned the hospital again, but it didn't seem necessary. I'd left my number and assumed that if anything went wrong they would ring me. I'm always assuming that what should happen, will. I really ought to know better.

4

The visitors' car park was full, and I had to risk leaving the Volvo on a yellow line in the main road. I didn't really believe Ashe would be able to leave the hospital, but it was obvious that I couldn't expect him to walk far if he insisted on going.

The long ward was busier today. I was late, and the support staff were already wheeling trolleys up the center of the room, dispensing early dinner trays and cups of teas from a big urn. I angled a look at one; despite the heat, we were having some kind of light brown stew. Obviously they wouldn't let Ashe pack up and leave in the middle of a meal. I wove a path among the trolleys and headed towards his bed.

It wasn't until I was close that I realized it was empty. The bedside table top was also clear. Even the visitor's chair had gone.

I stopped one of the student nurses, flying past in the direction of a winking light. "Where's Mr. Ashe? He isn't worse, is he?"

She looked vague and paused long enough to say, "I don't know him. Can you ask in the office?"

Of course it wasn't possible that he had died. Not without her knowing about it. I retraced my steps to the little room in the corner where Sister still seemed to be shuffling papers. Presumably an occupational hazard. I thought she stiffened when I appeared in her doorway.

"Where is he?"

"Mr. Ashe left two hours ago." The exasperation was unmistakable. "He discharged himself after the morning rounds."

I got myself in hand enough to demand details. Yes, she told me, he had woken in a bad mood, passed the morning in what sounded like alternating temper tantrums and sulks, and (obviously) tried everyone's patience a little more than was acceptable. In the end the doctor had given him a prescription but advised him to stay for another day.

"But he made a phone call after breakfast, and his son came . . ."

"His *what?*"

"Well, I guess it must be his son. They talked for a minute, and then the man went and waited in the smokin' room. Then Mr. Ashe got his clothes and signed the form, and he left."

"With this other man?"

"I was busy, myself," Mrs. Fletcher told me unnecessarily, "but I guess so."

It seemed likely. Though unexpected. "So he was all right today?"

No, she hadn't thought he was really well enough to leave. Nor had Dr. Aziz. Ashe himself had decided differently.

Groaning silently, I asked, "Where was he going? I'd better make sure he's all right."

I could see her wondering where I came in. I didn't explain and after a moment she riffled through a stack of big cards and produced one which looked newer than most of them. "Arlington House."

It rang a bell but I wasn't sure why.

"Arlington Road. Camden Town. It's a hostel for homeless men."

Of course it was. I remembered the big brick building just off the street market. "Of course. Thanks. I'm sorry . . ." Why did I feel that I had to apologize for him? The erratic behavior of Tom Ashe was hardly my responsibility.

We parted on coolly cordial terms, and I'd taken a few steps towards the main door when I heard her call, "Miss?" and turned back. She was following me quickly, holding something out. "I nearly forgot—I didn't give this back. It was in his pocket when he came in. Would you give it to him?"

She held something towards me: a big screwdriver,

maybe fourteen inches long with a thick black plastic handle. The flat tip had been filed sharp.

I said stupidly, "This was in his pocket?"

She nodded silently.

"How could he carry this thing in a pocket? . . . Is there something wrong?"

"There was a little hole in the lining."

I let her see that I didn't understand.

"The blade pokes through a hole, hangin' down inside the lining, and the handle is in his pocket where he can reach it. Be careful you don't cut yourself! They carry that on the street, some of them, for defense. See, some of them think it's better than carrying a knife. Just as useful, and less trouble for them—if the police find it, they don't make a fuss, they just take it away."

I closed my mouth before it could say something really stupid, like that Mr. Ashe wasn't that kind of person. What did I know about him? Maybe he spent all his nights in street brawls. Or doing woodwork for a hobby.

I stomped back to the car before it had been presented with a parking ticket, turned around by means of a bad-tempered half-circle across the road, and made off in the direction of Camden Town, where I was lucky enough to find an empty meter only two streets away from the hostel and so was feeling a little more cheerful when I arrived opposite the council depot and climbed the cracked steps to the door.

Ninety seconds later, I was descending the same steps into a recurrence of bad temper. The man at the reception window had just informed me in definite terms that no Tom Ashe lived there, or had ever stayed there, or was known to him even slightly, and there was no point begging him to check his register because he knew this already. Apparently Ashe had given the hospital a false address. Of course, if I wished I could stand in the street and watch the door for a few hours in case he was on his way here now. Or I could let the old man fend for himself since that seemed to be what he wanted. Next time he was ill he could find some other muggins to cart him around.

There was a stall in the market selling nectarines at seven for a pound. I bought fourteen of them so that my journey wouldn't have been entirely wasted. The sun was blasting down again today and I began to yearn for my own pleasant, shady shop where I could sit like a lady with the front and back doors open to create a gentle breeze, waiting for intelligent and book-loving customers to come in and buy books. Serious, valuable, antiquarian books that brought in some real money, unlike student texts or travel paper-backs.

Drops of sweat were rolling down my neck. I turned back to the stall and bought a watermelon.

And then I caught a glimpse of somebody who could have been Ashe himself walking away from me through the milling shoppers. He vanished when I tried to follow him.

Not my business!

I wiped a trickle of sweat from my jaw line, turned myself around, and got back to the car just as my meter time ran out. I could do with not seeing Tom Ashe again for a while.

PART 2

Looking for Tom

1

On Sunday morning I was pretending that I had important work to do and decisions to make. At eleven o'clock I stopped pretending and reviewed the situation. It had taken me four hours to feed one baby and one cat, and wash up. I seemed to remember that I'd done a fair amount of coffee-drinking and lots of stumbling around the flat opening windows, staring out at brick walls which were already baking in the heat, and flopping into chairs with my eyes closed and my head a blank.

The worst ghosts are the ones that hang around saying that you should have done better.

Not far away, the bells of St. Mary's gave a couple of tinny clangs. They'd stopped ringing them for a while under the impression that the steeple was about to fall down; but just recently calmer counsel (or divine optimism) had prevailed, and we got the occasional discordant reminder of time passing.

There was something, somewhere, that I needed to do soon.

I went into the bathroom to wash my face and

wasted another few minutes inspecting it critically in the mirror. I examined my dark, rather wild hair for signs of premature gray, but all I could see was that it needed cutting. Pointed chin, neat mouth, nose unremarkable, eyes a kind of bloodshot hazel, teeth all present . . . I looked at myself sternly. Thirty-three years old last February and on the downward path into middle age, what was I doing standing in my cramped bathroom trying not to think about Tom Ashe?

I could hear Ben waking up again in the bedroom and deciding to grumble. He was teething. I wasn't so sure what accounted for my own tendency to grizzle.

"Hang on," I yelled at him. "We're going out! Push-chair! Highbury Fields! We'll sit under a tree and I'll eat ice cream and you can have a taste." Just making decisions felt like a step forward.

When I walked out of my door I did intend to turn north up the back streets. I hadn't actually changed my mind even when I found myself directing the push-chair in a wide circuit which ended in the broad, traffic-choked, sun-battered stretches of Upper Street.

Upper Street at midday during a record-breaking heatwave was hellish. The area had become fashionable since I moved in, and sweating pedestrians in designer sunglasses were window-shopping through the exhaust fumes despite the fact that they obviously didn't need to be there at all. Ben fell silent. I was afraid at first that he'd been overcome by carbon monoxide, but when I looked he was staring around us in amazement. Probably debating crowd psychology, I decided. It wasn't until I'd swerved in through the gate to St. Mary's churchyard that I realized I'd been heading this way all along, chasing that dim memory of having once seen Tom Ashe here.

We entered the graveyard that surrounds the church on three sides. The headstones have been removed and stacked around the edges, leaving only open lawn still bumpy with what lies underneath, and a few table tombs behind the eastern wall. Old lime trees cast wide stretches of shade. From inside the church, a hymn tune floated faintly across the grass. To my left, a shallow oval pit had been dug out, paved, and surrounded by stone benches. On and around the bench at the top I found what I'd been looking for: the little group of resident drinkers. Even from the gate I could see that Tom wasn't among them. On the other hand, someone there might have seen him since the hospital episode, and I was hoping they could tell me where I'd find him. I hesitated, but only for a moment, and then humped the push-chair over a kerb and down into the arena.

I might have guessed that Ben would be my passport. Police officers and social workers probably don't turn up accompanied by small babies. Two of the dozen weather-beaten, drunken figures lolling around the bench were women. A girl with spiky blond hair, so thin that you wondered how she could lift her arm, spotted us first. She squatted in front of Ben and reached out a grimy, bony hand to touch one of his bare feet. It was a careful gesture, as though she was afraid that her fingers might hurt him, and I couldn't bear to imagine what was behind that gentleness. Then some of the others were leaning forward, and there was a babble of greetings: wasn't he a sweet, a bonny child, look at his blue eyes, how old is he, love?

One of the men, a sweating, broken-nosed drunk with a purple birthmark down one side of his face, carefully positioned his can of lager out of the way under the bench, lurched to his feet and tucked a ten-penny coin unsteadily into Ben's fist. "For luck," he said, in what sounded like the remains of a Geordie accent.

An old woman with stringy gray hair called, "You don't want to keep him out too long in this sun, love. Not even in the shade, 'cos they burn easy at that age."

It was my opening.

"I'm just here to find somebody. A friend, An old man called Tom. Tom Ashe. Do you know him? I was wondering if anybody had seen him today . . . or yesterday?"

The older woman was looking at me, puzzled. One of her eyes was milky and unseeing. "Tom?" she said loudly. "Anybody here know Tom?"

A voice said, "I know Tom. Kid works a corner by Angel Tube usually."

"Works"—did he mean begging? "My friend is an old man. Seventy or so." I thought quickly. "White hair. Short—only a little taller than me. He likes books. He reads a lot. He was ill a couple of days ago; he had to go into the hospital for two nights. I'm worried whether he's all right."

The man with the birthmark shook his head. Being ill, going into the hospital for a couple of nights: everyday matters. The others muttered, shrugged, and began to lose interest.

The two women weren't finished. The old one

had also shaken her head, but she was still looking at us. I spoke to her directly. "If he does come here— Tom Ashe—tell him that the woman in the bookshop was asking for him. Please."

She looked away from me to Ben. "He doesn't come here. We don't know him."

I was ready to believe her, because Ashe wasn't really like these people after all. I couldn't bear it: they were too sad.

She found her place on the bench again, pushing one of the men who had encroached on her space. One of the others passed her a bottle and her whole attention shifted to it. Somebody said something I didn't catch and there was a spurt of laughter.

The skeletal girl was left crouching in front of Ben, the two of them staring solemnly at each other.

"I'd better take him home now," I mumbled. "It's too hot here for him. See you later."

She didn't move. I pulled Ben gently away.

2

"Leave it alone!" Barnabas snapped. "He won't thank you—this Tom Ashe. Who the devil is he?"

Who *was* he? "I don't know," I said. "You must have seen him—he's been here a few times when you came in."

My father looked obligingly reminiscent.

"An old man. Your age, white hair. About five foot seven or eight. He looks like somebody who sleeps rough—you know?—layers of shabby old clothes. He comes in and reads and doesn't talk much." I stopped. What else could I say? He was like almost any old, impoverished, casual customer, and it struck me that he might never actually have crossed my father's path. "Barnabas, he reads Latin and Greek fluently—for pleasure. He was really ill when I took him to hospital, but two days later he gave a false address and vanished. I just wondered whether he's all right."

My father looked at me with an expression in which affection and exasperation fought to inform me that I was a well-meaning child who should learn to mind her own business. I agreed, though at my age that's unlikely. I have my fair share of responsibilities, which seems to encourage nosiness.

We were in the office at the back of the shop. My father was ensconced at the packing table, surrounded by the tottering piles of books I'd selected for my autumn catalogue. I was pulling more books off the shelves to add to the piles while I listened with half an ear to the baby alarm connecting us to my bedroom where Ben had been—and luckily still seemed to be—sleeping the triumphant sleep of somebody who has just achieved a new tooth. My relief was shadowed by the realization that we'd been going through the same experience together another two dozen times. You'd think that by now our species would have discovered a better system.

Even in this heat Barnabas wore his old-fashioned tweed-jacket-corduroy-trousers academic uniform. His single concession to the day's un-British weather was abandoning his tie and leaving the top button of his white shirt undone. I'd propped open the door into the yard in an attempt to keep him from heatstroke.

In the intervals of complaining about my reckless-ness, Barnabas was composing catalogue entries on three-by-four index cards. I mail out four or five cat-alogues a year, mostly for the benefit of the British and foreign university libraries which form the back-bone of my customer list. I also sell books in the shop and by taking them to book fairs, though since long before Ben's birth I'd been able to stop doing the out-of-town fairs and concentrate on the big monthly ones in Russell Square. I'd sold a sixteenth-century Plutarch last year for a great deal of cash, which was the reason for my current prosperity. My bank man-ager has recently become courteous. My accountant has stopped marking his bills "Very Overdue." I'd restocked the shop and transformed it into an ade-quately capitalized and profitable business capable of supporting not only an adult and an infant, but a loud-mouthed ginger cat.

And Barnabas was doing all my catalogues. He's worked with old books all his life. Having finished his edition of Tudor love poems last November, he appointed himself my assistant manager and head cataloguer. I'd assumed at first that he was feeling at a loose end because it was the first time since about 1945 that he wasn't involved in a research project. More recently, it had struck me that he was amused by the trade. My catalogues were beginning to get a reputation in the trade for a quirky wit which didn't hurt postal sales one bit.

I decided to change the subject. "Ernie was sup-posed to come in this morning, approximately. He's only about ninety minutes late so far."

"Should I buy him a wristwatch?" my father

inquired mildly. "Or just teach him how to tell the time?"

"It's because he walks," I said. "I told you he walks everywhere. He's probably walking from Kilburn this morning."

"Peculiarly old-fashioned for one so young," Barnabas said half-audibly. "Never mind, go away, I'll deal with him when he arrives. You aren't doing any good here. In fact you're distracting me, shuffling around like that. Go and make sure that baby is all right. Or buy yourself a new frock. Do something that will cheer you up."

"I am cheerful," I lied, and went.

Ben was still sleeping. I turned off the alarm and got a glass of mineral water out of the fridge. Mr. Spock had curled up in the armchair in the sitting room keeping cool and for once had nothing of any interest to say. I joined him, closed my eyes, and asked myself why I was feeling so moody when everything in my life was obviously going well.

Nobody feels right in this weather.

I only went to the window to see whether it could be opened any wider. The sun was beating down into George Street from a position almost overhead, and there was barely a shadow along the front of the buildings opposite. Light glared on the pavement, and the haze from car exhausts sat trapped between the buildings.

At the end of the street a figure with white hair was vanishing round the corner. I leaned out precariously but he was gone. It had been Tom Ashe.

Then why hadn't he entered the shop?

Having stopped long enough to remind myself

that it didn't matter to me in the least what he did, I phoned Paul Grant.

I've known Paul for more than a year. He's a detective inspector in our local CID who turned up after a break-in at the shop and got off to a bad start by making it a little too clear that he suspected me of insurance fraud. Later, our relationship had become a lot more than professional. But Paul was married. More or less. It had taken me a while to find out about that, and afterwards I'd felt as though I'd intruded into other people's troubles. Also an awkwardness had grown up between us recently. Maybe he also felt that our relationship was an unmanageable complication. Or perhaps he'd just found it too hard to cope with the fact of my pregnancy. The fact of Ben.

Being put on hold by the switchboard while they tried to locate him gave me the chance to brood over whether I was being honest about my motives for contacting him.

"DI." For a moment, that familiar, barked greeting startled me. It sounded more brusque than I remembered. "Hello?"

"Hi. It's Dido."

He barely hesitated. "Hello. How are you? It's good to hear from you." His tone said that he was in the middle of something and couldn't say much. Well . . .

I told him that I was fine, that we were all fine. "I need some help, if you have a moment."

He said, "I'm in a meeting. I'll have to phone you back. Can you give me half an hour?"

I could, and spent the next forty minutes waiting uneasily, probably because we hadn't seen one another for a little while. When the phone finally rang, Paul's voice said without preliminaries, "We've had a shooting, and we're all going crazy. What's wrong? What help?"

I decided that his tones expressed a satisfactory concern and relaxed a little. "It's not as serious as a shooting, but I hoped you could help me. I'm trying to find somebody. A customer. An old man called Tom Ashe."

He listened without comment until I'd finished my story. "The name doesn't ring a bell. I can contact the hospital when I have a moment and ask a few questions."

I told him that I didn't think the hospital knew anything they'd been unwilling to tell me. "What I was hoping," I explained, "was that you could ask your uniformed branch to keep an eye open for him on the streets." I told him of my excursion to the churchyard. "It's just that your people are more likely to come across him than I am."

"Maybe." He sounded unenthusiastic, and I had a moment to remember why I don't really enjoy asking him for professional help. "Look, do you have any real reason for finding him? If he's stolen a book from you and he hears we're asking questions, he'll probably just take off. You say you've just seen him outside?"

I assured Paul that my motives were benevolent, and that Tom hadn't done anything wrong that I knew about unless you counted his unmannerly escape before he had thanked me for looking after him. "It just niggles," I grumbled. "He seemed so ill. I'd like to know that he's all right."

Paul promised to pass the word around, but I

could hear his doubts. He asked about Barnabas and Ben, and we fenced around politely for a moment or two before I hung up.

Right, then. I'd forget Ashe now. I'd done everything that I could for him, enough to make me feel stupid and more than he'd wanted me to. If the police didn't turn him up he would presumably wander into the shop one day to look at the Classics shelf or the travel books, and he would be perfectly all right.

Talking to Paul Grant had been a mistake.

On the basis that the devil makes work for idle minds, I charged into the kitchen feeling bad-tempered. Mr. Spock woke up and followed me to inquire about the possibility of a snack, but I shooed him out the window onto the flat roof and set about washing dishes, wiping old grease out of the oven, and scrubbing the floor. By the time the room was looking unnaturally clean I was wet with sweat, but my temper hadn't improved. Was I really reduced to *doing housework?* I peeked into the bedroom and stood by the crib for a moment, watching Ben sleep, pink and naked except for his nappy, and felt happier, as I knew I would. He blew out his lips in a magnificent raspberry. I took it as an unconscious but valid comment on my bad temper and told myself to be thankful for my good luck. And went to run myself a bath.

3

By late afternoon the shadows had spread across the road, but it was no cooler. I was in the shop. I'd made

Barnabas go upstairs to drink a cup of tea and lie down. I'd assured him that Ben needed company. Now I slumped at the desk trying to concentrate enough to write prices on the cards he'd been preparing. When I yawned, the white rectangles danced in front of my watering eyes. I was nearly asleep, and it must have taken me a full minute to realize somebody was rattling the locked door.

A square, thuggish figure stopped knocking and pressed a nose to the glass. Ernie had arrived at last. Ernie Weekes.

He had turned up last autumn on the recommendation of my old friend Susie Bates. Ernie was taking a business course at the technical college where she teaches. I'd been complaining about not understanding computers and being at my wit's end, two weeks overdue with my winter catalogue. I might even have been going on and on about it? I was certainly in full flow when Susie informed me that she had the answer: a nineteen-year-old student from Sierra Leone who was just the man I needed to do my computer work for me as I was so obviously incompetent. Ernie, she had explained, could make computers sing. As opposed to me, who seemed only able to make them freeze in justified terror. Ernie needed money for his tuition fees. It was appropriate for me to give him some.

When I was introduced to Susie's wizard my immediate reaction was that her soft heart had overcome her common sense. My potential employee looked like the bouncer at a low drinking club. He stood roughly five foot nothing in his trainers and was as wide as he was tall; and the width was all bone and muscle. Alarm bells always rang when you met Ernie because he was black, and dressed in the season's streetwise costume of baggy denims, trainers, and short hair shaven into stripes. This was not a figure you would want to meet on a dark night. At closer range you would see that the wrestler's body was topped by a round face with little-boy eyes and the apologetic grin which said he knew what kind of impression he made and hoped that you wouldn't hold it against him.

Half-reassured, I'd agreed to give this unpromising-looking character a trial: and I scarcely had time to turn around before I found that my customer lists and stock records had gone into the computer in a form which was so sensible that even I could work the system. Not only that: Ernie had an artistic eye which meant that the pages of my catalogues began to look as though they'd been designed, rather than stuck together with blind hope and flour paste. I'd been impressed despite myself. So this was what they call the "information revolution"? Ernie's timekeeping remained individualistic, but on the other hand he was usually able to decipher the writing on Barnabas's stock cards, which is a thing to wonder at.

I unlocked the door and flung it open for him to bounce into the shop. He gave me a smack on the cheek and a "Howzit going?" and I said it was going all right but slowly, and I desperately needed his attentions in order for it to go better because I still had the notion that a printed catalogue ought to be ready to mail out in three weeks' time at most. His look said it was a piece of cake. Then he was suddenly transformed into a well-mannered boy in the presence of a revered elder, and I left him in hard-working silence at the desk while I set about a systematic trawl of the shelves.

Bookshops, like public libraries, are always sinking into chaos. The end of July and August is the quiet time in the trade, the time to close up and go on holiday or, in my case, get around to the tasks I'd been too busy to do over the last few months. Having Ernie clicking keys in the office seemed to help. I could hear him whistling through his teeth as I moved down the southern side of the shop, shifting volumes that had been misplaced and making a little collection of the ones I wanted to check for damage and possible repair, or to reprice. I was on my knees looking through the pages of Opie's *Illustrations of Lying* and deciding that it was worth more than the £125 I'd pencilled in, when the little Nepalese bell above the door chimed and I realized that I'd forgotten to relock it when I'd let Ernie in. I opened my mouth to challenge the invisible customer, stopped myself—after all, a millionaire collector is always welcome, even when the shop is closed—and stretched to peer around the central bookcases. And held my breath.

Tom Ashe stood there. He was wearing his shabby mac. It must have been killing in that heat. One hand dangled a plastic shopping bag, one of my own bags that I'd been handing out to customers last spring, in a rather pretty burnt-umber color with a black-line drawing of the shop front on it. A corner of my consciousness reminded me that I'd been meaning to order some more. Ashe stood for a moment looking as though he had briefly forgotten where he was, then sidled towards the illustrated books in the far corner. I almost spoke, but there was a kind of dreaminess in his face which stopped me. I had the feeling that if I said anything he would turn and vanish. He moved forward stiffly, which reminded me again that he was quite old as well as ill.

I stayed where I was and whispered, "Hello, Mr. Ashe. How are you?"

He stiffened, threw a quick glance in my direction, and found me kneeling on the floor. I must have managed to look very unthreatening. I watched his pale eyes flicker in and out of focus again and settle on my face.

"Yes. Thank you, nearly well," he said at last. His attention was caught by the noises Ernie was making in the office. For a moment he looked as though he would retreat, but then apparently he identified the sound.

"Ernie and I are having a sort-out and getting the next catalogue ready," I said quietly. "Let me know if you want help; otherwise, I'll just carry on."

He said, "I'm looking for something that might be lost," and shuffled towards the central bookcases. I watched him pull down a volume and bend over it, slowly turning the pages.

I'd better be doing something so he wouldn't see me watching him. I couldn't say why, but I *was* watching him. There was something strange about his movements. Not exactly furtive . . . I pulled one or two books off the shelves and put them back again, my ears tuned to the slow movements on the other side of the shop.

"Your father."

I heard the words, but at first I thought I must have missed something. "Barnabas? He's upstairs."

"Barnabas," he said. It sounded like an echo. "Barnabas Hoare."

I stopped pretending to work and straightened up very slowly. There was something wrong with him, something really wrong. I moved carefully to my left so that I could see the old man more clearly and thought that he had aged since our last meeting. Grown fragile.

"Do you want to see him? To see my father?"

He shook his head.

"Would you like to sit down for a while? I can get the chair out of the office. It's so hot . . ."

"All right," he said.

I shot into the back room, grabbed the spare chair, shook my head at Ernie when he opened his mouth, and went back.

"Put it there," Ashe said. His voice was stronger. He indicated the corner next to the office door, and I set the chair down. When he walked to it, his steps were stronger too. He settled himself with care, placed the bag on the floor between his feet, and began to read. I recognized a cheap anthology of nineteenth-century poetry and shrugged mentally. After a few seconds I went and snicked the lock of the door so that no other unexpected customer could ignore my Closed sign. Then I went back to my work halfheartedly.

I turned again when I heard him stir. He was on his feet holding out the shopping bag, thrusting it at me.

"For you."

I said, "Oh . . . thank you," and took it uncertainly.

"A present," he said. "A thank-you."

At first I thought the thing in the bag was a rather light, square-shaped book; but when I slid it out I held a box made from some soft, unpainted wood. It exuded a musty, slightly scented smell that reminded me of old ladies' clothing. The lid was held down by a fine brass hook. I inserted a thumb nail and levered it up.

"Careful!"

I'd needed that warning. A handful of yellowing newsprint scraps threatened to spill onto the floor. I juggled the box, the scraps, and something hard but flexible which was buried in their protective packing.

"Be careful," he said again; and I saw his eyes intent on what I held. "It's old."

I balanced the box gingerly on the palm of my hand, dug in, and hooked the thing out. I could feel my jaw drop. I was holding a piece of jewelry, a necklace. Two rows of grayish-blue oblong beads were joined together at regular intervals by other, rounded beads, some dull red and others made of a yellow metal from which dangled little yellow leaves. The clasp was missing. The piece looked both dainty and slightly crude, like one of the concoctions of hand-made beads that you see on sale in street markets. It was a delicate thing, quite pretty. Well, fairly pretty. Unusual, anyway.

I said, "Good heavens. How remarkable! Is it Indian?"

"Middle Eastern," he said briskly. He shot a quick glance at me. "Old. Quite old. I picked it up in Egypt after the war."

I started to push the beads back in among the newspaper scraps. I said, "It's very nice of you, but I didn't do anything that anybody else wouldn't have done."

He laughed sardonically. "Are you afraid to accept jewelry from an old man? I assure you, my intentions are honorable." He made it sound like a sneer. "What use is it to me? It should be kept in a safe place."

I had a sudden vision of him carrying this antique around with him in a blanket roll from one shop doorway to another, wherever he was living at the time. "I could keep it for you," I said slowly. All my instincts were screaming, *Dido, what on earth are you saying? You don't know where he got this!*

He was looking at me, and there was nothing unfocused now. He might have been reading my mind. "It's my own property, and I can give it to you if I like. Keep it. Wear it. There is only one thing." His shoulders seemed to slump, his face grew—blank? No, evasive. "A favor." He took half a pace towards me and held out a hand as though he wanted to touch me for emphasis. "A condition. You should keep this packed in its box, just the way it is now. The box was made for it. It belongs there. Will you do that?"

I opened my mouth to tell him either that I would do as he asked, or maybe that I couldn't accept this from him or didn't want it. The telephone rang in the office. I handed him the box and pushed past the chair. I had to edge past Ernie at the keyboard and abstract the telephone carefully from the orderly piles of cards that filled the desk top before I could lift the receiver.

I gave the name of the shop. There was a moment's silence: the call was from a pay phone, and everyone forgets to push the button.

"Is that Miss Hoare?"

I said that it was, and spent the next minute informing the nameless caller that although I wasn't open for business until Wednesday, I would be happy to see him on that day between eleven and six. There was a little silence. I sighed mentally. "Is there anything special that you're looking for?"

The voice said, "History books," mumbled something, and broke the connection. Somehow it didn't sound as though it was going to be the sale of the year.

As soon as I hung up Ernie asked me to interpret a particularly annoying squiggle on one of the cards. It took me several minutes to spell out that Barnabas was referring to the 1809 *Liber Facetiarum*. Latin wasn't Ernie's strong point.

When I went back the chair was empty except for the book Ashe had been nodding over and his little box. The old man and his carrier bag had vanished. There was no sign of him in the street; he had moved quickly, and so quietly that I hadn't even heard a jangle from the bell above the door. As I locked up after him I was wondering just what kind of game was being played.

"I di'n't hear you," Ernie informed me apologetically from the other room.

"I didn't say anything," I retorted. "I might have been swearing, but it's not your fault."

"That old guy take something?" Ernie asked, popping into view. "Want me to catch him?"

For a moment I was tempted.

"He didn't take anything," I said. "In fact, the opposite. He's left something."

Ernie looked at the box in my hand. "I could take it back to him."

I said, "Forget it. I'll give it to him when he comes back. Or maybe I will keep it."

I pushed past Ernie into the back room and opened the deep bottom drawer of the desk. As I was shoving the embarrassing packet inside, I saw that Ashe's screwdriver was still there. Something else I had to decide about returning to him. I was still thinking about it when Ernie yawned, stretched, switched off, and departed. I bolted the back door, set the answering machine and the alarm system, and locked up. There was a bottle of white wine in the fridge which would make a good kir, and it was beginning to call to me.

It wasn't until I'd unlocked the door of the flat that I remembered about Paul. I ought to phone and call off the dogs. Assuming that he'd actually done anything about my request. But Barnabas was upstairs and I didn't feel like having him eavesdrop on my apologies. Feeling slightly martyred I let myself back into the shop and went to the phone.

For once, he answered immediately. "I wanted to thank you and tell you not to bother about Ashe," I said quickly. "He's turned up."

I thought there was a second's silence. "He's all right?"

"I guess so. More or less. Not actually well . . ."

"Did you find out where he went from hospital?"

The question had come just a little too eagerly. I said, "No, we didn't discuss it."

Again there was a silence.

"Why?"

"I guess I'm curious. Were you telling me the truth about all this? I mean, he really hasn't lifted anything? Or anything like that?"

I thought I was beginning to understand. "You've run his name through the computer, haven't you? Are you people looking for him? Does he have a record?"

"I can't say."

Oh yes, something was wrong. "Can't, or won't?"

This time I caught a chuckle. All he said was, "Yes."

I thought about it. "You aren't going to tell me?"

"No, it's just a bit odd."

I said patiently, "What did you find out about him?"

This time there was no hesitation. "Nothing at all. His name is in the computer but there are no details. I don't think I've ever seen it before; it's what's called an SO 12 entry."

I waited.

"Basically it's a 'Refer-to' note. Anyone who has a query about him is asked to think twice about whether it's necessary to proceed."

"And if it is?"

"I'd have to contact a department at Scotland Yard."

I discovered that I was tapping my foot. "What on earth does that mean?"

I heard him chuckle. "I'm not allowed to tell you." He laughed when I groaned at him. "It's no big deal. He probably worked for us at some time. An informant, maybe."

I put on my Humphrey Bogart voice. "A grass? A stoolie?" It didn't especially fit my picture of Tom

Ashe as the retired classics master.

"Dido, what about meeting for a drink? Do you remember that pub over towards Barnsbury with the model aeroplanes hanging over the bar?"

I admitted that I did.

"I'm going to finish late this evening, but what about tomorrow? Six? I could take you for a meal afterwards. If you like. I haven't seen you for a long time."

It was my turn to hesitate. Presumably the marriage was going through one of its periodic rough patches. Well, what the hell, I'm old enough to take care of myself. Confusingly vivid memories offered to interfere with my common sense.

"Will you pick me up, or shall I meet you at the pub?" I asked. Having arranged it, I relocked the shop and waltzed upstairs to inform Barnabas that he was scheduled for a little extra babysitting. I reckoned that it would suit me very well to have him in the flat tomorrow evening, because I wasn't intending the drink to lead to any more than a pleasant couple of hours and an explanation of what an "SO 12" really meant. It didn't make much sense attached to the old man. Not really.

PART 3

Dead Past

1

Light footsteps crossed the pillow and a whiskered face lowered itself inquiringly towards my nose: Mr. Spock, commenting on such matters as the weather and the inexplicable absence of breakfast. I could hear Ben muttering to himself in the crib beyond the chest of drawers, but he sounded content, so I shut my eyes and thought about things.

From one point of view last night had been a failure: I was no wiser about police procedures, computerized or otherwise. My suggestion that Paul might actually get in touch with Department SO 12 hadn't been welcomed. Apparently my curiosity wasn't proper grounds for an enquiry. I tried to appreciate that point of view. Beyond repeating that the marker on Tom Ashe's entry probably meant that he had worked for them at one time, Paul had been evasive.

So we'd spent an almost entirely pleasant hour talking about other things at a table on the patio overlooking a potted bay tree. Then we'd moved to the garden of a Spanish bistro near Camden Town where we drank sangria, ate from little dishes of calamari and chorizo, and found it almost possible to imagine ourselves sitting under a tree in Spain. It was like old times. I got to bed late and alone.

And at seven a.m. wasn't quite ready to face the day. The bedroom was already stuffy, even with its window open. Mr. Spock bunted my nose and I raised myself gingerly to a sitting position, decided that I might not be hung over after all, and surrendered to the necessity of getting on with my life.

It being a Wednesday, I opened the shop. Barnabas arrived at eleven and vanished into the back room to write catalogue cards, and I was passing time by standing on the rolling steps and dusting the half-forgotten volumes on top of the central bookshelves when Ashe sidled in. He was wearing his grubby mackintosh and the same shopping bag was in his hand. I watched his eyes identify me and then flicker around the shop.

"You're back," I said unnecessarily. "How are you?"

When he tilted his head I could see the answer to my question. His watery eyes looked at me, not through me, today. "Better. It never lasts more than a few days."

That wasn't quite what I'd meant but I let it pass. "You frightened me," I offered. "It seemed bad enough when I found you on my doorstep."

He dismissed that with an irritable shrug. "I'm used to it. Had it for a long time, but not for a while." He seemed to notice something wrong with that sentence, and shook his head irritably. "I thought it was gone, but it stays in the blood. I picked it up in the Middle East when I was there in forty-six."

Even then it struck me that this was only about the

second thing he'd ever volunteered about his past.

"Anyway," I said lamely, "I did take you to Horsell Road, but you couldn't tell me the house."

His face changed. "Horsell Road? What's that?"

"Where you live," I said, watching him.

He turned away. "You're mistaken. I live in Camden Town. In a hostel."

I opened my mouth. And closed it again. I couldn't imagine why he was lying unless my original instincts had been right after all, and he was one of those obsessive shoplifters who live secretively in a rat's nest of stolen books. There have been one or two cases of people caught with thousands of stolen volumes—all antiquarian book dealers know the stories. But I could swear I wasn't missing anything, or not anything I could attribute to his visits.

I decided not to push it and imitated his shrug. "You're better, that's the important thing. But about the necklace . . ."

He glared. "It's yours. I pay my debts."

There was a sound behind me, and we both turned nervously. I'd forgotten about Barnabas, but he had heard the voices and was standing in the door of the office, staring at Ashe.

"This is my father," I said. "Barnabas, this is Mr. Ashe, who . . ."

I stopped. Something in Ashe's face had closed up and his eyes had started to flicker again. The feeling came to me that Ashe knew my father. Yet I could swear that Barnabas was puzzled. He stepped forward, peering down at the visitor.

And then I remembered Ashe asking me about Barnabas.

Ashe turned his back sharply on us both and shuffled to the door, where he stopped for a moment without turning and said something so unexpected that I thought I hadn't heard him properly: "Hut 8—remember?"

He must have left then, but I was staring at Barnabas, who'd put out a hand to steady himself on the nearest bookcase, so that my own heart skipped a beat and I flew to him down the steps.

"What is it?"

"Don't break your neck!" He was all right. He looked as though he was listening to an internal voice. "*Tom Ashe* . . . Good God—I knew him!"

The old man had vanished into the street. I went to snick the latch on the door and flip the Closed sign. Hang the business, there weren't any customers around anyway. Then I said, "What is Hut 8?"

Barnabas said slowly: "Another lifetime."

2

We sat upstairs with the fan coaxing a stir of air from the sitting-room windows and the answering machine switched on and the bottle of Irish whiskey which I keep for my father's benefit on the coffee table. It didn't seem like the weather for whiskey, but apparently Hut 8 demanded respect.

"You do know about Hut 8," he muttered, "you've forgotten. Lord, I'd almost forgotten it myself."

I picked up the rather hefty shot that Barnabas had poured for me and waited.

"Bletchley. Fifty years ago—more. When you were little you were fascinated by the story."

Of course! *Tell me about the war, Daddy.* . . .

"I went up to Oxford in forty-one. I'd wanted to join the Air Force, but they said I had a problem with one lung, so your grandfather decided I might as well get on with my studies. I sat Mods, and then my moral tutor . . . we had moral tutors in those days, and just this one time old (I can't remember his name now) the old fellow was useful."

I was remembering. "He recruited you. You're talking about working for Signals Intelligence. Is that where you met Ashe?"

"Obviously. I was at Bletchley Park by the end of May. The big thing then was Enigma, the German U-boat codes. Dozens of us were working on those signals. Hut 8 was the center of it. We lived nearby and most of us came from the same kind of background: academics from Oxford and Cambridge, all either linguists or mathematicians, so you tended to get to know people pretty well."

"Did you know him well?"

"Not as well as others. He used to chum around with a chap . . . Marlowe? Mallow? Now *there* was a queer one. Anyway, Ashe left Bletchley before I did. I've been trying to remember what the story was—I think they'd assigned him somewhere abroad. I went home when Germany surrendered, and I started at the university again in the autumn. The rest, as they say, is history. But Tom Ashe . . ." He shook his head as though he was trying to shake his brain into remembering. "Ashe was a

Cambridge man, but I don't believe he went back. I seem to recall that he was particularly interested in the Middle East. Presumably he knew Arabic or Farsi. Perhaps he went in there at the end of the war. I think . . . There was an Intelligence section that specialized in the Middle East and Central Asia. They called it MI2 for a while, before it vanished in some reorganization. I've been racking my memory, but the best that I can say is that I *think* I remember hearing that he had gone for that as a career. I have a . . . no, I won't even call it a memory, but perhaps I remember hearing something of the sort."

"He told me he was a retired schoolmaster."

Barnabas laughed and drained his glass. "He might have been that, too. Cover? He might easily have had humdrum periods of staying out of sight, teaching at a school . . . who knows? And who knows what he would have done after he got too old to go on playing?"

I looked at him down my nose. "I'm learning things about you," I said. "You aren't going to tell me that you . . ."

My father smiled and shook his head. "No. I had a real profession, remember. I always felt wonderfully lucky to be able to work in a subject I loved at a place as congenial as Queen's was then. As a matter of fact, I believe that I was once sounded out in the mid-fifties about going back. Somebody I hadn't seen for six years turned up in the senior common room and engaged me in a very long conversation which I felt, at the time, moved in rather puzzling directions. But, as I say, I'd got my fellowship, the big Spenser project was going well, and I had no desire to be doing anything else, however melodramatic."

He was silent for a long time. When he spoke again, he was talking mainly to himself. "For me, the war was over and there was no longer the same motivation that some people seemed to feel. I stayed out. But Tom Ashe wandered off to . . . whatever it was. Until today I hadn't thought about him for nearly half a century."

"He remembered you," I told him. "When he came in and gave me the necklace, I realized then that he knew your name." The thought came to me: "I think he was checking to make sure that my father really was the man he remembered. But then when he saw you today he ran away. That was how it looked to me."

"I'd better see this necklace," Barnabas frowned.

"He said it was Middle Eastern. I chucked it into the drawer in the office. If you'll keep an eye on Ben . . .

But at that moment, the object of our attention awoke and explained in forthright tones that he required care. . . .

Motherhood is odd. Something like changing a baby's nappy or warming a bottle of milk will automatically take precedence over matters of art, faith, justice, high finance, and knowledge. Though even if Barnabas had inspected Ashe's gift that afternoon, it wouldn't have helped. It was already too late. It had been too late for years.

3

When the doorbell rang I assumed that Phyllis, who had just left with Ben in the push-chair, had come back for keys or some piece of forgotten baby equipment. I was head-down over the bath tub at the time with my hair full of shampoo, so I half-rinsed it, wrapped a towel around the mess, and flung myself down the stairs with rivulets of soapy water running off my chin. But when I opened the door I faced not an apologetic Phyllis, but the familiar chest regions of Paul Grant.

He took in my soapy drip. "I hope I'm not too early for you."

Struggling with the knowledge that something wasn't right, I used a corner of the towel to remove most of the streaming water from my face and explained, brilliantly, "I was just washing my hair. Would you like to come up?"

"Please. We need to talk."

His tone made me look at him carefully. I'd seen him only thirty-six hours ago, yet he'd changed again. I recognized the glaze of business on his face. I was being visited by a detective inspector in the local CID and the invisible wall had gone up between us again. I led the way upstairs and into the sitting room, offered him a seat and settled myself opposite, feeling at a damp disadvantage.

"I've come to tell you that your old man, Ashe, was found dead early this morning. It looks as though he was on a binge and his heart gave out. I guess you can stop worrying about him."

Well. I struggled. *Well, that's that. Problem solved.* Something was bothering me, but for the moment I couldn't think what. Anyway, I'd stopped worrying about him since last Monday when he had reappeared in the shop. Hadn't I?

I mopped uselessly at the soapy water dripping off my chin. "I saw him." My head still wasn't working. "He was here just yesterday morning and he seemed all right. Well, he was old. The fever probably weakened him."

Paul nodded.

I said, "Well—thanks for letting me know."

But that was a part of what was wrong. Why should Paul Grant turn up on my doorstep during working hours to tell me in person about the death of one of my casual customers? It would have been nice to think that he felt a passionate desire to see me. A little nervous buzzing located itself under my breastbone.

I took a deep breath and let it out slowly. "What's wrong?"

As I spoke my memory nearly located what was bothering me, but it had escaped again when Paul replied, "Nothing as far as I know. I should explain that he died in the Northwest Division and they're handling it at Kentish Town. They got on to me because somebody knew I'd been asking about him. They're wondering whether you can give them any information. You might know his home address, for example? Relatives' names?"

My mental alarm bells jangled. I said, "You know I don't know where he lived! I was asking *you* a couple of days ago."

"I know you were." It struck me that Paul's voice sounded cool. "And you told me he was just a casual acquaintance, remember?"

I shrugged defensively. "I've known him as a customer for almost a year. When I say 'customer'—he didn't have much money, of course, but he bought cheap books occasionally, after he'd got his pension check I imagine. So?"

"So according to him, you're his guardian, or something."

After a couple of moments I got my jaw under enough control to screech, "*What?* You're joking! What do you mean?"

Wordlessly, Paul handed over what looked like (probably was) one of the cards Barnabas used for cataloguing. Somebody had printed on it the words *In case of trouble please notify Dido Hoare, the Book Shop, George St., N.1.* "This was in a pocket. I knew that you'd been anxious about him, and I wondered whether there was something you hadn't told me." He extracted the card from my fingers and returned it to his breast pocket. "We'd like to find his relatives. We need a formal identification."

I repressed the impulse to say that men like Tom Ashe don't have any family. But of course that could be wrong: there was the supposed son at the hospital, for example. For all I knew, he might have a wife, children, and grandchildren anxiously awaiting his return. He could be an obscure royal duke for all I actually knew about him.

"This is some kind of joke, isn't it? I've told you: I don't know where he lived, I don't know anything about him . . ." Except of course that I did. I decided to keep my father's story to myself for the moment. That was a long time ago, and I couldn't see that it was necessary for Paul to go and bother Barnabas about Ashe's death.

Ashe's death . . .

I said abruptly, "How did he die? Where? When?" I was chasing my uneasiness.

Paul grimaced. "When? Sometime last night. It must have been after dark, probably after the Tube stopped. There's a covered space by Kentish Town station with a bench or two. A group of homeless men had been drinking there most of the afternoon. They were moved on once or twice by the local police, but they drifted back a couple of hours later. You can't keep that type off the streets."

Something in me noted that Tom Ashe was "that type."

"The station staff noticed him when they arrived this morning to open up. He was slumped against the wall near the entrance. The local constable knows the regulars there and asked. They said Ashe had been at it for hours. His heart gave out. He was an old man."

That was wrong. I said, without thinking, "No, it shouldn't be that."

"Why not?"

I was angry, and the words came out clipped: "He didn't drink. I've never known him to take even one drink, not even at the New Year. He told me . . ." it sounded silly when I set out to say it, but I went on regardless ". . . that he never drank because he was an alcoholic."

Paul made a face, pulled a notebook from his pocket, and scribbled. "Well, he was drinking last night. The others said that he and a mate had a whole shopping bag full of lager cans. They were handing them round. It sounds like quite a party. And he'd been sick; the body stank of lager. If, as you say, he normally didn't drink, he certainly slipped up yesterday. Look: I think that somebody from Kentish Town is going to want to have a word with you."

I wasn't really listening, because I'd tracked down what I'd been trying to remember. "The second thing is that there was nothing wrong with his heart."

"What do you mean?"

"I think they ran tests when he was in the hospital. The ward sister told me his heart was fine. Hadn't you better check?"

"I'll pass the message on, of course. Can you give me the doctor's name?"

I gave him Sister Fletcher's.

We exchanged ideas on why Tom Ashe had been carrying my name around with him on his little card, but I was deciding that he'd had some kind of fantasy connected with having once known Barnabas. I'd spoken up firmly for his sobriety and his healthy heart, but I couldn't be so sure about his sanity. We spent another five minutes exchanging speculations, but even I knew that we weren't going to get anywhere with this. Besides, I was bothered by something about Paul's attitude. His body language. I filed it away to worry about.

At the door, I said, "I'd like to know what happened to him even though his emergency-contact business is nonsense."

Paul turned on the pavement and looked down at me. "I told you this case is nothing to do with Islington or with me. I've already had to try to explain to my Super why I'd been asking around."

Ahh. He was caught on the wrong foot, and he blames you for it. He thinks you've made him look silly.

"I'm sorry about that," I said, not meaning it.

"Don't let it worry you," he said politely. "Anyway,

somebody from Kentish Town will be contacting you. You can ask them about the post-mortem."

"When?"

"It depends how busy they are and what the results are."

But I couldn't leave it like that. I took a deep breath. "I'm likely to be in and out. Will you give them the number of my mobile, please?"

He said, "If you like," and smiled in a slightly more human way. But when the door had closed behind him, leaving me to go back to my hair-rinsing, I found myself instead leaning on the wall trying to think. There were questions. Had Tom Ashe named me as his emergency contact because he expected *me* to find answers?

4

I'd made the mistake of driving up to Hampstead Village. The parking regulations there are so incomprehensible that the visit to my customer took three times as long as I'd intended. I'd just got back to my car with its expired parking sticker and a traffic warden approaching purposefully, when the mobile warbled inside my bag. I turned on the Volvo's engine to demonstrate law-abiding intentions before I dug it out, and switched on.

It was Paul. Still sounding unhappy, I thought—no messing.

"For what it's worth, I've heard something."

I eyed the approaching warden and wondered whether being in the process of speaking on the phone to a policeman constituted a defense against a parking fine. "Can you hang on for ten seconds?"

I put the phone down, extracted the car from its place at the kerb, and inserted it into the stream of traffic which was moving sedately towards the lights. "I'm back. What was it?"

The reason for the unhappy note became clearer. "You were right, the hospital was right: his heart looks perfectly healthy. There's no doubt he'd been drinking heavily, by the way—but that doesn't seem to be any reason for his heart to stop. Apart from a graze on his arm, there's no sign of external trauma. They're still looking."

"It couldn't have something to do with the malaria, could it?"

"I told them about that. They've sent samples off to a lab for testing, but they don't think so. It will take time to get the toxicology results, depending on how much other work they have on at the moment. Look, the old boy was sleeping rough."

It took me a moment to interpret that statement; I thought about it while I was negotiating the right turn at the lights in the middle of the Village and edging the Volvo into the stream of traffic heading down the hill.

"Are you saying that you don't bother about somebody who's sleeping rough?"

"No." He had taken offense. "I'm saying that the Met's resources are limited, and they'll get to the bottom of it in time."

"And nobody knows why he died."

"Yes . . . all right. But that's no reason to think there's anything wrong—not yet. Anyway, it's down as suspicious circumstances, so they'll go on looking for answers."

I took a slow breath and considered the situation. "Will you hear about the lab report?"

"I have an old friend at Kentish Town. He'll probably let me know. Not before next week."

I took the plunge. "I don't know whether you're free, but I could cook us a meal one evening, if you like."

I could hear the hesitation. It made me angry enough to add, "No strings!"

It was a relief to hear him laugh.

PART 4

A Truth

1

We never open on Mondays. Anyway, business was nonexistent: even the tourists must have fled town. But Ben had gone to Phyllis for the whole day, and Barnabas had phoned to say he was taking refuge in the British Library for a morning's reading, so I was alone for brunch. Unless you count Mr. Spock asleep and uncommunicative on the settee. I'd got a bottle of freshly squeezed juice and two big butter croissants from the bakery around the corner. Bliss.

And yet, after I'd put my glass and plate in the sink and the melting butter back into the fridge, and wandered into the sitting room with the noble intention of doing something about the place, I found myself holding a stuffed yellow elephant and realized that I'd been standing motionless for about five minutes.

Damn Tom Ashe!

I will not even think about him.

My phone was ringing but I was in such slow motion that it took me half a minute to pull myself together and find it under the mess on the sideboard.

"Hello?" I heard the electronic hum of an open line. *"Hello?"*

He said at last, "It's Paul. Did I wake you up?"

I told him only a little inaccurately that he hadn't, and we exchanged small talk, but I could hear that his heart wasn't in it.

"What?"

"You were right after all."

I said stupidly, "What about?"

"The old man. Ashe. Somebody phoned half an hour ago. You were right." His tone suggested that this was rather tactless of me. "He was injected with something called pentobarbitone. They'd missed it at first because it was injected through a graze on his forearm. Or perhaps the injury was made afterwards to hide the puncture mark. The stuff isn't that hard to detect, but maybe whoever did it hoped we wouldn't look. Stupid of them."

I said very firmly, "Pentobar-what?"

"A barbiturate. They use it to put animals down. Apparently there was enough in him to kill a cow. . . . Sorry. It attacks the central nervous system. I am told that the victim stops breathing. His heart forgets to beat." Paul sounded depressed at the thought.

I missed what he said next, but there was a pause at the end of a sentence and I said into it, "Where would the killer get hold of that?"

"Who knows? Vets use it."

"You mean he was killed by a vet? There were witnesses, the people he was drinking with. Can't somebody identify . . ."

Paul laughed shortly. "Witnesses? The local CID has been talking to everybody who was there on the night, everybody they can locate, all permanently paralytic. Apparently the old man's 'friend' was about twenty-five. Or maybe fifty. He was tall, or maybe medium height. He had blond hair, red hair, or brown hair. Nobody mentioned that he was a vet, though."

"But he might have been?"

"Unless the killer stole the stuff. I don't suppose that veterinary surgeons are as careful about their drugs as doctors are. You don't expect people who steal drugs to be looking in an animal practice."

"But it does suggest special knowledge."

"Or just opportunism."

"Is Islington going to be involved in the case now?" I was going to suggest a visit to Horsell Road.

"No." His voice was flat. "The file's gone to Scotland Yard. Special Branch is taking it."

"*Special Branch?*"

"They say it's to do with the SO 12 on his name. Look, I just thought I'd warn you that when somebody is assigned, they'll want to talk to you. You're going to be around?"

I explained that I had no plans to flee the country, and then regretted the flippancy. "I may have an idea where Ashe was living. It's worth looking at least. I wondered whether you . . ."

"Weren't you listening? It's nothing to do with me. Somebody will get in touch with you." There was another of those buzzing silences. "Sorry, I didn't mean to snap. Listen . . . would you like to meet me for a drink? Maybe that wine bar off Camden Passage?"

It sounded like a peace offering. I hoped so. But it was also a change of subject, and it felt as though we still had things to resolve. "I'd like to, but I'll need to check babysitting. Can I phone you back?"

"Use my mobile number. Do you still have that?" It was an idiotic question that I didn't bother to answer.

It left me on my own. Common sense told me there was nothing I could do about Ashe's murder and I certainly hadn't any illusions about going into competition with Scotland Yard. But I did have two overwhelming feelings. One was just outrage at the image of an old man being put down like an old dog in a dirty corner up the road. The other, let's admit, was naked curiosity. Barnabas calls it mind itch.

2

Horsell Road is a short turning east of the Holloway Road. Apart from the Victorian terraces with their flights of cement steps rising from the pavements, there was nothing in the street but a corner convenience store and a pair of run-down prewar factories that seemed to have been converted into workshops. It wasn't exactly fashionable, and I could just about see Tom Ashe having a room somewhere here, though why he'd tried to lie about it was the question. I hadn't asked for any of this, but Ashe had gone to the trouble of involving me and so I thought I had the right at least to know what was going on. Apparently he was about to cause me as much trouble as if we had been lovers.

The convenience store was the obvious starting place. It was the usual inner-London, Asian-run corner shop that stocks everything from cigarettes to washing powder and stays open eighteen hours a day. I found a middle-aged couple inside using the mid-morning lull to restock their shelves, so I picked up a couple of tins of the kind of food that all cats are supposed to prefer and made my way to the cash desk. A neatly lettered card by the register informed me that checks should be made out to A. R. Shah, so when the female half of the partnership slid behind the counter, I pushed my tins forward and said, "Mrs. Shah? I hope that you can help me. I'm looking for my grandfather. He told me that he lives on this street, but I've lost the house number."

The woman tilted her head expectantly, and the eyes that looked out from behind a pair of clear-rimmed glasses missed nothing. "Your grandfather?" she repeated. "Oh yes, we may know him. We know most people in this street."

Perhaps it would be easier than I'd thought. "Ashe," I said expectantly. "His name is Tom Ashe."

The man spoke from behind me. "We do not know all the names. Perhaps if you could describe this gentleman?"

I did my best. They exchanged a long look.

"I think we have seen your grandfather," Mrs. Shah said eventually. Mr. Shah nodded. They both looked at me. "The old gentleman who always wears a coat, you say?"

Under the gaze of these respectable citizens I became aware of my T-shirt and old jeans. At least they matched my "grandfather's" style.

"An old gentleman in a coat." They were nodding at each other.

"So, do you know which house he lives in?" I'd nearly said, "lived."

The nods turned to slow frowns. "He did not buy on credit," the man explained. "He did not chat. He paid in cash, and there was no newspaper delivered . . ."

At least I was in the right place, but I was going to have to ask at every door after all, so I paid them for Mr. Spock's dinner and headed back into the sunshine. *It isn't a long street, Dido; so don't hang about. . . .*

But by the time I'd made my way down the western side ringing every bell I could find, I'd made the door-to-door salesman's discovery that mid-morning is the time when nobody is ever at home, unless you count one fat, sweating man wearing nothing but a pair of jeans, who was already so drunk that I fled.

The only other response to my ringing came from a child, a small girl in red dungarees who looked about six and was certainly too young to be alone, though she said that everybody was out. I was turning away when the thought struck me that I might do better with a child than with adults. Children notice things that adults choose to ignore. I lowered my voice confidentially and told the story about my missing grandfather.

The child grinned. "I know him. He's . . ."

She stopped abruptly.

I could guess what she'd wanted to say. "He's sort of funny, isn't he?" I conceded.

I could see her thinking about it. Frankness prevailed. "Is he crazy in the head?"

"Sometimes. But he doesn't mean any harm. He's just a very old man."

She nodded understandingly.

"So-o, d'you think you can tell me which house he lives in?" I prompted.

"He doesn't live in a house."

Oh, wonderful. I nearly turned away, but she hadn't finished.

"He lives there."

She was pointing at the factory buildings.

"I didn't know that anybody lived there," I said carefully. "I thought it was just for working in."

But she was sure. "Your grandad does. In the basement."

Light dawned: caretaker? I tried to ask her when she'd last seen Ashe, but she hung her head and turned silent so I suggested that her mum might not like it if she opened the door to strangers, and left. Children usually survive. At least I hope so.

Numbers 23 and 25 adjoined one another on the eastern side of the road. I climbed a short flight of steps to the door of 25 and found it locked. The name cards beside a stack of doorbells listed a caretaker. I rang the appropriate bell vigorously and uselessly.

Through the open window to my left I could see rows of metal shelving with people moving to and fro, so I made a guess that this was Freedom Distribution in Unit B, and rang their bell. A tinny voice said "Hello." I stabbed at the speaker button and told them I was wondering whether they knew where I could find the caretaker.

There was a pause. "Nobody's seen him lately."

But have you seen him since last week? I asked silently. I pulled out my second story. "I was wondering whether there was a small unit for rent. Do you have any idea when he'll be back? Mr. Ashe, isn't it?"

After a pause, the little speaker crackled at me. "Dimond," it said disappointingly. "Somebody did see him going out before nine, so he might be back at dinner time. You could come back then."

I agreed that it sounded like a good idea and thanked the voice lamely. I almost asked whether it knew Ashe, but decided to leave that until I could talk to Mr. Dimond. If somebody like Tom Ashe was wandering around the building it must be with the caretaker's knowledge. Of course I only had a small child's word for his presence, and small children fantasize. I used to.

I scrabbled around for another idea. Now that I looked more carefully, I could see that number 23 appeared deserted, and there was a notice-board attached to the wall on the first-floor level which described it as "Commercial Premises of 1,300 square metres For Sale or To Let." The sign had the dingy appearance of something that had been there for months. Token inspection of the door revealed half a dozen bells, but the name holders were all empty on this side, and I got no answer to all my ringing. It had already occurred to me that the windows were closed, and in this weather that had to mean number 23 was unoccupied. Probably waiting hopefully for the economic upturn that would make redevelopment viable. As a home for Tom Ashe it looked even less likely than number 25.

I wandered fruitlessly to the end of the road and back; by one o'clock I was sitting on a low wall opposite the workshops. Nothing interesting happened and went on happening.

How long are you going to sit here like Humpty Dumpty?

Not much longer, actually.

Good. Because if you had any sense you'd come back early this evening when any self-respecting caretaker is watching television. In fact, if you really had any sense, you'd tell the police and then forget about it.

It was stubbornness, not inspiration, that carried me back across the street for a last, restless look at the two properties. I rang the caretaker's bell once in case some fairy had spirited Mr. Dimond invisibly inside. An unexpected breeze stirred the length of the street, raising the dust and litter that had collected in the gutter and flapping a plastic shopping bag that was caught under the railings of number 23. It was a burnt-umber bag with a black-ink picture on it: the outline drawing of my shop.

I retrieved the bag Tom Ashe had been carrying the last time I'd seen him and held it, empty, in both hands.

A flight of crumbling cement steps led down into a narrow space below the pavement which ran along the front of the empty building. Four tall windows along the front were defended by rusting bars. To the left of them was an old door with flaking paint and a bulky padlock on a rusting metal hasp. That too seemed old. And yet . . .

The thing that caught my eye was a pale gray length of insulated cable. It emerged from the outside corner of the padlocked door, stretched along a course of mortar just above ground level, and headed towards the adjoining building. I followed the line along the wall, lost it briefly where it dived under the stairs, and then found it again as it reappeared next door. It vanished there into a big junction box that bore the electricity company's logo.

I delved back into my murky student past: somebody was stealing power from next door.

Ashe.

At the end of the sun-drenched street, two delivery vans had met between the lines of parked cars and were trying to edge past one another. A horn blared. Two boys came out of the doorway of the shop and stood watching the show. If anybody else happened to be around they would presumably also be watching, because there is nothing as riveting as the possibility of crumpled metal. I slipped down the stairs into the shade, sure that nobody would notice me. Dust and litter gritted under my sandals.

And when I touched it, the hasp shifted. I tugged and the whole thing came away in one piece: somebody had unscrewed it and then pushed the screws back loosely into their enlarged holes. I could imagine Tom Ashe at work with that big screwdriver of his. For some reason or other, my heart was pounding.

Then I realized that there was also a lock in the door itself. Damn!

In detective stories, they always go house-breaking armed with a set of picklocks and a thin metal strip for springing latches. Personally, I wouldn't even recognize picklocks, though I picture them as a set of giant's toothpicks on a steel ring. I'm probably wrong about that. A hammer and a really stout chisel would probably solve my problem, but unfortunately these are things I don't carry around in my shoulder bag.

I pressed my face against the bars on the window to the right of the door. Through the grimy glass I could see empty space, dusty and littered with a drift of old cardboard boxes and a broken chair.

But it wasn't dark. A faint, yellowish light outlined a door across the room. I squinted. That wasn't daylight. An electric light was burning somewhere beyond this room.

I stopped long enough to force the screws of the padlock back into their holes and had just got everything looking untouched when the door of number 25 banged over my head. Voices. Two men began to trolley cardboard boxes out onto a pile on the loading ramp. I could see blue labels with the name of the Freedom Distribution Group on them—probably one of the men heaving out boxes had been the voice on the entry phone.

Keeping my face casually averted, I ascended the stairs and crossed the road to take refuge in the Volvo. I walked in a ladylike manner. My heart was still pounding, and a quick glance in the driver's mirror revealed that dust was coagulating in the sweat running down my face, and one of the window bars had left a vertical streak on the side of my nose. I looked less than respectable and felt worse. There had to be a better way to go about this business.

My eyes fell on the agent's flaking sign. Phone number. And my mobile, tucked into the door pocket. I dialed.

A voice trilled, "Dover and Parker. How can I help you?"

"My name," I said thoughtfully, "is Dido Hoare. I just happened to notice your board on Horsell Road.

I own an antiquarian book business down Upper Street, and I'm looking for storage space." I considered the face of number 23, which was looking even more disreputable than mine did, and thought quickly. "I'm looking to rent some inexpensive entrance-floor or basement space for a period of about six months, and I see that your property in Horsell Road looks appropriate. I'd just like to make sure it's dry. Could I inspect it tomorrow morning?"

The voice said, "I'm sure we can arrange that," in tones which, even over the phone, sounded too eager. Before I drove away I'd arranged to meet her at nine o'clock in the morning. If I'd thought that I could have insisted on an immediate visit, I would have; but the urgency would have seemed odd, especially from somebody who so obviously needed a good wash.

I drove south to pick up Ben and arrange with Phyllis for an early-morning start. There was an open bottle of white wine waiting in my fridge, and a third of a bottle of sparkling water beside it. I reckoned I'd done enough to merit a spritzer with my evening salad. In fact I was so sure about it that I managed to bathe and feed both Ben and myself before I could bring myself even to check the answering machine. When I did, it poured out messages from Barnabas (thrice), and Ernie saying that he would phone me in the morning about coming into work.

The final message was different: a stranger's voice. *Inspector Diane Lyon, Miss Hoare—Scotland Yard. DI Grant at Islington probably told you we'd be getting in touch. In the matter of Mr. Ashe's death—I'll call around to see you at ten-thirty in the morning. Thanks.*

I took a soothing sip of my spritzer. Sometimes I think that the police spend too much time with criminals, which gives them a narrow view of other people's convenience. I even considered phoning Scotland Yard, but it wouldn't be difficult to get back by the time she'd given. If I wasn't, she could wait for me. That matter settled, Ben and I dozed. Unanimously.

3

Dover and Parker sat conveniently on the main road just south of my goal. I judged that there wasn't much hope of finding a legal parking space, so I inserted the Volvo into a row of cars parked nearby on a single yellow line and walked back. When I arrived, I discovered that the entire staff consisted for the moment of a twenty-year-old redhead with a low neckline who was sitting at the front desk in the full blast of an electric fan. She slammed down a copy of the *Express* as I opened the door, reinforcing my feeling that the property market was a bit slow. If my business had been legitimate I would have decided on the spot to offer a rent at least twenty-five per cent lower than whatever was being asked.

"Miss Hoare?" she asked, with a probably unnecessary glance at the appointments pad in front of her.

I confirmed my identity.

"I am *so* sorry." Her face expressed deep professional so-sorriness. "Mrs. Parker was supposed to be here, but she's phoned to say that she has a puncture, and she's asked me to ask you whether you could *pos-*

sibly wait for a while because she will get here as soon as the AA changes her wheel."

My internal voice said, *Bingo!* I adjusted my face to mirror her regret, then added frustration and a tinge of impatience and explained that while there was nothing I'd enjoy more, in the usual way of things, than waiting for Mrs. Parker, I was alas booked to view some storage space near York Way in an hour's time. I allowed my expression to modulate to lingering regret, and added that I was sorry not to see the space in Horsell Road before making up my mind about the other one. "I'll leave my card," I concluded. "What a shame."

At that point I plonked one of my special business cards down on her desk. At the beginning of the year I'd blown real money on a hundred of these things with the name, address, phone number and sketch of the shop on heavily embossed cream cards so thick that you could use them to tile a roof. Up until now I'd handed out exactly one of them—to an American collector of great wealth and self-importance. It seemed to intimidate even him, and I thought the present recipient turned pale, which was exactly the effect I'd hoped for.

I frowned again. "Actually, isn't there a caretaker on the site? Why don't you phone and ask him to show me around?"

She looked even more flustered. "He only has keys to the units next door. We've—um—got a couple of places available there. Maybe you'd prefer to lease there anyway . . . It's . . . mmmm . . . better looked after. With the caretaker on the spot, I mean."

I digested the news that Ashe, if he had indeed

been resident at number 23, was unofficial, and said innocently, "Oh, I thought somebody told me that there was a caretaker in both the buildings."

"Not in 23," she said promptly. "Not exactly. They do have somebody living on site, but he isn't a caretaker, more a sort of building-sitter." She giggled at the wit of her description. "In case of fire or vandals. Not an employee. He doesn't actually *do* anything. So I *was* wondering whether you wouldn't prefer next door? With services? Central heating and cleaning?"

I shifted so as to edge myself further into the blast of tepid air from the fan and said, "I didn't realize there was ground-floor space available in the other building . . ."

"If it *has* to be on the ground floor . . ."

"Or basement."

I repeated my prepared story about having bought thousands of books at country house sales, and needing a convenient space to store and sort them before selling them on. "You see," I pointed out gently, "one wouldn't want to have to carry them up and down staircases." Well, one wouldn't. Books are heavy. I came visibly to a decision. "Why don't you let me have the keys to number 23? If I go over there now, I'll at least be able to see whether the place is secure and dry enough for book storage. If Mrs. Parker arrives in the next twenty minutes, perhaps you could ask her to join me there? Otherwise, there should be just enough time for me to drop the keys back here before I go on to my next appointment."

I was gambling on not getting a refusal. What possible harm could be done in an empty building by a potential lessee with such superior business cards? She hesitated almost invisibly and handed over a fistful of assorted brass keys on an old bit of string in exchange for my signature. I fled to the Volvo. While I was prepared to settle for a tour of number 23 in the company of a letting agent, it would be much easier to poke around on my own without having to keep up any pretences. I should be able to check out the building in ten minutes. If the place was empty I'd be ready to admit that I'd sent myself on a very wild goose chase and that Tom Ashe had simply been mad. Let somebody else find out what kind of game the old man had decided, in his cracked mind, to play with us all. But if he'd been living there . . .

I turned the Volvo at a convenient junction and headed back onto the main road, where as usual there was a slow-moving, fuming traffic jam. It wasn't far to Horsell Road, but five minutes of stopping and starting left me thinking again of taking off to the country.

Talk about cracked: me, not Ashe.

Ten minutes later I stood in a corridor at the foot of a flight of cement stairs leading upwards in an airless gloom. I poked my head through the door of an ancient lavatory with broken fitments and checked out the big room which ran the length of the entrance floor, but everything had been cleared barring a pile of yellow newspapers in one corner and the grit on the cracking gray floor covering.

I flicked a couple of wall switches to confirm that the electricity was off. There was enough light seeping in that it didn't really matter, and I didn't think I'd have to go very far. I was betting on the "building-sitter" being Tom Ashe, and his headquarters being where I'd seen the light yesterday. There should be a door somewhere here in the entrance hall that would open to the basement.

At first I thought I was wrong. I poked my nose into the long, empty room and hesitated at the foot of the stairs. In the washroom I could see a dripping tap—the place had its water supply connected, if not its electricity. I wandered in to use the toilet. It was when I was coming out again, with the rumble of the flush echoing through the silent building, that my eye fell on a door tucked under the staircase that led to the upper floors. I tried the handle and it refused to open. Of course.

I straightened out the agent's string of keys and began trying them. On the third or fourth attempt a key went in and I felt the tumblers shift grudgingly. *Good.* I'd just look quickly, and then I'd be out of here and back to sanity. I could already see myself double-parking the Volvo outside the agent's office, pushing through their door to fling the keys down on the receptionist's desk with a breezy, "Thanks! I'll let you know . . .", rushing off to the appointment with Scotland Yard. . . .

The door wouldn't open. My attention back on the job in hand, I went through the motions again. Key. Lock. I concentrated, and my ears and fingers agreed that the key was working and the catch was moving back stiffly into the body of the door. I turned the handle slowly. And the door stayed solidly shut.

I pressed my face against the door frame and tried uselessly to see something through the crack. The door was old oak, solid. And still locked. No: bolted on the other side, of course.

Stepping out onto the pavement was like moving from a tomb into the real world. A van had drawn up next door, and two men, stripped to the waist in the heat, were carrying bundles of magazines up the steps and into the building. My wristwatch told me I'd been inside number 23 for ten minutes. I was beginning to wish that Mrs. Parker would arrive and give me some help. The men emerged, slammed the door, and hauled themselves into the front seat of the van. I slipped down into the basement area and stopped by the door. The padlock and hasp pulled away again without any trouble and I began the process of trying each key in turn. It was a while before I stumbled across the one that not only pushed all the way in but turned easily.

More easily than the others. Very easily. The lock must have been oiled.

Yet the room where I stood when I'd got the door open looked as dusty and abandoned as the floor above. An ancient wooden chair sat against the front wall—too old, too broken for anyone to bother taking it away. A few cardboard boxes and sheets of paper littered the floor.

The door on the far side of the room was shut and the space beyond it seemed dark today. Perhaps some light bulb had burnt out at last. I flicked the switches behind me with no more effect than upstairs. Then what about the cable I'd noticed, the amateur wiring? I located it again at the edge of the door frame where it descended loosely to the floor and dived into a hole in the boards. Somebody had cut into a plank and run the wires out of sight. The edges of the cut looked jagged but clean. New. The board shifted when I pushed a couple of fingers underneath; but it was too heavy to raise without a tool of some kind. Somebody had gone to a lot of trouble to hide the course of the cable.

I listened again. A car passed in the road, and upstairs the water was still running into the cistern. One corner of my mind wondered whether I'd broken something and started a flood—not that there was much to damage. I moved across to the door, which opened into a corridor stretching from a blank wall at the far right to a flight of stairs at the left. Only the bottom dozen steps were visible: the bolted door from the entrance hall was up somewhere just out of sight. Three doors punctuated the opposite wall. The nearest was open, and I could see yet another of the building's lavatories. There was nothing to suggest that it was in use. The second door led to a storage cupboard with empty shelves. The third, at the end, was closed. I reached it and turned the handle gently. Those oiled hinges again . . .

It was a space about ten foot deep and twice as long, and it wasn't empty. Windows on the back wall had been boarded up, but enough light slipped between the cracks for me to see rubbish spilling across a floor-covering of ancient linoleum, a bed overturned. . . . It was just a moment's vision.

Behind the door—movement. I shouted, holding my bag by its long strap and swinging it hard at the blackness before something exploded against the side of my head. No time even to think, just register outrage, *this kind of thing doesn't* and pain but no time to be frightened or . . .

4

Time passed. A huge and cruel fist was battering my skull.

The next time I woke up nothing had changed except that the pain was steadier. I was lying on something hard. When I told my muscles to move they refused; so I lay quietly with my right eye open, sighting along the dusty floor beyond my nose. It was covered with things I couldn't identify.

After a while my eye and my brain were ready to focus. I started to make an inventory. Keys on a string, fallen in front of my face. Beyond them, my shoulder bag gaped, contents scattered. I ought to pick it up and put everything away. I ought to try to sit up. I couldn't remember what had happened.

Something had fallen on me . . .

The pain had settled into a dull, space-filling ache and I knew that my head would drop off if I tried to move. There was a cool stickiness under my cheek which I wasn't particularly anxious to identify, but it might be related to the little sharp agony above my ear.

I understood that somebody was going to have to help me because I couldn't help myself.

Then I thought about dying. I wondered about it for a while. Barnabas would have to tell Ben I was dead. Would he be able to look after Ben properly? Would Ben have to look after him? A spark of anger suddenly flared and I found I could move after all. I scrabbled for leverage, pushed, and was sitting up.

Then I was sick.

When I'd stopped vomiting there was a faint,

intermittent ringing sound which I'd thought was in my ears and only slowly understood was somewhere outside me. I stared lopsidedly until the slow and swollen thing that my head had become finally identified the sound and then it took me forever to reach my mobile phone and switch it on with hands that scrabbled clumsily, and I was so far out of it that Paul Grant seemed to have been repeating, *"Hello? . . . Dido? Dido?"* forever before I coughed, with the sour smell of my own vomit everywhere and, wondering whether he could possibly hear me, whispered, "I'm in the basement at 23 Horsell Road—I've had an accident." And kept on croaking the same words over and over again, trying to make him listen, when all he seemed to want to do was ask questions I couldn't even begin to understand.

PART 5

Some Consequences

1

My left eye refused to open, but my right eye registered Mr. Spock's desperate bound onto the bed. This was a cat enraged by hunger and neglect. His arrival told me that it was morning, and the light on the ceiling informed me that it was late. The sound of unfamiliar voices drifting into the bedroom warned me that something unusual was happening.

I focused painfully on the door as it swung wide in front of a tray. The tray was followed by Barnabas, who was uttering a string of threats about cats underfoot.

I pulled myself together. "You'll find his food in tins under the sink." Talking was surprisingly painful. "Is Ben all right?"

Barnabas stood puffing benevolently. "Phyllis is giving him his bath. I've made you tea. How do you feel?"

Difficult question. My impression was that some bits weren't working, but that I'd regret it if I tried to explore them. I raised my hand to my blind side anyway and encountered tender swelling and a rough line above the ear which was distinctly painful and strangely prickly.

I said, "I need a mirror," and Barnabas passed me the little one from my chest of drawers without comment.

There wasn't a lot to say. My left eye was buried in a swollen, blackened area extending up and down the left side of my face. Some kind person had shaved a patch of hair over my ear, in the midst of which the ends of blackened stitches protruded from a line of dried blood.

"It didn't look as bad as this last night," I whined.

Barnabas seemed to be impelled to explain. "It's not as bad as it looks. The doctor is coming over later, you can ask her. You'll be fine."

I looked again and found it difficult to believe him.

Barnabas persisted. "You just need to rest. By the way, Pat is coming this afternoon—I think she wants to see you with her own eyes. Also . . ." and he was drowned out by the ringing of the doorbell, a shriek of rage from Ben in the bathroom, and the babble that rose suddenly in the sitting room as though a small crowd were quarreling. My father pushed a cup of tea in my direction, said, "Drink it," and went away.

I discovered that it was possible to sit up after all. Having manoeuvred the cup cautiously to my lips I also found that I was capable of sipping. As usual with my father's brews, it was cool and weak. I listened to the sound of feet thumping up my stairs, what sounded like protests from Barnabas, and unintelligible voices from another direction holding several loud and simultaneous conversations. The noise level was rising, and I'd swear that someone had just lost her temper. I put one experimental foot on the floor beside my bed, but the prospect of trying to stand up made the drumming start in my skull again. Minor riots would have to sort themselves without my assistance. I withdrew the foot, pushed Mr. Spock out of the way, and leaned back against the pillows feeling pale but not very interesting. And the riot arrived.

Ernie Weekes led the way. He was wearing camouflage-pattern trousers, a red beret, and combat boots, and looked like a cross between Che Guevara and a Boy Scout. There was something about his attitude that suggested he had fought his way to me against overwhelming odds. He paused dramatically, blocking the doorway, and inspected my face with a mixture of curiosity and alarm. Then he bounded swiftly to my bed, leaned over, and kissed me firmly on the mouth.

"Hey? You OK? What you been doing?"

Wondering whether it was true that I looked as near to death's door as his attitude suggested, I said that I was pretty much OK. Clearly doubtful, Ernie sat down on the edge of the bed with a bounce that rattled my back teeth and lowered his voice confidentially. "The professor says you been attacked in some old warehouse. If you wanna go digging around basements, you should take me with you. Nobody's gonna mess with you if I'm there." He glared.

Behind his head, Barnabas, supported by Phyllis and a towel-wrapped baby, loomed.

I waved reassurance at them and said quickly, "Ernie, believe me, next time I'm hiring a bodyguard, and I mean you."

"So who was it? I'll sort him out."

I looked at him. The face belonged to an eager ten-year-old, but the body on the edge of my bed oozed determination, reliability, and strength. It occurred to me that if he *had* been with me yesterday I'd almost certainly be a great deal healthier now.

I said slowly, "When I've got everything sussed, I'll tell you about it. Are you going to be working on the catalogue?"

"If that's OK. If the professor's got stuff for me."

Barnabas loomed again. I interrupted his protests at the invasion of my bedroom and arranged for him to supervise Ernie's working day. That accomplished, I received my son onto the bed and we examined one another thoughtfully. After a momentary doubt he reacted quite politely to the sight of his mother's one-eyed purplish face, merely remarking, "Ah-wa-wa-ba!" But could I count on similar tolerance when he was a year or two older? We said a few things to each other privately before Phyllis removed him.

"We're going out with the pram," she said. "Give us ten minutes. He'll never get to sleep around here. As for you—don't take any nonsense from those people. And I mean your father as well as the others. Barnabas says your sister's calling by later, so if you want to go back to sleep now, I'll get rid of them."

Her words reminded me of the undiminished babble in the next room. Barnabas had joined in. Then I realised that I was hearing Paul Grant's voice rising above the rest. The others didn't sound familiar.

Forgetfully, I tried to raise my eyebrows in inquiry. It was a mistake. I squeaked.

"Three of them," she whispered. "That detective,

your friend—the one from the local station. Two others, a man and a woman. They've been in there for the past hour, but we've made them wait until your father thinks you're ready. He keeps arguing with them."

"Why three?" I wondered aloud. Then I remembered. The strangers would be the ones from Scotland Yard whom I was supposed to have met yesterday. Apparently there was no escape.

I could see Phyllis examining my face with a nurse's cold eye. "I'll tell them you aren't up to it. They can come back."

I told her that I doubted whether postponing them would do much good. "Besides," I confessed to myself as well as her, "I want to know what happened. I know that Paul rang my mobile, but after that I was out of it. I'd better get it over with and have a nap before my sister gets here. She's a bit over-protective."

Phyllis had met Pat, who is a couple of years older than I am and can't forget it. She and Ben vanished without further comment, leaving me temporarily on my own. I was tempted to hide my head inside a pillowcase, but reminded myself Paul had seen my battered face yesterday, and there was nothing I could do at this stage to disguise the fact that I looked like a fourth-rate boxer. I pulled the sheet up straight, leaned back, and watched Barnabas usher the next contingent into the room.

There was nowhere to seat even one visitor, much less three. You could describe my flat as "cosy"; the top floor of the little terraced cottage with a sitting room which stretches the width of the building in front, and the rest of the limited floor space divided between my bedroom, a small kitchen, and a cramped bathroom. I happen to like the place: the shapely Georgian proportions of the front room and the windows, the early Victorian furniture picked up piece by piece in little antique shops and street markets. It suits me. My bedroom, on the other hand, was never intended to hold receptions, not even before I'd slotted Ben's cot and cupboard into the last free floor space. The police organised themselves cautiously into a semicircle, with Barnabas hanging on in the open doorway obviously intending to see fair play.

I winked at him with my good side. "Hadn't you better go and let Ernie into the shop?"

My father ignored the wink. "You may need something."

I assured him that I didn't, and that when I began to feel tired the officers could see themselves out. Barnabas glared at me, growled, "You and I must have a talk," and left extremely slowly. I could hear him stopping to speak to Phyllis before he and Ernie descended to the street. I concentrated on this next segment of what looked like being a busy day.

Inspector Lyon, whose voice had been on my answering machine two days before, was a woman a little older than me with mousy hair, colourless eyes, and the unmemorable face of somebody who based her career on not standing out in the crowd: you might misbehave in her presence out of sheer forgetfulness. She crammed herself in against the chest of drawers, and I could see sweat trickling down her cheek, making a porridge of her foundation make-up.

Her companion, DS Pickles, was a big man with a square, fleshy brown face, thinning brown hair, and dark eyes which gave very little away. His body had thickened; I would say he was probably a beer-lover. Despite the heat he was correctly dressed in an uncreased gray suit. A solid gent. Paul introduced the two of them, his eyes on the damaged side of my face. He looked unhappy. I hoped that it was guilt. It was going to take me a little while to forget that he might have been with me yesterday, even if half of my mind said I was being unfair.

"How are you today?" His voice was formal, a reminder of the unofficial nature of our real relationship. He leaned a little closer. "It looks better."

"I haven't thanked you properly. I don't remember much about what happened, but there was some kind of noise . . . Did you have to break in?"

He nodded slightly. "Whoever attacked you must have left through the area door, and the lock had caught. I had to kick it in. Lucky the wood is old."

I was still remembering. "I heard noise, and then a light came and you were there. And the ambulance people."

I could feel Inspector Lyon bump the foot of my bed as she shifted position. The room really was impossible, but I had no desire to get up. She was asking urgently, "Did you see them?"

That was exactly where my memory failed. "I don't think so. No. I was . . ." But it felt too complicated to explain, so I stopped again.

Paul's voice said softly, "Tell us anything you can remember. Your father couldn't even say what you were doing there."

I shut my eyes and tried, with a brain that still wasn't working. Yesterday had somehow moved into a more distant past. I was just sharp enough to remember that Paul had a fair idea why I'd gone to Horsell Road . . . So he hadn't told them about our conversation.

"I was looking at number 23 because I thought there was a chance that Tom Ashe had been staying there. No, I forgot—the agency told me that he'd been living there. That's right. I got the key from them and checked the ground floor, but then . . ." I tried to remember . . . the sound of running water . . . "I flushed a toilet. That was it. Somebody must have heard it. They must have been hiding in the basement when I got there." Another piece of memory stirred. "Somebody had been going through his things. They were scattered all over the room, weren't they? Someone must have heard the running water, and when I . . ." I stopped again, because it was too difficult to sort out. "I can't remember."

The one with the comical name—Pickles—was trying to be fatherly. "You have a slight concussion. Everything will come back to you."

I opened my eyes and looked at him when he stopped.

"The sooner you can help, the better. We're in the dark right now."

I remembered again. "You're from Scotland Yard, aren't you? And you think that the person who was in the basement was the man who killed Tom Ashe."

The hesitation was so obvious that I could almost see their admission hanging in the air. I decided that I wouldn't say anything else until one of them spoke.

We listened to my clock ticking on the bedside table, and to the traffic in Upper Street. It sounded as though someone had broken down and every car, bus, and lorry in north London was in first gear, trying to get past. When Lyon spoke, I almost missed it. "Scotland Yard, yes."

But Paul had said something else: some other name. I'd remember afterwards.

Lyon said, "Could you start at the beginning and go slowly? Tell us whatever you can remember. You can fill in when you're feeling better."

I needed to sort out events just as much for myself as them, so I started with the night of Barnabas's birthday dinner, when Ashe had mentioned Horsell Road. I explained what I could about his disappearance and return. To me, it all sounded muddled; but the three of them listened as though it made sense. I told them about the little girl who had said that Tom lived in the empty building, then about getting the keys.

Somebody said "Good" in an encouraging tone. It was good. Things were coming back. The stuffiness of the empty building, the smell, the heavy silence. I explained about the locked door in the entrance hall, about going down into the area and entering by means of Tom's unofficial route.

"I didn't hear anything. I just assumed the basement was empty. I went into the back room . . ." That was where it got difficult. "I thought that the ceiling had fallen in on me. I remember being sick, and my mobile ringing. P . . . Inspector Grant came. I'm sorry, I just can't think."

Lyon said, "I begin to understand. You didn't actually see anybody?"

No. It felt as though a wall had been constructed across part of my memory.

"It may come back to you. You've been very helpful."

I couldn't imagine why they kept saying that, because it hadn't seemed particularly helpful to me, so I asked, "What did you find when you got there? Can you tell anything about what the . . . the intruder was doing?"

There was a kind of universal negative murmur, and Inspector Lyon said, "Our scene-of-crime people haven't been able to find much. As you say, the place was a tip. So . . ."

There was something else I did recall. "You were coming to see me. About Tom Ashe . . . Why? I don't know anything about his murder." I was leaning back on the pillows, watching the three of them between my eyelashes, and I saw the glance that the two Scotland Yard people threw at Paul. It reminded me that I wanted to know why two pretty senior detectives were running around London investigating the death of a crazy old homeless man, but something told me not to pursue it until I was feeling less hazy. Instinct, or the thump of a headache. I said, "I can't keep my eyes open any longer. I need to sleep."

Lyon and Pickles made polite noises and extricated themselves from the narrow passage at the foot of the bed. In the circumstances, there wasn't much else they could decently do, though they looked reluctant. I heard one of them speak to Phyllis, who'd obviously been standing guard outside the door. When I looked, I found Paul alone.

I gave him a cautious smile, but he was brooding. "You were lucky."

"I don't feel lucky."

"You might have got more than a headache, you know."

I said humbly that I did understand that much. I was awake enough not to add that if he had come with me he would probably have caught Tom Ashe's killer and I wouldn't be looking like Frankenstein's monster. I understood the rules all right, but I hadn't been very lucky if you looked hard at it.

"Are you all right?"

"I think I need an aspirin."

"They're on the bedside table," Paul said abruptly. He hesitated, and I was already stretching for the bottle and glass when he said, "Wait, I'll get them," so as it happened my hand reached them before his did. When I'd swallowed, the pounding seemed to fade but the tiredness increased.

He was still standing at the doorway, and I could see the funny expression on his face; but I wasn't prepared to hear him ask under his breath, "Why are you so *fucking* stoical?" Nor for him to vanish quite so quickly afterwards.

I said, "What's that supposed to mean?" But he didn't hear me, and I listened to footsteps clattering down the stairs, and to the front door slamming. Then the stoical person leaned back on her pillow. Crying was uncomfortable, but that didn't stop me.

Footsteps came into the room. Phyllis. She said, "Oh." At least, it was the word that's written "oh," but there were some Australian vowels, some "ah"s and "oo"s in the sound, that under any other circumstances would have made me laugh. At the moment it sounded comforting. She was slipping an arm under my shoulders, removing two of the pillows so I could lie flat, and pushing a box of tissues into reach. Then she said, "Bloody men, eh?" and I fell asleep.

2

A clear voice in my ear said, "Special Branch," and I opened my eyes. The room was empty, barring Ben doing waking-up noises in his cot, so I concluded that my mind was playing tricks on me.

Or not. Lyon and her partner were not just Scotland Yard, but *Special Branch*. Paul had said so, but I'd been too groggy yesterday to remember properly. It must mean something. I'd probably have to ask him, if we were still on speaking terms. At least it meant that they were taking Tom Ashe's death seriously.

Good.

Anyway, it was none of my business. Let Paul bloody Grant have his own way. What did he mean by calling me *stoical*, as though it was an insult? A tear of self-pity rolled down my nose.

I threw back the sheet and made myself sit up. When nothing shattered, I got to my feet, balanced successfully, and tottered a couple of experimental steps to the window. Every muscle I owned was sore. I asked myself how I was feeling and my answer was: awful . . . aching . . . depressed . . . and not as bad as yesterday. My left eye was willing to open, and though my vision still blurred it was usable. I tried rolling my head both ways. Warning throb just above my left ear, but acceptable. Everything else seemed to be more or less working. I went on rolling, relaxing sore shoulder muscles, and then hung over the cot for a moment. Ben was kicking thoughtfully, first one leg and then the other. He crowed at me and went back to his work, so I left him and went to face the truth in the bathroom mirror.

It was no worse than I'd imagined. The left side of my head was still swollen, the skin around my eye a puffy mixture of purples and reds just starting to fade to greeny-yellow at the edges. My hair would have looked worse if it weren't naturally curly and cut short, but it was matted with sweat. I twisted my head and rolled my eyes to get the wound over my left ear into my angle of vision. It looked as though it had oozed during the night—the ends of the stitches were matted with dried blood. What I wanted more than anything else was a bath and shampoo, but I remembered that I was supposed to keep the cut dry. Immediately my scalp began to itch. All over.

I applied my hairbrush cautiously while I was grinding coffee beans, boiling water, and opening a tin for Mr. Spock, who arrived hurriedly when he realised I was in the kitchen. By the time I'd drunk half a pot of coffee, successfully changed, fed, and rechanged Ben, then lowered myself into the bath, I knew I was likely to live.

Naturally the phone rang. I debated letting the answering machine have it, but the thought that it was Barnabas needing to know that I was still alive (and bound to assume the worst if I didn't answer) made me struggle out of the bath and limp, wet and cursing, into the sitting room. I caught it in the middle of a ring and growled, "Hello?"

"Miss Dido Hoare?" Not Barnabas.

"Speaking." And dripping on this carpet.

"My name is Leonard Stockton, of Wisby Finch, Solicitors. I am ringing you in connection with the death of a client, a Mr. Ashe."

I stopped feeling abused and began to pay very close attention. "Client?"

"We drew up Mr. Ashe's will."

I said, "Will?" and pulled myself together. The man must have thought I was half-witted. *Tom Ashe? Client? Will?* "I'm afraid that I don't know anything about this. But how did you know that Mr. Ashe is dead?"

"The police contacted us. Mr. Ashe made an arrangement several months ago for his post to come here while he was travelling, though he came in occasionally to pick up his letters. I believe they found some bank statements at his home with our address on them."

I came within an inch of repeating *Traveling? Bank? Statements?* but caught myself just in time, shifted onto a drier segment of the carpet and said instead, "I see. Um. How can I help you?"

"I would appreciate if you could call in to see me as soon as possible. We are on Essex Road, quite close to you, I believe. I hope it won't be inconvenient."

I consulted the little clock above the fireplace. Nine-fifteen.

"I can be there in an hour," I said, "if that's convenient for you."

The formal voice became warmer. "Very satisfactory, thank you. The police are calling here at noon, and I ought to explain the situation to you before then. I look forward to meeting you, Miss Hoare."

I told him it was mutual, memorized the address, and limped stiffly into the hallway asking myself just what the hell was going on. I was standing outside the sitting-room door in a brown study when a key grated in the lock downstairs and I had to take refuge in the bathroom before one of my minders walked in on me. I splashed back into the tub.

"Dido?"

"Barnabas, I'm in the bath. Don't wake Ben!"

"What are you doing in there?" His voice advanced rapidly to the bathroom door and lowered to a whisper. "Why aren't you in bed?"

"I am all right," I decided aloud. "I'm feeling fine. Look, Barnabas, I have to go out."

Barnabas exhaled audibly and said, "I want to talk to you . . ."

"I have an appointment with a solicitor," I interrupted. "Honestly. I'll take a cab. But I need you to babysit for a while."

Even through the closed door I could hear him snort.

3

The offices of Wisby Finch occupied the first and second floors in an early Victorian terrace halfway up the Essex Road. We had barely made ourselves

known to the receptionist before Mr. Stockton himself appeared: a little, pale man much younger than
I'd been expecting from his measured, rather formal
way of speaking on the phone. He nobly avoided any
expression of horror at my appearance, and managed
to look splendidly unsurprised to find me accompanied by an aged father and a small son. He shook
hands gently and ushered us down a narrow corridor
painted and carpeted in Georgian green and into a
wide front office whose book-lined walls, Chinese
silk carpet, and gleaming mahogany furniture suggested that, whatever else Wisby Finch might be,
they were certainly not a budget firm. Which left me
wondering how Tom Ashe could have been a client.

Stockton steered me into a leather armchair while
Barnabas was coping with the baby seat. "Will you
have coffee?"

We made the polite responses and I added, "I'm
curious . . ."

He interrupted me with a raised hand. "I should
explain before you begin that I really know nothing
of Mr. Ashe personally. He came in unannounced, off
the street, about a year ago."

I couldn't prevent myself from saying, "You must
have been startled."

I caught a quick flash of amusement in those gray
eyes. "You could put it that way. I happened to be in
the outer office when he arrived, so I had the opportunity of speaking with him. I was intrigued by his
manner and his speech. I presume you knew him
quite well?"

Barnabas said, "No." His tone was forbidding.

I decided to be honest. I told him about Ashe's periodic visits to the shop, and about finding him slumped in my doorway needing help. I even told him about "Dido, Queen of Carthage." The rest could be kept for later.

My anecdote obviously amused him. "The Latin tag and the evidence of an old-fashioned schooling— I know what you mean. He told me he'd been educated at St. Paul's and Trinity College Cambridge, and I thought it might well be true. I am an Old Pauline myself, but I've never made any attempt to check up, although I suppose I could have done."

I decided to be blunt. "I don't understand how he could afford this firm's fees."

Instead of answering, he hesitated and seemed to be staring through the cover of a yellow folder which he had positioned squarely on the desk in front of him. Eventually he said, "Our charges for drawing up and storing a simple will are reasonable. And Mr. Ashe had some kind of civil service pension, I believe."

"Is that all you've done for him?"

"There was a previous will, which is now invalid; and we allowed him to have his post sent here for collection, as I believe I explained."

"But how did you get my name?"

He untied the tape and opened the file. From across the desk I could see a folded document tied with another tape and a large white envelope without any inscription. He was unfolding the document, flattening it on his desk, and passing it over. "You'll want to read this. It's very straightforward, but let me know if you want me to explain anything."

It was indeed straightforward.

> *This will is made by me Thomas John Ashe, c/o*
> *Barclays Bank, The High Street, Camden Town,*
> *NW1.*
>
> > *1. I revoke all earlier wills and codicils.*
> >
> > *2. I appoint as my executor Miss Dido Hoare*
> > *of 3 George Street . . .*

I groaned, "Why did he do that?"

Mr. Stockton was watching me keenly. "Appoint you executor? He didn't say. I assumed you were related."

I suppressed the impulse to say what I thought of Tom Ashe's fantasies and went on reading, only slightly hampered by Barnabas hanging over my right shoulder. Having appointed me sole executor, and instructed me to have his body cremated, Ashe had bequeathed me free from all taxes "one gold, lapis lazuli and carnelian necklace with its own box and packaging, already in the safekeeping of Dido Hoare." Then: "*I give to my wife Emma the whole of the rest of my estate.*" There was nothing else of significance. I looked for the date. The will had been signed the day after Ashe had come in with the necklace. He had written his signature, *T. J. Ashe,* in a small, cursive hand with long ties between each letter, and it had been witnessed by two people described as legal secretaries: Wisby Finch had supplied not only a solicitor but witnesses.

I passed the document over to Barnabas, whose face was a study. "What am I supposed to do about this? He had no reason to do this to me. What was he thinking of?"

Mr. Stockton hesitated visibly. "I did ask him whether he had obtained your consent to act. He assured me he had. But you should know . . ."

"What?"

He stared at me with narrowed eyes, as though judging my reaction. "You can refuse. In that case you may renounce the obligation—I can provide a form of renunciation, if you wish. Or you could ask either your own solicitor or myself to act on your behalf. The estate will pay any fees. You're under no obligation."

I stared at him, at the document on his desk, at my knees. *Of course I'm under no obligation!—I've done enough for Tom Ashe already. I have a life I need to get on with . . .*

"I gather," the dry, polite voice was saying, "that Mr. Ashe was murdered. You—ah—have had an accident yourself? I was wondering whether they were connected. Perhaps I should tell you that a detective from Scotland Yard has an appointment at noon to discuss Mr. Ashe. It would help me know what to say to him if you were willing to come to a decision about your position. I would recommend that you consult your own solicitor."

I could hear Barnabas clearing his throat and jumped in first: "I don't actually have a solicitor. My father hired somebody when I was divorced, but . . ." I couldn't even remember her name, and I wasn't sure that a family lawyer was what I really needed now. Unless you thought of murder as the ultimate divorce.

My heart sank a little further, and I said, "If I were Tom Ashe's executor, I suppose it would give me some . . ." What did I mean to say? More to the point, what did I really want? I thought of him put down like an old dog in a corner. And I remembered something black moving in the basement room.

Any sane person would say thank you Mr. Stockton and goodbye. I refused to catch my father's eye.

"If I were Tom Ashe's executor," I said aloud, "I suppose I would have some kind of status in all this." I looked at Stockton. He didn't understand. Never mind. I said, "I'll do it. Of course I'll need your help, because I've never done this before, but I'll take it on. Just don't ask me to explain."

"There will be papers for you to sign to set the probate in train. The police will not release his body for cremation in the near term, so those arrangements can wait. We can recommend a local firm if you wish, when the time comes. If you can make an appointment with Miss Aitken for tomorrow I will have everything ready."

Barnabas cleared his throat explosively, signaling his entry into the argument, but all he actually said was, "His wife. Emma, was it? Have you told her he's dead?"

I misinterpreted Stockton's stare. "I suppose I should do it. Will you give me her address?"

"We have no address."

We all stared at one another.

Stockton said gently, "I'd recommend a word with the police. I'm sure they will be only too eager to locate her. But probably this will help." He handed me the large white envelope. It was sealed, but I could feel a thickness of papers inside. "You'll find an envelope addressed to you: he left it with us when the will was witnessed and I imagine it contains information you'll need. There's also a letter from this firm confirming that you have been appointed Mr. Ashe's executor by his valid will, a bank statement which came here two days ago, and a letter which arrived at about the same time. And of course a photocopy of the will."

I said, "I must be doolally," and we left him with only the smallest of cracks in his professional gravity. As for me, I was all too aware of Barnabas simmering behind me along the corridor and down the stairs, but that wasn't the reason why I really didn't feel like laughing.

PART 6

Trust

1

Blowing the dust off the surface of my little Victorian writing desk, I made a mental note that I ought to clean the sitting room and then threw the note away because I recalled all the others I'd made recently. At my age I have to accept my own bad habits.

I stopped for a moment to listen to the murmur of Barnabas's voice in the bedroom. When we'd got home, I'd pretended to be feeling exhausted and accepted my father's offer to get his grandson off to sleep: I needed time to think. Furtively I prised up the flap of Wisby Finch's big envelope. Maybe it held something that would give me a clue to what was going on. I wasn't going to be allowed to escape the paternal lecture Barnabas had been composing ever since Paul Grant had phoned him with the news that I was being patched up in the emergency department of the nearest hospital. Long experience had taught me I'd better be ready with a full account of my dealings with Tom Ashe. I could already imagine the outraged cry, "My dear Dido, you are *mad!*" when he heard the whole truth. Secretly I was hoping that I might find something interesting to distract him.

A sheet of paper and four envelopes slid out onto the desk: the photocopy of the will, which I put aside for the moment; an unsealed business envelope containing a single sheet of Wisby Finch's headed notepaper stating as promised that I was the executor of the estate of Mr. Thomas John Ashe; the window envelope with his final bank statement; a grubby manila envelope with a second-class stamp; and the thing I was looking for: a long envelope with my own name handwritten on the front.

I tore open my letter from the dead man.

I don't know why I expected an explanation. Some practical last word, preferably along the lines of *Dear Miss Dido Hoare, Thank you for agreeing to act for me, and I hope you will not be too inconvenienced. My entire estate consists of £20 which should be posted in a strong envelope to Mrs. Emma Ashe, residing at Dunroamin, Clacton-on-Sea . . .*

I pulled out two sheets of cheap blue notepaper covered with the odd, fluid handwriting of the signature on the will and looked at them with increasing panic.

Dido, Your Majesty, There is nobody else.

Samarkhand is the most beautiful city I have ever seen, but I always preferred Cairo for everyday. Have you ever gone south from Cairo? You can go by road or river, let's say traveling by car maybe through El Minya, Asyut, Sohag? I went there just after the war. You could do anything then. Barnabas if he remembers those days will tell you to trust nobody in this matter. I am very serious, you must trust nobody trust nobody . . .

The handwriting began in an orderly fashion, with those curious long ties between the letters, but as he repeated the phrase down the page time after time, like a forger practicing a signature, the lines began to straggle and sag downwards to the right. When I looked at the second sheet, he had carried the same phrase a quarter of the way down the page, then apparently pulled himself together, slashed a line through his scribbles, signed the sheet *TJA* and stopped.

The hairs were standing up on my head. This was a letter to forget about. A sensible person would say, *Poor old man, I hope I don't live so long that my mind goes . . .*

I was still staring at the pages when I became aware that I was no longer hearing Barnabas's voice in the bedroom and looked up guiltily: my father stood silently in the doorway. "You're looking better today," he conceded grumpily. Presumably that meant he was allowed to attack me. "Now, start at the beginning. No, start at the end. What was Tom Ashe thinking of? What are *you* thinking of?"

I told him humbly that I had no answers.

"He was insane. Obviously. What possessed the man to put you into his will and ask you to look after things? I can't imagine why any solicitor would allow it. Off his head. Though not as mad as you are to agree."

He confiscated my copy of the will and reread it twice with pursed lips. "I suppose his wife must be very old, and perhaps incapable of dealing with an estate. Presumably there are no other relatives and he got it into his head that you are a kind person. You were kind to him." He threw me a glance of pure affection which had the effect of lowering the defenses I always raise against his meddling. "It's perfectly straightforward: if you phone Stockton and tell him you've changed your mind, the courts will appoint some professional to act."

I opened my mouth and said, "I'm going to do it." When Barnabas scowled, I reminded him that Wisby Finch would do the work and I'd just sign forms. "It doesn't seem much, considering Ashe gave me that necklace. It's probably quite valuable. At least, he says in the will that it's gold."

Barnabas hesitated, looked at me, and finally shrugged. "Perhaps we shouldn't have raised you to pay your debts." He sniffed. "I don't like it, you know. The man was murdered. And have you forgotten that you've also been attacked?"

Hardly. I turned the bruised side of my face on him. "I guess . . ."

"What?" Barnabas asked after an impatient minute.

"The last time we saw him he was behaving very oddly." I was thinking on my feet, trying to work out how much I could say to Barnabas without causing panic. "At the time, I thought he was a bit dotty but harmless. Now I wonder. I think he knew he was in danger, and I . . . I think he was hoping I'd make sure that the police didn't let it rest if something happened to him. They almost did, you known. People who sleep rough are always dying on the streets."

"Why you?"

Why me? "Because," I was working that out, "because there's nobody else." The words in his note.

"And I suspect it's your fault."

"*Mine?*"

"Yes." I'd said it almost frivolously, but there was a reason. "The more I think about this, the more I believe he was looking for you. He said something the day he spoke to you—remember? Ours isn't a particularly common surname, and as soon as he saw it on the shop last winter, he must have wondered. When he recognized you, I think that settled it for him. He mentioned Bletchley to make you recognize him. He'd just made this new will. He wanted us to look after his interests."

Barnabas looked at me sardonically. "Then why wasn't I named executor?"

I'd said, "You're too old," before I could stop myself. Barnabas sniffed. "You know what I mean. He was ill and tired, he thought of you as being his own generation and . . ."

Yes, that was right. As though responsibility was something that got passed down like the family silver.

"Well," my father said reluctantly. "Well, I don't suppose it will do you any harm to make sure your solicitor passes on the wife's inheritance. It will be practice for you when you have to do the same for me." I looked at him quickly, and found him glaring. "However, you'd better not undertake any more curious solitary escapades. Apropos, will you kindly start at the beginning and explain what the devil you were doing being beaten up in the basement of a disused factory in Holloway?"

I rebelled. "It's a long story, and I'm tired."

Barnabas said grimly, "So am I. I will accompany

you to the kitchen while you make us both a pot of tea. Come along, I'm listening already."

I walked ahead of him meekly and, filling the kettle, began with the night of his birthday party.

"That's all?" Barnabas asked in the middle of his second cup. "Good lord, what a mess. I need to think about this. There must be something you've missed."

I was jolted by a memory. He noticed. "What?"

I went back to retrieve the papers from the flap of the writing desk, and handed him the crazy letter. He read it through several times. Finally he refolded the sheets and handed them back. "Good lord."

"Barnabas, why would *you* tell me to not trust anybody?"

"I really don't know."

"You must. Are you sure you didn't know him better than you told me?"

"Absolutely."

I persisted. "But it must be because of the old days that he mentions you. Will you try to think?"

I scratched away at this for a while because it was Ashe himself telling me to trust nobody, and in the circumstances I would scarcely need my father to back him up. But he had chosen to word it that way. There was something in the background.

"Unless . . ."

"Unless?"

"There was the general principle of Intelligence that they dinned into us all: keep your mouth shut about your work, don't trust even your closest friend, even your wife, your mother, your child . . . I don't know what that tells us, though."

I wanted to do something. Not just sit arguing

with my father, or hanging around the shop waiting for casual customers and watching Barnabas write catalogue cards. I'd already started investigating Tom Ashe, and now I'd received the genuine authority for poking my nose into the case.

Barnabas would never approve.

"What else do you have in that collection of papers?" he demanded abruptly.

I shuffled out the remaining envelopes: bank statement and . . . what?

That brown envelope bore the signs of long travel. The original address had been obliterated with a black felt pen. The same pen had readdressed it to the bank, and a cramped ballpoint had scratched that out and inserted Wisby Finch in the last available space near the top edge. At least three postmarks had overstamped one another, but it seemed that one of them dated as far back as April. I found a kitchen knife in the table drawer and slid the tip of the blade under the flap.

The only thing inside was a yellowing cardboard rectangle with deckled edges. On one side it displayed the outline of a crucifix with lilies and a bleeding heart at its center, and the motto *Repent for the Kingdom is at Hand*. It looked like a bookmark or a Sunday school prize. There was no writing.

Barnabas was turning it over and over. In the end he said, "I'm not sure that one would welcome finding this in one's morning post. Your friend was religious?"

I said that Tom Ashe had shown no signs of bursting into prayer in my presence. But that wasn't saying much: I didn't *know* the man. The whole business was beginning to depress me again. None of it made sense.

Barnabas muttered, "Nonsense, it's just that we don't see it yet. But . . ."

"But what?" I demanded.

"I was going to say that I'm sure the very competent pair from Scotland Yard will be able to work things out. There is no need for you to be involved."

I said, "No." But I hadn't spoken quickly enough to suit him.

"And what exactly is it that you intend?"

"I'll talk to Scotland Yard again." I knew enough about procedure to understand that the police would have taken a team to Horsell Road. Scene of the crime. They would have gone through the contents of the basement with a fine-tooth comb and then sealed it up. Assuming they were finished by now, Tom Ashe's executor might be able to visit. One thing I had grasped from Stockton's briefing is that almost the first thing an executor does is to list the dead man's possessions for valuation. That room was full of his belongings, wasn't it? Duty called. And where my previous investigations had been stopped was the place to start again.

Barnabas, looking thunderous, was making an effort. Sometimes I'm almost sure he can read my mind. "Dido, I won't ask you not to inspect cemeteries or arrange funerals, or whatever comes next. You may even make yourself a nuisance to the police and I won't say a word. But I do ask you to promise me— most solemnly—that you will not go out searching basements. If somebody manages to kill you next time, you will be leaving both Ben and me to the tender mercies of an orphanage."

Barnabas understands me. Motherhood has made me delicate about certain things. "I promise," I said, "that if I do something crazy I'll take along somebody I can trust." I meant it.

Trust nobody . . .

Maybe my attacker had just been a casual intruder. But who would burgle an empty building? *Trust nobody.*

Ideally, I ought to arrange a visit and then persuade Paul to accompany me. Only something told me, quite firmly, that this would be interfering in the work of another department. As the sign over the bar says, *Kindly do not ask for credit as a refusal often offends.*

I remembered that Superintendent Lyon's number was on my telephone pad, but I would swear that I hadn't moved a muscle when Barnabas squinted at my face and asked, "What are you scheming now?"

So I told him truthfully I was only scheming to spend the next three hours on the telephone asking, persuading, cajoling, and insisting on my legal right of access to Tom Ashe's lair, and threatening the full powers of the Registrar General if Special Branch attempted to refuse me. In response, Barnabas asked me what good I thought I would do, and insisted that if I went anywhere near Horsell Road it would be over his dead body. I consoled him with the promise of letting him have Ben for the afternoon.

As for the rest, my prediction was accurate enough. I practiced saintly patience; and a phone call to Diane Lyon from Wisby Finch did the trick in the end. By teatime I had been promised that the door under the stairs on the ground floor would be left locked but unbolted by the morning, received by motorcycle courier two newly cut keys, and then used the telephone for the last time to arrange a bodyguard for the main event: Ernie, rarin' to go.

By the time that Barnabas had brought Ben back from a stroll round the corner into the churchyard, I felt as though I'd spent hours in physical combat. I roused myself to give my delightful son a bath and a meal: and the three of us slumped in the sitting room in front of the open windows. A tiny breeze stirred.

"I have some chablis in the fridge," I said tentatively. "We deserve it, don't we?"

We contemplated Ben's progress with his own bottle and agreed without speaking again that we did.

"I'll put your papers away," Barnabas said significantly. "I don't suppose you've thought about eating?"

"Salad," I said promptly. "Bread and pâté. It won't take a minute."

But Barnabas was holding out the final envelope. "You haven't opened his bank statement?"

I remembered. "Mmmn."

"Should I have a look?"

I laughed. I'm not the only one in the family with a bump of curiosity. "If you like."

When I returned ten minutes later carrying a tray with a bottle and two wine glasses, a rather tired green salad and the remains of quite a nice slab of liver pâté which surprisingly smelled all right, I discovered my father still standing in front of the desk where I'd left him, and the desk still covered with papers. I angled the tray onto the sideboard instead. "Do you mind eating off your lap?"

He was contemplating the wall. "You haven't

asked. Don't you want to know about the bank statement?"

I said, "Do I? All right, then. But I know he had a
pension of some kind."

Barnabas said, "He has over thirty-two thousand
pounds in his current account."

Curiouser and curiouser, as it says in my favorite
book.

2

Somebody had been at work in Horsell Road, so that
the lock on the door under the stairs turned uncom-
plainingly and nothing prevented it from swinging
open at a push. A naked cement staircase descended
into the dimness.

Ernie said, "You wait here—I'll check it out," and
I stood aside and admired his galloping descent. He
had turned up that morning full of determination,
dressed in the usual semi-military outfit of black
boots, army trousers, and a white T-shirt with a curious design of a winged pyramid with an eye in the
middle. My guardian angel. He poked his head
through each of the doors in the passage, then turned
and grinned up at me. "All clear."

I hadn't expected anything else. Whether it was
Ernie's presence or knowing that the police had been
there with their own particular method of steriliza-
tion I couldn't say; but the place felt empty.

At the door of Ashe's lair I halted and clicked the
light switch uselessly.

"I got it!" A small searchlight beam swept over the

room, and I realized that Ernie had produced a huge torch from one of his innumerable zipped pockets.

I produced my own more modest one from my shoulder bag. "Wait! I saw something . . . on the floor beside the bed. Turn your light there."

Ernie complied, and our two beams focused on a tangle of electrical wiring and an ordinary three-way adaptor with an old desk lamp plugged into it. The adaptor was attached to the business end of that familiar electrical cable which had emerged from the floorboards and was snaking around the edge of the room. I climbed over a semi-visible pile of rubble and tried the switch: a naked hundred-watt lightbulb suddenly flashed into life. The brightness was welcome but what it revealed was not particularly illuminating.

Somebody, presumably the old man himself, had furnished the room with things out of dustbins, skips, and the abandoned rooms upstairs. An old folding camp-bed made of canvas on a wooden frame lay tumbled in the corner; the pillow and an aged khaki sleeping bag had both been ripped open, and handfuls of wadding littered the floor. Aside from old boxes, the room contained several bits of office furniture, probably pieces so old and shabby that the departing tenants had abandoned them. A metal cabinet stood against one wall with its doors dangling. It appeared to have been Ashe's wardrobe and bookcase: at any rate, a mound of what looked like rags lay on the floor in front of it, mixed with tumbled secondhand books. I recognized the cover of the Thubron paperback. The only other pieces of real furniture were a typist's chair with its back missing and an old oak desk without drawers which was in use as a table for a rusty electric hotplate and a plastic bottle half full of water. There was a scattering of battered cutlery and crockery shards under foot.

"He's been turned over," Ernie commented, sounding subdued. "You think the plod done this?"

No, I didn't think it was them. Or at least, not all of it. I remembered my brief sight of the room on my last inspection. No doubt the police had searched the place. They might even have searched it carefully. But so had somebody before them. There wouldn't be anything interesting here now.

The air in the room was stuffy and there was an unpleasant smell of unwashed clothing. I gritted my teeth. "Look, I know it's no good, but we have to search the room."

Ernie grinned. He'd been looking forward to a treasure hunt. "What'm I looking for?"

Good question. "Papers," I said firmly, just as though I knew what I was doing. "Anything with writing or typing on it, even just a scrap." An idea rose to the surface. "Or anything about Egypt."

"Egypt?" he blinked.

"Right. So look at the books too. No, I'll look at the books. I'll start with the stuff that's fallen in front of the cupboard. You begin on the other side of the room. See if there's anything underneath the cot."

I checked that there was nothing left inside the cupboard except dust, and then turned to the tangle on the floor. My books were all there, every one that he'd bought from me as well as others that he must have picked up from stalls or charity shops. I checked each volume separately. They were almost all either Greek and Latin texts or travel books. A couple were about North Africa, and I angled those up to the harsh light from the old lamp. Apart from what looked like a shopping list on one endpaper, they were unmarked: Tom Ashe had not been a book defacer. If only.

Well, I could estimate the value of this part of Ashe's estate: about five pounds on a good day at a car boot sale. I made a mental note and turned to the scattered clothing.

He hadn't been a smart dresser. I picked up old garments one by one, trying to ignore odors as I emptied the pockets and tossed everything as quickly as possible into the bottom of the cupboard. I was left with a little pile of bus tickets, a cheap ballpoint pen, a crumpled, empty super-glue tube, and a Yale key. It didn't seem promising, but these were the only individual possessions I could find, so I tore a sheet from an old copy of the *Telegraph*, wrapped everything up, and stuffed the parcel into my bag.

Ernie was prowling the rest of the room turning things over, picking them up and shaking them, putting them down again. Occasionally he would mumble to himself, and at one point he said plaintively, "*Somebody* been looking for something here. The old guy didn't rip this up himself: looks like a knife to me."

I went over and inspected the pillow that he was holding and I could see what he meant: the tear that was leaking lumps of kapok crossed the weave of the fabric on the diagonal.

"Wouldn't be the cops?" he asked tentatively.

I shook my head. "The person who hit me was probably doing this when I walked in." If I'd interrupted a search, that would explain what had happened: the shadow who attacked me had merely been trying to get away without my seeing him. Perhaps I had been lucky after all.

Ernie grew solemn. "Somebody thought he had money, right? But they didn't find it on him when they stiffed him, right? So they come here for it."

"Maybe." That reminded me. "Ernie, have you seen any sign of bank statements?"

My guardian angel looked incredulous.

"Oh, he did have a bank account," I assured him. "I suppose the police have taken them."

Ernie's expression lightened. "There was an *envelope*," he said hastily. "I put it on the cooker." He had straightened up the desk and its contents, and I saw the envelope sitting on the hotplate. It was an old window envelope, empty but identical to the one already in my possession. I added it to the meager gleanings in my bag. It was the only thing in the room that suggested Tom Ashe had any contact with the normal world. There were no other envelopes, no scribbles, notes, letters, lists . . .

Not any more, or not ever?

If only I'd got here before my attacker, not to mention the police . . . If I asked them, would they tell me what they'd found?

After an hour and a half I took pity on both of us. The room had achieved a more orderly look, though nobody could claim that we'd been tidying it up. Ernie had set the sagging cot on its legs, and we'd searched the bedding carefully, folded and replaced it. It was impossible to tell whether Ashe had ever been so conventional as to hide something in his ripped-up bedding, but there was certainly nothing there now. The clothes and books were back in the cupboard, the eating things on the desk. We checked Ashe's collection of cardboard boxes, and Ernie found a bag of mouldering oranges, but the rest held nothing but old newspapers. He seemed to like collecting old newspapers: you could have built a hut out of what he had there. Or barricades.

"That's it?" I asked.

Ernie scowled. "We haven't checked the floor."

"You mean, under the boards?"

"That stuff," Ernie said.

The floor covering was an ancient, brown patterned lino, dim with cracks and worn patches. I stamped my feet: the floor itself felt solid, but the lino provided a practicable hiding place, and it looked as though that at least had not been disturbed by either the shadow or the police. I found a cracked patch in front of the door and got my fingers under the edge where it was broken. The stuff had once been stuck down, but it cracked loudly and began to pull off in an irregular sheet.

"Lemmee," Ernie said, bundling me out of his way, and set to work. I took refuge in the passage and watched while he puffed and sweated and pulled. It took him about ten minutes to rip most of the stuff up and pile it outside the door. The old floorboards were sound and showed no signs of disturbance, but where the lamp had stood, a small rectangle of dirty paper was left. Ernie pounced and retrieved it, stared, and handed over the receipt for a year's rental of one "mini-compartment A34" in U-STOR of Barnet, dated the previous September.

Ernie and I looked at each other. His grin would have lit a bigger space than Tom Ashe's little den, and it felt as though mine matched it.

"Time for a beer. Come on, my treat," I said and waited in the passageway while Ernie switched the light off, but it didn't need more than the faint daylight that was making its way through from the other room to realize that no publican would let a filthy tramp like Ernie into his establishment. And judging by the look of embarrassment on Ernie's face we were two of a kind.

"Home," I said. "I have a bottle of lager in the fridge, and maybe if we're lucky nobody will recognize us."

"We got it, though," he consoled me.

I hoped that he was right.

3

I sat in the front room, watching Ben fall asleep with his left fist in his mouth. Pure satisfaction.

When the phone rang he woke, momentarily outraged, so that I made soothing noises and let the answering machine pick up the call. The little voice so barely audible above Ben's said, "... *Pickles. Will you phone me at Scotland Yard as soon as you get this? Something has happened, and we need to ...*"

I hoisted Ben over my shoulder and got to the receiver.

"I'm here."

Ben informed him of his presence also.

"Sorry, it sounds as though you're busy."

"He was just going to sleep."

"Oh lord. Sorry." He sounded as tired as Ben and just about as happy.

I sighed. "Don't worry. What's wrong?"

"You were at Horsell Road today?"

I agreed cautiously that I had been there.

"What time did you leave?"

I told him I hadn't noticed.

"There's been a fire."

I opened my mouth, closed it, and thought furiously. Tom's amateur wiring hadn't looked safe. Had we . . . no, I distinctly recalled Ernie switching the light off. Maybe the hotplate?

"Is there much damage?"

"The flames only reached one corner of the room. There's smoke damage."

I thought of the newspapers. It sounded like a miracle.

He was saying, "It would really help if you could tell me when you left, even roughly."

"Sometime between noon and one?" I guessed. "I'm sorry, but by the time we'd finished I was too hot and filthy to worry about anything except getting home for a wash."

"Somebody was with you?"

"A friend was helping me. We did turn off the lights and lock up. I'm certain of that."

"Your friend—would she know what time you left?"

I examined Ernie mentally. I'd discovered by bitter experience that he didn't own a wristwatch. It seemed to be a matter of principle. And no, his wrists had been bare.

"I think not, but I'll ask. As I said, the place was all right, locked up all right, when we left. Was it that amateur wiring?"

I listened to the electronic hum of the telephone line until eventually his voice said flatly, "Somebody broke through the board on one of the back windows. There are bars, so they couldn't get in; but they smashed the glass and stuffed some old petrol-soaked newspaper through the gap and tossed in a match. The caretaker next door noticed smoke at about three o'clock, but by that time it was almost out."

I thought again about Ashe's newspaper collection. Wondered whether anything had been secreted among those pages and if so whether it was gone now.

It was only after I'd hung up that I remembered I should have told him about the U-STOR receipt. Well, I'd certainly have another chance.

PART 7

Negative Evidence

1

I clawed my way out of sleep. London is never silent, but in summer there's a time around dawn when you can hear sounds that aren't drowned in the general hubbub. I listened to Ben's breathing.

There'd been a dream. I couldn't remember details, but I thought it had included Tom Ashe's charred body moving and speaking to me, burned but still horribly alive. I pushed the image away by planning my day. Phyllis was due early by special arrangement, and with any luck I'd escape before Barnabas or the police arrived with good advice or questions. The clock radio beside my bed told me that it was almost six. I pressed the button to listen to the news and fell asleep again before it started.

But at a quarter past ten I was in the Volvo heading back from my first errand, full of a depressing certainty that I hadn't got anywhere and wasn't likely to. U-STOR had turned out to be a huge tin shed next to a football stadium on the northern outskirts of the city, its oversized green-and-yellow hoarding advising me and most of the rest of north London that we could hire secure storage space from ten square feet upwards at very reasonable rates. After a sharp argument with a yob at reception, whose eyes seemed incapable of focusing on anything except my breasts, I'd been allowed in and given directions to locker A34. The key from Tom Ashe's pocket fitted the lock on its slatted door, which had opened into a walk-in space about six foot square containing precisely nothing. Unless you count dust; and I never do. I'd persisted against the odds, threatening lawyers, police, and the army, until the yob had allowed me to look through his register unmolested. Tom Ashe's familiar signature and the letter W revealed that he had been there on 3 April and withdrawn his locker's contents, whatever they'd been. I'd locked up and come away.

I was just turning off the North Circular when the Volvo suddenly emitted an ear-shattering grinding noise from somewhere in front of the steering wheel, and lost power. The sound of an engine trying to eat itself stopped after a few seconds and the old car trundled on towards Archway, but I stored the experience as one more thing to worry about.

I had kept the key to Ashe's empty locker. The space was paid for until September, and if it all got too much for me I could store myself there for a few days. In the meantime I had a catalogue to finish. But curiosity demanded a couple of detours. At the Archway roundabout I turned towards Kentish Town.

There was space outside the underground station so I stopped, switched off the engine, and wondered about my next move. Just to the north of the station entrance, between the pavement and the brick wall above the railway line, was the spot where Tom must have died. A glass canopy on iron supports sheltered a bench. Nobody was sitting there today. Litter had drifted up against the wall, and a stray dog nosed at it without interest and then trotted off into the side road. I don't know what I'd expected to see, but there was no sign that anything had ever happened there. Vaguely depressed, I decided to drive on.

In Horsell Road I stopped in the middle of the roadway and sat with the engine running. The face of number 23 was blind. Somebody had boarded up the doors and windows with chip board, and the building looked more ruinous than ever. Whatever Ashe had kept locked away for six months in storage could well have been here since April. If it had ever been real, and not just Ashe's fantasy, then the black shadow might have discovered it before I ever arrived. *But then why had he come back and set the fire?*

Unless that had just been casual vandalism, nothing to do with Tom Ashe's murder or the attack on me or anything else.

And pigs might fly.

The half of Islington that wasn't away on holiday was shopping in Upper Street, so I had trouble at home. By the time I'd squeezed into a residents' space about five minutes from the shop I was hot-faced and cross, and the sun was near enough overhead that my walk back to George Street was a sweaty business. Seen from the street, the book shop looked dim and cool. Inside it was just stuffy. There were no customers, which perhaps excused the babble of voices in the office suggesting that people were having problems keeping my business ticking over while I went on wild goose chases.

Barnabas popped into the doorway. "You're back," he announced unnecessarily. "It's been a madhouse here."

"Obviously," I agreed, giving a wave in the direction of Ernie's attentive voice. "What's been going on? Do I hear Ben in there with you?"

My father nodded and allowed a smug expression to cross his face. "Just dozing off now. Phyllis had to go. She's taking her husband to the doctor—he had an asthma attack. I'm looking after Ben until she is free again. What about you?"

I brought him up to date on my wasted journey.

Barnabas suggested that he'd told me so, which wasn't entirely fair. "And Ernie has two hundred volumes in the computer. All you have to do is sit down for two minutes and price them."

I nodded. Barnabas's two minutes was actually three hours' work, but it was certainly overdue.

"And the boy detective dropped in for a few minutes." This is my father's occasional way of referring to Paul Grant, whom he blames for being a person under the age of fifty with serious responsibilities. "There was also a phone call from Scotland Yard saying that they must talk to you, and your Mr. Stockton wants you to phone him . . ."

"I have the picture," I assured him. "What did Paul want?"

Barnabas wrinkled his brow and said if anybody could be expected to know that, it was me.

"Are you all right if I leave Ben here for a little while?" I asked humbly. "I'll make phone calls upstairs so I don't disturb you."

My father indicated forcibly but probably inaccurately that he'd had more experience with babies than I. "And Ernie has two younger brothers," he remarked to my back, "in case I am at a loss."

I said over my shoulder, "You're never at a loss," and retreated upstairs with the feeling that I'd had a very rare last word.

I should have begun with a bath, or at least the cold drink I'd been promising myself. Instead, I rang the switchboard at the local station and was informed that DI Grant was out somewhere on business. I started to dial the number of his mobile but left off halfway. He might not thank me for a friendly call in the middle of a drug bust or whatever he was doing these days.

Stockton was in a meeting. I left the number of my mobile so that he could reach me even in the bathroom. As for Scotland Yard, either Lyon or Pickles would ring again: I can recognize gritty persistence when I meet it.

In fact I'd been in the tub for two whole minutes before the phone rang and my answering machine picked it up. Even with the door closed I could hear Lyon's businesslike voice. I leaned back, closed my eyes, pinched my nose, and submerged in tepid bubbles. With luck I could postpone returning her call by at least ten minutes.

The doorbell rang.

I considered pretending I'd drowned. Then of course I struggled into my bathrobe and dripped out to the sitting room to identify the visitor from a window. I wouldn't have turned a hair to see Special Branch surrounding the building: I watch too many old FBI movies. But in fact it was Paul Grant who was standing stiffly on my doorstep in low-voiced conversation with Barnabas. I couldn't hear what either of them was saying, but there was something about the way they were facing one another that suggested that the conversation had become abrasive. Barnabas had been forming his own conclusions about Paul's recent absences. I felt my heart thump, told myself I'd better remember to be stoical and leaned on the windowsill, clearing my throat. They both looked up.

"Give me a minute. I'll dry off and get some clothes on."

Paul smiled politely. "Don't worry. We're chatting."

Which presumably meant that Barnabas was trying to pump him for information. I went at a businesslike speed to pat myself dry, brush my hair over the stitches, and slide into a sea-green sun dress that set off my tan rather nicely I thought. There was no sound from my visitors during this time, and I found Paul still at the foot of the stairs talking to Barnabas and looking, it struck me, evasive.

"I thought you might like to come out for a drink," he said. "Do you fancy the pub off York Road?"

I said that I did.

"We'll be quite all right here," Barnabas said comfortably. "You two probably have a good deal of business to get through."

Did we? I thought I caught a ghostly wink and wondered whether my father believed he was matchmaking. I'd have to ask him later.

2

We settled at a table on the petunia-decked terrace under the shade of a striped umbrella, and I waited while Paul went back for his lager and my spritzer. The heat bounced off the unmoving water of the canal basin; even here there was no escaping it. I closed my eyes.

"Penny for them."

I said, "What am I doing in London when I could be sitting in a lemon grove?"

"You have a lot on at the moment," he replied, and there was something in his tone that hinted at an agenda. When I looked at him directly, he raised his glass. "Cheers. It's nice to see you."

I said, "It's nice to see you too. But?"

"What?"

"It sounded like 'but'."

He put his glass down. "It's just that . . ."

I waited.

"It's none of my business."

"As a friend," I suggested. I was beginning to feel edgy.

"Tom Ashe."

Oh, really? I waited.

He shifted on his chair. "Look, you know what kind of work we do at Area level. Most of the violent crime is dead ordinary: you know who did it, and most of the time they were out of their heads with drink or drugs. Or just out of their heads. A lot of what we do is social work of a kind. We're always short-handed and we have to cope; and we do solve a surprising amount of local crime. And we spend a lot of the time on paperwork."

I can recognize public oratory when I hear it at a pub table. What had I done to deserve this? I went along with it. "You make it sound boring."

"It is. A lot of the time."

I looked at him carefully. Nice brown eyes. "But?"

He laughed. "Barnabas was trying to get me to tell him what's going on and I can't. It's strange, the kind of silence that's settled over the old man's death. I told you I have a friend at Kentish Town? We worked together for a while in west London, so it goes way back. I gave him a call yesterday and he told me that they've been instructed by their own Super to forget the whole business. As a result, of course, they aren't talking about much else up there. But they've handed over the papers, and the local newspaper has been told that Ashe died of a stroke."

I considered this for a moment. The only thing I could think to ask was, "Why?"

"Because Special Branch is looking after everything. Lyon has overall charge. Pickles is doing most of the running around, and seems to have as much back-up as he needs—which is odd these days. All over the death of a homeless old man?"

"They keep phoning. They want me to go down there and talk to them."

"You might want to take a solicitor."

I gaped at him. "Why?"

He laughed shortly. "I don't mean they're going to arrest you. I just mean that you may need a solicitor who knows the ropes. Or . . ."

He stopped. I waited. He fumbled with his glass and seemed to have come to a dead halt. I waited. Two people can play the waiting game.

"You know I wish you'd just answer their questions and then forget about it."

I glared at him.

"I worry about you. All right. Scrub that. There's no reason to worry about you." He scowled. "Why do you have to push it all the time? I just don't like the feel of this. I hear that Lyon is very good—very ambitious. Whatever needs to be done about Ashe, she'll make it her business to do, especially if there's the kind of top-down interest in this investigation that I think there is. Why don't you take Barnabas and the baby and get out of London? Weren't you saying that you needed a holiday?"

Why didn't I? I worked out two possible motives behind this conversation. I preferred to believe Paul did care what happened to me. But I also had to consider the possibility that somebody had told him to have a word. "I'm not going to push anybody. But I can't go away—we're doing a big autumn catalogue this month. Also I am Tom Ashe's executor. The lawyer's doing most of the work, but I have to be around for a while to sign things."

"You could get hurt again."

"It wasn't really like that," I said slowly. By this time I thought I remembered the details of the incident, just the way everybody had said I would. "I walked in on somebody who was where he shouldn't be. He panicked—he was trying to get away before I saw his face."

"You're probably right, but that doesn't change anything. Do I have to point out that you might not be so lucky next time?"

"Why should there be any next time? Why

couldn't it have been just one of the people on the streets who thought he could rob the place because Tom was dead?"

"It could be that," Paul agreed. He hesitated. "Would you like another one? And they do sandwiches."

It was the lunch hour now, and the terrace was getting busy. A couple of girls leaning on the railing over the water looked hopefully towards our table but gave up when they saw me settle back ostentatiously. By the time that Paul returned with seconds and a platter of triangular sandwiches garnished with the compulsory tomato segments and frilly lettuce leaf, I'd had the time to work up half a dozen new questions.

"What do they think at Special Branch? Do you know why they want to talk to me?"

Paul lowered the tray hard onto the table.

"Didn't you hear me? Nobody's telling me anything about it! It isn't my business, it isn't Islington's business, or Kentish Town's!"

He stopped again. I looked at him, but he was looking at the water. Or maybe the two girls. "All right. I've been told not to talk to you about Ashe."

"*What?*"

"Don't pretend you're dim: I was *instructed* by my Super not to talk to you about Tom Ashe! He asked me what our relationship was and I said that we'd become friendly last year. He stopped short of telling me not to see you, but he wanted to. Something has come down from Scotland Yard, or he wouldn't bother. If you really have to get answers you'd better talk to them. They *want* to talk to you anyway. What's your problem?"

I looked at the sandwiches and wasn't sure I felt hungry any more. "That's why you said to take a solicitor." I could feel a little trickle of anger, like bile in my throat.

He said abruptly, "I *can't* help you. It isn't that I won't. Nobody likes this, but I can't do anything about it. I'm just a humble district DI myself."

He was right, but a part of me had been counting on some support here. I tried to look at it from his point of view. I tried to see myself as this *stoical* woman who kept making ridiculous demands on him and then backing off and going her own sweet way regardless. Whoo! I said, "I understand, of course. Are those chicken?"

He said, "Chicken tikka salad," and we talked about the weather.

3

When I got back, Ernie was alone in the back room with the flickering computer screen and the remains of a take away kebab. He confided that he thought "the Professor" and his grandson were probably taking a mutual afternoon nap. I heaved an inconspicuous sigh of relief and said I hoped Ernie had been all right on his own and hadn't had any trouble with customers.

He grinned proudly. There had been two: one old fellow who had "hung around" for half an hour and bought a five pound book, and a young one who chose a pile of things and then, when Ernie had added up the marked prices, asked for a trade discount.

My anxiety levels rose. "Who was it? What did you do?"

Ernie favored me with a reassuring smile. "Just what I saw you do last week. I asked him for his business card, and it said he was from a book shop. It had the symbol on it that you got on your invoices, PBFA, right? So I said he could have ten per cent off. I let him pay by check, but I kept his card. And," he added in a final report, "there's been two phone calls, on the machine. I didn't answer, 'cause it was just the cops. That woman."

I smothered a groan. DI Lyon was growing insistent. "Look, I'd better go and talk to them. I'll be away for an hour or two. Will you hang on here and mind the shop? You can get Barnabas down if there's a problem. Is it all right for you to do some more hours for me today?"

Ernie grinned and said simply, "I gotta save up for when college starts."

I got Stockton's secretary, who told me he was in court until five o'clock at the earliest. Despite Paul's advice it didn't seem worth delaying; and DS Pickles, when contacted on the number he had left, admitted they were anxious to see me at my very earliest convenience. Naturally the excursion took closer to four hours than the two that I'd been planning. When I fell out of the taxi after struggling back through rush-hour traffic, I found the shop closed and an unlikely quartet in the sitting room upstairs: Barnabas on the settee; Ben and Ernie sprawled on the floor where Ernie was feeding Ben a bottle with what looked like a practiced hand—his claim to a couple of younger brothers was obviously accurate; and Mr. Spock giving the impression of overseeing them all from a seat on the mantel, despite the fact that his eyes were closed. There was a jug containing the dregs of some iced lemonade. I confiscated Barnabas's glass and finished it.

"Hot?"

"Unspeakable," I assured them.

My father demanded an immediate and accurate account of my doings, but the truth was merely that I'd spent two hours in an inadequately ventilated office with one full wall of overheated glass window, being interviewed by DS Pickles with an occasional intervention from his boss who had wandered in apparently by chance, if you could believe it. It had been perfectly friendly, but they'd left me with the guilty feeling that I was suspected of a dozen misdemeanors.

I'd repeated the story of my original visit to the basement in Horsell Road. They'd asked precisely what Ernie and I had seen and done on the second visit, and I'd reminded them carefully of my duty as Ashe's executor to provide a valuation of his property. Nobody was so rude as to exclaim, "Excuses, excuses," so I volunteered an account of the U-STOR receipt and the empty storage locker, which seemed to interest them more than it had me. I'd come away minus the receipt, with a clear impression that the yob in U-STOR was about to suffer a police raid because Lyon was the type who wouldn't believe in the existence of the sun and moon without three kinds of corroboration including a written confession from the

Astronomer Royal. In the end I'd signed a brief statement: if it contained any single fact that was useful to
anybody, I couldn't imagine what that was.

"Hey, we di'n't start that fire." Ernie hesitated.
"They don't wanna talk to me, do they?"

Barnabas understood the problem and said,
"Probably not, but if they do I will go with you. I'll
see to it that there isn't any trouble."

Ernie flashed a grin and proceeded to burp Ben. I
expelled my own sigh of relief; like any working
mother, I'm always on the lookout for emergency
babysitters. I began to dream of Ernie teaching little
Ben to use the computer.

The phone rang.

"Leonard Stockton here. A problem?"

I said that I hoped not, and told him about Paul
Grant's advice. He heard me out, paused, and said,
"How interesting! But there wasn't a difficulty?"

The question made me hesitate in my turn. "Not
as far as I could see." What had worried me was the
way that somebody had been able to *instruct* a man I'd
thought of as a friend not to help me. But I was conscious of two pairs of ears listening to my end of the
conversation.

His voice came through again. "I phoned you
originally because I've been on to the bank to notify
them of Mr. Ashe's death. I asked them to let me have
copies of his statements for the past twelve months,
and they turned up in the morning's post. Curious
things they are. I think I'd better send them on to
you. You don't by any chance have a fax machine?"

I told him that by some chance I did, in the office
downstairs, and he promised to send them straight

through. And as I stood in the office five minutes later, looking with increasing surprise at the long trail of paper unrolling from my machine, my respect for his sharpness grew. When the machine gave a final ping and switched itself off, I tore the flimsy stuff off the roll and sat down with it.

Each month's statement had consisted of a single sheet addressed to Tom Ashe care of Wisby Finch. They were basically identical. There was one deposit, made each month on or about the tenth, for the sum of £301.52, rising in April to £310.38. The source was identified by the initials TPA. All the other items were cash-card withdrawals, mostly for twenty pounds at a time. The machines that Ashe had used were identified by their locations, and the odd thing was that he had rarely revisited any one cash machine more than two or three times in the course of a year. In geographical terms, the withdrawals had been made from Enfield to Kingston upon Thames, and from Uxbridge to Greenwich. You would have thought that he spent his whole life travelling on buses.

The most extraordinary thing, though, was that he had begun the period which the statements covered with a balance of nearly thirty-one thousand pounds, and ended it over thirty-two: savings of half his income. If only I could manage that . . . Of course it didn't imply a very high standard of living.

I went back to the beginning and read through the smudged lines again. There had to be some kind of pattern? There was. Ashe had been withdrawing at a higher rate before the end of March than since. Once during every week, until the last occasion on March 24th, he had withdrawn at least sixty pounds, sometimes a little more. This was in addition to smaller, more irregular drawings on other dates. I leafed back through the desk calendar and found that the big withdrawals had been made on Fridays.

Rent! He had been renting bed and breakfast in some hostel or cheap lodging house. Towards the end of March those withdrawals had ceased. Presumably that was when he had moved into number 23.

It seemed as though I really needed to find out where he had been living, whether he'd had friends there, and why he had left. It wasn't because he could no longer afford it. The picture came to me of Tom Ashe furtively bundling up a couple of books, a few bits of old clothing, and a cash card backed by thirty thousand pounds, and creeping out of a crumbling common lodging house in a midnight flit.

If Paul Grant hadn't warned me off, I would have phoned to ask for advice. Instead I phoned Wisby Finch in case Stockton had not yet left and was relieved when he answered.

"I see what you mean. It would be nice to know where the income came from and who he was paying rent to, in cash, last winter."

Stockton's little voice came back warmly. "I thought you'd see it. Look, I can tell you about the income as it happens, because my mother was a school teacher. TPA is the teacher's pension scheme. If you wish me to, I can contact them. His wife should be in their records as a dependent: as she'll be entitled to a widow's pension, they will probably have a current address."

I said, "Please!" with a rush of relief. At least one thing might turn out to be simple.

"As for the other," he was going on, "may I suggest something?"

I urged him to.

"If he left lodgings suddenly, it is possible that he may have owed some money there. We should advertise for creditors immediately, don't you think?"

Oh, yes, Mr. Stockton!

"The only problem is, where?"

We tossed suggestions back and forth and finally agreed that Ashe's frequent visits to my shop during the winter suggested local connections, and that modest display advertisements in two local newspapers and the *Evening Standard*, under the name of Wisby Finch, would be the best way of getting news. When I finally hung up, folded the fax paper neatly, and placed it in a brand new folder in the bottom drawer of my desk, it was with a feeling that things just might be moving now, despite the fact that almost everything I'd found out so far had been negative: no addresses, no checks written to named individuals, no records, nothing in storage.

He had emptied the locker at the beginning of April, just after those regular withdrawals had ceased. Something had gone wrong in March. Something or someone had turned up and Ashe had run away.

I was still sitting at my desk stirring through my speculations when the bell rang. I ignored it until it became clear that the visitor was going to persist. Then I craned my neck and peered around the edge of the bookcases. The arrival was a stranger, a solid man about fifty years old with faded ginger hair, wearing a creased shirt open at the collar and carrying a briefcase. My first thought was that he was a plainclothes policeman. They could have chosen a better moment.

I extracted myself from the desk chair and went reluctantly to open the door. The little Nepalese bell jangled over my head.

"We're closed, I'm afraid."

"I know. I was here earlier, but you were out. You're Dido Hoare."

I agreed, wondering why Ernie hadn't mentioned him. Or had he? Looking through Ernie's eyes, I could see that this might be the one he had described as an "old fellow" who had bought a book for five pounds.

"You bought a book?" I suggested. "I hope there's nothing wrong with it."

He made what looked like an involuntary gesture with the briefcase, and I knew I was right. "No, it's fine." Now, how did I get the impression that he couldn't even have said what the title was?

I said, "Good. Then what can I do for you? I was just leaving." I reinforced the message by standing firmly in the doorway.

He said, "I can come back tomorrow, but it would be better if we talked now. My name is Dennis Ashe. You knew my father."

PART 8

The Honey Pot

1

"But she's dead," the ginger man said harshly. I'd taken him into the office. We were facing each other across the desk top and the piles of cards which Barnabas and Ernie had been working on.

"Dead? Then why ..." I stopped myself and instead said carefully, "I'm sorry, I didn't know that."

"My mother died five years ago."

"I assumed she must be alive because she's your father's legatee." I was searching the square, slightly jowly face opposite me for some trace of Tom Ashe. "I should explain that he left everything to her. You weren't mentioned in the will, that's why I was so surprised."

He shrugged slightly. He was sweating, and there were wet patches at the armpits of his green shirt. "We were never close. I always thought everything would go to her, but now it'll come to me and my daughter, won't it, whatever was left."

I thought there was some kind of question in that, which was understandable, so I told him: "His pension was paid into a bank account. I suppose you realized he was living on a small teacher's pension? So far, we haven't found anything else." My necklace was no business of a disinherited son. "The solicitor is still looking."

"Nothing? Not even personal things—souvenirs? Books? My father always had his books."

"Nothing that I've found out about yet, except for old clothes and a few paperbacks." I could have sworn that his face stiffened. "What kind of thing do you mean?"

He hesitated. "I don't know. I wish I had just—you know—something to remember him by. A watch? Cufflinks? Some kind of souvenir?"

A funny looking old bead necklace? I added mentally. Maybe the thing really was worth something after all. On the other hand, it *was* strange that somebody who had lived out his three score years and ten, and wandered over large portions of the globe, should end up with thirty-two thousand pounds in the bank and no proper possessions at all, not even an ashtray with *A Present from Blackpool* outlined in seashells.

I thought I'd covered my hesitation pretty well by pulling over a blank card and a stray ballpoint pen. "You might be able to help. The solicitor will need to know your mother's last address and the date of her death. Also your father's previous address—where he was living before last March. And the name of his last school."

"Why?" He seemed amazed at my irrelevant questions.

I straightened my shoulders and tried to look as though I knew what I was doing. "It's to do with his debts. Probate won't be granted until we've made a proper investigation of all his affairs and advertised for creditors."

The ginger man smiled bleakly. "I'm not bothered. Tom never gave me anything. He wasn't even around when I was a boy. I don't need anything from him now, I can tell you that."

But that isn't what you told me a minute ago. So what are you doing, hovering around like a wasp at the honey pot?

What I said was, "Do you remember your mother's address?"

"I remember it all right. She was living with me and my wife when she died." I poised my pen significantly, and he gave me an address in Hampshire.

"Oh. You're just up here for the day?"

He shook his head. "We don't live there now. My wife and I split up a couple of years ago. My daughter lives abroad."

I wrote his name on the card under the Hampshire address and said, "While I'm at it, I'd better have your current address."

"Unh-hunh. It's 14 Station Road, Willesden."

"Phone?"

"Not connected yet. I've only just moved in."

I persisted, "What about your father? Do you know where he was living last winter?"

A rueful shake of the head.

"Or his last school? I suppose that must have been a long time ago."

He shrugged. "The late seventies. I don't remember—some secondary school in south London. It can't really matter."

I was inclined to agree, but as I'd invented the

question for some reason I couldn't quite say, I just shook my head and put down the pen. "Had you quarreled?"

I could have sworn that he looked at me speculatively. "Like I said, he was away all the time I was growing up. We never got to know each other. I think that's what bothers me most. I didn't really know him, and I have nothing left now that belonged to him."

We sat for a few minutes with our own thoughts. His presumably were the hard memories of a man who resented everything his father had never done for him and was facing the fact that there was nothing he could do about it now. Mine, as I was slowly realizing, were focused on the feeling that I didn't like Dennis Ashe. But then if we were being honest I hadn't liked his father very much either.

I heard myself say, "You saw him a couple of weeks ago, though. You were at the hospital."

"Hospital?" He seemed to stammer. "What hospital?"

Had I got it wrong? I looked hard, and noticed the sweat on his upper lip. No, I'd guessed right. "You were at the Whittington the day Tom discharged himself. The ward sister told me about you."

"Oh, then. Well, he phoned me and I dropped in on the old man to make sure he was all right. I didn't see you there."

"Where did you take him when he left the hospital?"

"Nowhere. I gave him a lift to Camden Town. He wanted to go to some hostel."

"Was that where he was staying?" *Go on, lie to me.*

"Well, I left him there."

Well, maybe. I was saying, "I'll let the solicitor have the addresses. There is one thing." I'd been saving it. "Why did your father write a will leaving everything to your mother just before he died? Didn't he know she's dead?"

Dennis got heavily to his feet, his face pink and damp and stiff. "Oh, he knew all right. He was gutted. I'll tell you something: I think his mind was going. When I saw him at the hospital he talked about her all the time, like she was still alive, and when I told him to stop he kept forgetting what he'd said."

He'd spoken faster and faster, as though the memory was running out of his control. I remembered Ashe's eyes flickering and focusing behind my head, and I knew what my visitor meant. Maybe after all the problem was all just an old man's senility. Maybe.

At the door I said, "Will you call me as soon as your phone is connected? I'll be able to tell you then what's going to happen about the will."

He mumbled something and left me in the doorway, and I watched him walking towards the end of the road. He was twenty feet away when I remembered, and called after him, "Who gave you my name?" He didn't hear me, and rounded the corner without breaking his stride.

It was late and they would be waiting for me upstairs, but I went back into the shop to check the bolts on the door into the yard. The *London A to Z* was in its place above the desk for once, and I took it down without any specific reason, unless you count the buzz that our meeting had left me with. There is a Station Road in twenty-two numbered postal districts in London, and also in a lot of suburban areas stretching all the way from Barnet to West Wickham. But not in Willesden. Not as far as I could see.

And then, about five minutes too late, it struck me. *"Well, he phoned me and I dropped in on the old man to make sure he was all right. I didn't see you there."* It was wonderful that Ashe had managed to phone him from the hospital although Dennis didn't have a telephone.

I set the alarm system. These days I don't always bother.

2

I woke up again with a voice speaking loudly in my ear. The voice belonged to Tom Ashe, and it had been saying *"I give to Miss Dido Hoare, free from all taxes, one ancient necklace with its own box and packaging on condition that she will trust nobody."* If I'd believed in ghosts I would have got up and looked into the hall and the bathroom to find out whether Tom Ashe had really materialized to bellow at me. Instead I lay still, waiting for my heart to stop its pounding and asking my subconscious for an explanation. Not that there wasn't enough reason for me to be having nightmares. After a few minutes the echo died out of my head, leaving behind the feeling that there was something I ought to do.

When I'd lain for ten minutes listening to the sound of Ben's breathing, I turned on my side. The clock informed me that my subconscious had chosen to shout just before five-thirty. Softly I swung my feet to the floor, grabbed a handful of clothing from my bedside chair, and crept barefoot out of the room. In the kitchen I splashed water onto my face and slipped into a T-shirt and red cotton skirt. I'd dumped my bag on the settee in the sitting room the night before. I scooped out the keyring and padded down the stairs to the street. In my need for silence I'd left my sandals in the bedroom, but I didn't think there'd be any customers around just now to worry about eccentric booksellers with naked feet.

When I opened the drawer the tang of old dust that had gathered there made me sneeze. The box which contained the necklace was hidden in the bottom under a file of receipts awaiting the calculation of my quarterly VAT returns. I hauled it out, along with my copy of Ashe's will.

My subconscious had remembered the wording inaccurately. The will read, "one gold, lapis lazuli and carnelian necklace with its own box and packaging . . ."

Every time I'd seen the words they'd looked odd, but the oddness of everything else had distracted me. All right then, let's see. I levered up the little brass hook and pushed at the unpainted lid. The musty smell filled my nose. I stirred into the paper and lifted out the necklace. The dull red and blue beads lay cool in my hand. The edges of the little leaves were outlined by small beaten ridges, and the tip of one of them had broken off. When I turned the broken leaf over I could see tiny marks of hammering, and I found that it was easy to leave a scratch in the metal with the tip of a straightened paper clip. Whatever that yellow material actually was, it was certainly soft enough to be pure gold.

I keep a small mirror on the wall above the sink, and I went over to it and held the beads against my throat so that I could see what the thing looked like against my skin. I'd stand by original impressions, I thought: delicate but unattractive. I hadn't the foggiest idea where such a thing had been made or whether it was valuable. Middle Eastern, according to Ashe. But I couldn't tell whether it was the sort of thing some veiled lady wore to display her husband's wealth, or just the equivalent of beads for wearing to an Istanbul disco. Some kind of professional judgment was called for. But anyway, the clasp was missing and the thing wasn't wearable now.

There was perhaps something that I could do myself to work out where it had come from. I shook the scraps of paper onto the desk and turned the box upside down, searching for a stamp or label. The only marks were dirt and a faint smudge of purple ink. I pulled out the magnifying glass that I keep in the long drawer of the desk for inspecting a flaw or inscription in books that I'm offered. Magnification revealed that the smudge was exactly what it appeared to be.

Start again. The will had left me the necklace, also the box and the packing. *Don't lose anything. It's very important*, he had told me. The necklace had been bedded in torn scraps of yellowing newsprint. I switched on the desk lamp and brought out the magnifying glass once more. There's nothing more incomprehensible than jigsaw scraps of old newspapers, but it was easy to see that they would have been of limited value to me even in one piece: I can recognize Arabic but I certainly can't read it.

Barnabas had told me that he wasn't sleeping well in the heat, so I decided to gamble he'd be awake and breakfasting. The voice that answered the phone was, as I'd expected, thoroughly alert.

I said, "Barnabas, how's your Arabic?" and explained.

"I shall take a taxi." He cut me off before I could tell him I'd be upstairs with Ben, who'd been left on his own for long enough. I abandoned the scraps where they were—the paper was brittle with age, and the less handling they got, the more legible they would be—and lowered the beads into the empty box. After a moment's uncertainty I put that out of sight again in the bottom of the drawer. If the necklace turned out to be in the diamond rather than cut-glass category, I'd put it somewhere safer, but for the moment I just set the alarm system carefully and then found myself looking furtively left and right over my shoulder as I locked the door. But George Street is not full of early risers, and there was nobody in sight to wonder at my furtive exit from my own shop.

3

"The thing about this," Barnabas said abruptly, "is that it's Arabic. Your gentleman admirer could have bought the necklace anywhere from Morocco through to the Gulf States. He could have got it in Cairo, certainly. Or stolen it. Or whatever he did."

I said, "I know it's Arabic. What I was wondering is whether there's something odd about these scraps of paper."

"Odd?" Barnabas said. "What kind of odd?"

I explained again about the wording of the will, and about Tom Ashe's curious injunction.

When I'd finished he looked doubtful. "I wouldn't want to rely on the scrupulous textual analysis of his every syllable—would you? It's not as though the old man was rational. His mind might have been just unstable enough for him to feel it important that your memento should be kept just the way it was."

"It isn't rational that he should have left the necklace to me at all," I pointed out sharply. "Not if it's really made of gold and semi-precious stones. It could be worth a few thousand pounds."

Barnabas looked amused. "I suppose that a court might regard the whole thing as proof upon proof of mental incompetence, casting further doubt on the will. If anything more were needed, I mean, in view of his carefully leaving his estate to a dead woman."

"Or living in a pile of rubbish in an abandoned factory when he had thirty-odd thousand pounds cash in his bank account."

Barnabas raised a warning hand and looked pompous. "One should never make assumptions based on the style of people's lives. It is possible that he was an eccentric millionaire, just as it is possible that I have always considered your preference for an independent life running a bookshop, when you could be safely and respectably acting as my housekeeper in a comfortable villa near Kew, proof of *your*—Dido do *NOT* make that face at me just because I offer this as an exemplary warning against assuming that just because Tom Ashe was hiding in a basement, he was necessarily insane. Judging by what happened to him, I'd think it obvious that he was as sane as anybody in trying to keep out of sight."

I took a deep breath. "All right. Let's argue backwards. Somebody did in fact murder Tom Ashe."

Barnabas nodded. "Four or five months beforehand, he abandoned his old haunts, wherever they were. He was hiding, giving false addresses . . . either he was paranoid or he knew he was in danger."

"And since in fact he *was* . . ."

"*Mortal* danger," Barnabas interjected dramatically.

". . . We have to assume he was acting perfectly rationally?"

"Crafty as a fox," Barnabas muttered.

"Because the danger was real, there might even have been a reason for *everything* he did—for leaving hospital with his son, for vanishing, for giving me the necklace, for making the point about the box it was in, for leaving his estate to his wife . . . Barnabas, I'm not sure about that."

"You have her name, her last address in (where is it?) Lymington, and her son's statement that she died about five years ago," my father said mildly. "I presume that this solicitor of yours could send his clerk down to the Public Records Office and get her death certificate without much trouble. In fact, he will need to do just that at the first possible moment."

It hadn't even occurred to me. I said quickly, "I'll phone him . . ."

"We're not finished yet," Barnabas interrupted in an annoyingly tutorial tone. "The careful wording—we are assuming that it is deliberate, remember?—about the necklace, the wrapping, and the box . . ."

I turned and looked again at the three components laid out in the space he had cleared on the desk top. It struck me that my father had been playing with the scraps of newspaper, which were laid singly in rows. "You aren't trying to put those together like a jigsaw puzzle, are you?"

"I was wondering about that, but I don't think it's practicable. Nevertheless, most of them seem to have been torn from the same newspaper. The typography seems consistent, and so is the age and quality of the paper. If we could read Arabic, we might be able to see something that would illuminate things. I think we ought to take them to somebody who can help us. The School of Oriental and African Studies at the university seems the obvious choice."

I said craftily, "It sounds like your kind of thing. The bits aren't all from the same paper, though."

"No, I saw the scrap of English, too. Now that is interesting. If you look, you'll see an inch of sub-heading." He pointed. A wedge-shaped scrap held the words . . . *jesty King Farou* . . .

I looked at Barnabas. Interesting?

"Farouk, I presume. Egypt. He reigned from before the war until he was deposed by Nasser in the early fifties."

"They're *Egyptian* newspapers?" I didn't even have to pull out the note Ashe had left me. *I always pre-ferred Cairo for everyday* . . .

It was the first thing that really suggested a method in Tom Ashe's madness. If it was madness. "We have to get somebody to look at this as quickly as possible. There isn't anything else, is there?"

"On the contrary," Barnabas said. He leaned over

and picked out a fragment about an inch and a half square, a single piece of dark golden-brown paper which was sharply frayed, almost fringed, at the top and bottom. When I touched it with my forefinger, the flaking material felt powdery and soft."

"Better not pick it up," Barnabas said abruptly. "I can't be sure, but it looks much older than everything else here. It's a strange texture, fibrous, and the markings on it are handwriting, not printing. I don't know the language, but the lettering is Greek."

"Part of a certificate of provenance for the necklace, do you think?" I looked more carefully and resorted once more to the magnifying lens. What I was examining resembled a very coarse handmade linen paper with three lines of writing that had faded from black to an irregular brown tint. The square had been the corner of a page. The top and bottom had frayed into those irregular indentations. The right-hand side had been one edge of the sheet, with a narrow margin now fragile and flaking. The fourth side had been creased and torn vertically through the lines of writing, and unless my eyes deceived me this had been done recently, because the fires on the edge looked paler. I handed the magnifying glass to Barnabas and stepped back feeling a little bubble of excitement: this old browned scrap of torn manuscript was Ashe's real message.

Barnabas was hissing tonelessly through his teeth, an irritating sound which I knew meant satisfaction. "I have a feeling about this. It's old. Much older than I realized. I think maybe after all . . . the British Museum. Do you have one of those silly little clear plastic pockets that you use to hold the smallest prints?"

I found one in a box under the packing table and watched him slide the scrap gingerly inside. When it was in without further damage, we both breathed again.

"If you could do without me for an hour or two . . . ?"

"Ernie has enough to keep him going all day, when he finally gets here. And Phyllis is on her way."

He hesitated, looking like a truanting schoolboy. "You'd better put the rest of this away. It's not as though you have *no* customers, even on a day as warm as this is going to be."

"You wouldn't like to kill two birds with one stone?" I suggested. "The British Museum and the university are side by side, and you might be able to save me a trip."

"Just drop into SOAS on the offchance that somebody is around?" He contrived to look both dubious and excited, and we set about sliding the scraps of newsprint into a larger plastic pouch as gently as we could manage. At the back of my mind I was picturing Dennis Ashe arriving suddenly for another chat. Or Sergeant Pickles. In either case, I liked the idea of getting everything off the premises. Something in me wanted to know what I had before I passed on the news.

4

Then I was at a loose end. Luckily Ben was in a communicative mood, so we had a long conversation about his toys until Phyllis arrived. Then I went back downstairs and started up the computer, found the catalogue file which Ernie had kindly labelled "Yourcatalogue" so that even I could identify it, and set about proofreading entries and adding prices in the little boxes he had left for this purpose. Most of the volumes were familiar, so my mind kept wandering. By the time I pulled myself together I'd managed to deal with the last twenty entries in a dream. I'd priced a perfectly nice Zola novel at £3,350, which was pushing it for the twenty-third printing even though it was Swinburne's copy. I removed the first digit, remembered just in time to save my work, and switched off.

A couple of customers drifted in and out in the course of the morning. A pleasant Canadian whom I'd never seen before bought my two-volume 1851 Cowper for the two hundred pounds I'd marked in it without even trying to bargain—and paid cash. A year ago, a sale like that would have thrilled me for hours. I reflected ungratefully that my stock had improved so much during the past fourteen months, given the cash I'd invested after what I still thought of as the great Plutarch scam, that I was getting blasé. Either that or I was still worrying about other, unprofitable matters.

Some physical activity was what I needed. I found a duster under the sink and opened the door onto the sunbaked walled yard at the back of the shop to give myself something which might laughingly be described as fresh air. Twenty minutes later I found myself standing at the top of the stepladder. I didn't know how long I had been motionless, but I was getting a cramp in my left calf. It's in moods like this that people throw books, or even bombs.

I fell down the steps, staggered into the office, and dug out the notebook in which I'd written Inspector Lyon's telephone number. Her phone rang for so long that I was just about to hang up when she answered.

"It's Dido Hoare."

"Good afternoon, Miss Hoare." You would almost have thought, from her tone, that she had been thinking of me. "Is something wrong?"

I said, "Yes, there is. I seem to be wasting a lot of time with this Ashe business. I want to speak to the person who put Special Branch onto the case."

In the silence, I heard a telephone in the background ringing and ringing. Eventually she said, "Actually, I'm in charge of the investigation."

"That isn't what I mean. I want to speak to the person in the Intelligence Services who put Special Branch onto the murder. Assigned you, told you to investigate—whatever it was."

"What makes you think . . ."

I interrupted. "What makes me think that there's something weird about Special Branch investigating the murder of a homeless old teetotal retired schoolmaster with thirty thousand pounds in his bank account, who was murdered by injection in the street while he was boozing with a lot of homeless people?"

The telephone in the background stopped and then started again. She said, "Let me think."

"What do you mean, *think*? It's obvious to anybody that your department is only involved because of who Tom Ashe was, or used to be. I *know* that he was some kind of spy. MI6, was it? I'd've thought it was too long ago to matter now, but obviously I'm wrong, and the more you try to put me off the more obvious it is. I must talk to somebody who has the authority to tell me a few things."

"Tell you what?"

It was my turn to hesitate. What really worried me was the question why MI6 or Special Branch or anybody else could possibly be so interested in Tom Ashe nowadays. I couldn't tell her that I wanted to make a fishing expedition, but really that's all it was. I took a deep breath. "Look, I don't want to do anything that's going to create difficulties for you. It would be better if I could exchange information with someone in the Intelligence Services who really knows Tom Ashe's history." I thought that just sounded plausible, and hoped she would think that what I said actually meant something.

"All right, I'll make a phone call. I'll try to get back to you this afternoon." I was opening my mouth when she added. "There is one thing you'll need: I have Mrs. Ashe's address for you. She's in a nursing home in Brighton . . ."

"She's alive?"

I seemed to have caused another of those silences.

"I told you—she's in a nursing home just on the outskirts of Brighton. The place is called Clifftops Retirement Home."

I mumbled, "Let me get a pen," and stirred among the papers on the desk. I wanted to whimper, but after I'd scrawled down the information I managed to find enough voice to thank her. Then I hung up feeling as though I needed one of those restorative tumblers of Irish whiskey that Barnabas doles out in moments of stress.

If Tom's widow was alive, was I supposed to think that her son, with whom she had been living when she died—or when she *hadn't* died—hadn't known? I stopped and corrected that: if Mrs. Ashe was alive, why had her son told me she was dead? The nasty little thought popped into my head that he was expecting me to pay over the estate to him. But that was nonsense; any fool would know that I wouldn't hand over Tom's bank account without seeing his mother's death certificate. So it couldn't just be that. Could it?

Had he been setting up a con, with either me or his own mother as the victim? The false address he had given made sense in those terms.

Unless Mrs. Ashe was not the person she was supposed to be. That suggested a priority visit to Brighton. A day by the sea: just what I'd been longing for.

PART 9

Oh, I Do Like to Be Beside the Seaside

1

"But why you?" Mrs. Ashe asked with her gentle voice expressing naive astonishment, and a stare like a razor's edge.

I suppressed the temptation to simper guiltily and explained: chance, whim . . . or perhaps Barnabas and Bletchley . . . I thought the story sounded far-fetched, but her face softened.

"Yes—I can see that. Tom has been living so much in the past recently . . . If he noticed your name, your father's name, it might have seemed he had found somebody from the old days whom he could trust. He would have said, 'Somebody who wasn't compromised.' Would he really have recognized your father after so long?"

I told her that Ashe hadn't hesitated. She nodded, and we sat for a while in silence. I could see that she was remembering; and memories were just what I wanted from her.

We had left home early to avoid the worst of the traffic on the tedious route through south London shopping streets and bypasses. My foray had become a family expedition. Barnabas sat behind me, navigating. Ben was being closely watched by Phyllis in a holiday mood and carrying a picnic. I'd left the three of them encamped on a quickly filling beach under two vast beach umbrellas—Phyllis, being thoroughly modern, considers the sun mortally dangerous to babies. Barnabas, traditionally costumed in long beige cotton shorts, socks, and ancient sandals, showed signs of rebellion.

I'd abandoned them to their disagreement about healthy sunbathing, happy that Ben at least was going to be defended from all harm, solar and otherwise, and turned the Volvo along the sea front. The telephoned directions had brought me without difficulty to the big gabled brick house sitting on the clifftop as its name had promised, overlooking a flat blue sea.

There was a small parking area at the side and, at this early hour on a weekday, no competition for the visitors' spaces. And Mrs. Ashe had been waiting for me, sitting at a little table on the terrace above the cliffs: a shrunken woman in a lilac cotton dress, with a cap of dazzling white hair, bright gray eyes, and a wheelchair. We had shaken hands. There was no strength in her grasp, only warmth.

"I won't get up," she had said. "I'm afraid that I have cancer, and . . . No, no—when you are my age it progresses very slowly! Only it makes me feel tired, and the heat makes it difficult. I see you've had an accident—do sit down and rest. Would you like some coffee? I'm afraid I drink more of it than I ought to."

Somebody had left her a pot, perched on a little candle heater, with cream and sugar and two china cups, and she poured coffee and offered thin sugar biscuits and told me that she had been the head-mistress of a grammar school in Berkshire until her retirement. I'd almost guessed that. Something about her reminded me of difficult teenage interviews with my own headmistress back in Oxford.

I explained about the will. She listened silently, looking at the sea, and I told her, "I don't know why he took it into his head to make me his executor, rather than your son."

And she put her cup down gently in the saucer and said, "Our son was killed in a plane crash twenty years ago. Perhaps you remember an airbus crash at Birmingham airport? Everybody died."

I put my own cup down rather less gently. "But I met . . ." No, cancel that one. I took a deep breath. "Somebody came into the shop yesterday. I don't know how he found out about me, but he said his name was Dennis Ashe. That's one reason why I'm here." I struggled, feeling a fool. "I mean, I did real-ize. I've put this very badly. You see, he told me that *you* were dead."

She had pursed her lips and was looking at me as though I was one of her errant fourth-formers. "Our son was named Michael, not Dennis. Apparently your visitor wasn't aware of that. Who on earth could it have been? It was a cruel trick."

"I don't think it was any trick." I'd settled this in my own mind. "It must be some kind of attempt to get money from your husband's estate."

"I suppose so." She frowned. "Can you describe this person?"

I thought back to the interview and described the ginger man as well as I could.

She shook her head decisively. "I don't know him."

"Could it have been another relative?"

She shook her head again. "I have a brother in New Zealand, and my granddaughter, Christine—Michael's daughter—who is living in Vancouver now with her mother. There is nobody else."

I stored away the memory that "Dennis" had also claimed to have a daughter living abroad. If Mrs. Ashe didn't think she knew him, it still appeared that he might know her, or about her. "A friend of Mr. Ashe?"

"Not one that I'd recognize from your description."

I said, "I'm sorry to pry, but I don't quite understand the situation. How long have you been at Clifftops?"

"For several years now. I am two years younger than Tom, and in any case he was not the kind of man to cope with an invalid. So when it became clear that I was going to need help for the rest of my time, he arranged for me to come here. He took a little flat in town so that he could be near, but he was always restless. He gave the flat up about a year ago and moved to London. He still came every Sunday. Even quite recently, he rarely missed."

I looked around at the sea views, the tended gardens, and the solid house. There was a discreet sign at the foot of the drive, but apart from that, we could have been sitting in the garden of her private mansion.

I said, "I hope you don't mind my asking, but are you all right for money? I expect it'll take a while for the will to be sorted out because there are so many questions . . ."

She smiled. "I have my own pension, and I was getting half of Tom's, too. Then there is an annuity that he bought when we sold our house. I shall be perfectly all right for as long as necessary." She laughed. "I am even saving to leave something to Christine. She works with disadvantaged children, which is no better paid in Canada than it is here. I don't need many extras. It is extremely comfortable here, as you see."

The image of Tom's street garb, and the dark and littered den in which he had ended, swam into my head. So did the small fortune in his bank account. It was comfortable at Clifftops and apparently my task as executor would not be complicated by the needs of his widow.

And then, thinking aloud, she had added, "But why you?"

We sat for a while. I was thinking of the strange way in which events of half a century ago seemed to have led us both to this terrace. She said, "I should like to meet your father."

"I'll bring him the next time I come."

"Good. There aren't many people left with whom I could reminisce about the old days. In the meantime . . ." Her voice faded, but the look was sharp. "It's very kind of you to visit, and to fill me in on . . . on what Tom was doing in London. But I have a feeling that you wanted something from me. Perhaps we should get down to it? I am a little tired this morning."

"I don't know where to start."

"The police said that he was murdered, that there is no doubt about it. I hope he didn't suffer."

"I keep wondering," I said, "whether you might know why it happened."

"So do I, Dido, but during the last few months he told me very little about what he was doing. He said that he was looking after an empty house while it was being sold, that he read a good deal, that he was content—nothing important, you see. He was getting forgetful. There seemed to be nothing . . . extraordinary . . . in what he said."

He'd given her a highly sanitized version of the truth. I thought quickly. "When, exactly, did he move to London?"

"Last year at the end of August."

The U-STOR receipt had been dated September 6th.

"Was it only because he was bored down here?"

". . . Yes." She had hesitated.

"Anything else?"

"I would have said he was worried. I felt that something had come up, but he pooh-poohed that when I asked him."

"Why did he come to Islington? Did you live there in the old days?"

"We were never in London, except for a few months just after we married when we had a little flat near the Portobello Road. Near the market."

So Ashe had left Brighton and moved to temporary accommodation in an area of London with which he had no connections. The thought came to me once again that he had been hiding all year. When I suggested that, Mrs. Ashe admitted, "That is possible."

"Hiding from what? Or from whom?"

"He wouldn't tell me anything like that. He never did, ever. Should I explain? We were married in the winter of 1950, at a time when Tom was teaching. He had been working abroad for the Government, but there was an interval of several years when he was here in England. Michael was born then. Tom said that he wouldn't be working for the Intelligence Services again, so he talked to me occasionally about his earlier experiences. Nothing classified, of course—not about the business side of things—but stories about places he had been, things he had seen and done, odd characters he'd met. Some time afterwards, I think in about 1955, they employed him again suddenly, supposedly to work for the Foreign Office on various assignments. But from then onwards he would never tell me anything about what he was doing. For a while, he travelled a great deal and brought me presents from the Orient or the Middle East, but he would never talk about his work. Never."

"And that went on for a while?"

"Yes. For about twelve years or so. I stayed in England with the baby, and when Michael went to school I started teaching again. I ended as the headmistress of a very good girls' grammar school outside Newbury."

"He wasn't still . . ."

She laughed. "Heavens, no! Tom was long past tottering around in the Orient by then. No, he has . . . he was in England permanently from the late sixties. He worked at GCHQ for a while, translating, and afterwards they arranged a teaching post for him. But he was a classicist and that was not a popular subject by that time. Also . . ." She hesitated, and I saw a pink flush that came and faded suddenly. "Also he had a drink problem for a few years."

I told her that I knew about that. "But you lived an ordinary life after he left the service?"

I seemed to have amused her. "I suppose you'd say that. They were very generous to him after he retired, I believe, because there always seemed to be enough money and we lived surprisingly well."

The thought of Tom's well-furnished bank account came back to me. That money . . .

"And no more periods abroad?"

"He went off to the continent alone during term time once or twice, but only for a few days. Apart from that, we took family holidays like everybody else. We went camping in France with Michael on several occasions. There's nothing to explain why anybody would kill him. Is that what you're asking?"

I said, "Would you tell me about the time before that? Where did you meet him? Did you know him during the war?"

She laughed. "Didn't you know? I met him at Bletchley. I was in the typing pool. There were a lot of girls, and we managed to have a very good time. I left at the end of war in Europe and began my teacher training. My parents didn't think it was necessary for me to go to university, but I made them agree that I could attend a training college. And then I met Tom again just after I qualified, and we were married within a few months."

The necklace and the scraps of newspaper belonged to those years, and maybe the mad note Tom Ashe had left for me, and everything else too.

I said, "Tell me about the early years, will you?"

2

There were three of them, she said, always hanging around Bletchley together: Tom, Sammy Butler, and Peter Mellor. They were young, and therefore less intimidating than a lot of the older men who worked there, so the typing pool kept an eye on them.

Tom was the best-looking of the lot, but they thought of him as a bit "serious"—he read Latin poetry for pleasure and he was a whiz at modern languages too.

Peter Mellor had been unremarkable. Mrs. Ashe remembered him vaguely as dark, tough, and silent. Remote. Apparently he had ignored the typing pool. Tom had told her, years later, that Mellor had gone into the Church.

Sammy was a big redheaded man with an equally big voice who liked his beer and his women, but liked himself more than anything else. There was a story about Sammy: Sammy had decided there was going to be a silver shortage after the war, never mind whether the Allies or the Axis powers won, because new manufacturing techniques would require more than the industrialized nations had available. Sammy wanted to be rich, so he'd bought up all the silver he could afford and buried it in the bed of a stream near the Park, reckoning it would be safe there until he could come back and dig it up. Only when he got back there in 1950, the stream bed had been cemented over and culverted. He had never found his treasure—hadn't even been able to recognize the place where it was hidden. Tom had told her about the episode. A good story—they'd laughed about it.

All three men had been recruited to Signals Intelligence as Cambridge graduates, and all three had been recruited, or returned, to the Intelligence Services after the war ended.

"Did they still hang around together then?" I asked. "What kind of work did they do?"

She poured the last inch of coffee into my cup, and I added the final drain of cream.

Yes, they had been working for the same section for a while, both in London and abroad. Tom and at least one of the others had been in Palestine. After the end of the Mandate, they had been sent off in different directions, though they still met whenever they could. One year, she knew, they had gone on leave to Persia and taken some mad journey together. Probably their own idea, not official. They had ridden north in lorries across Afghanistan and crossed the border into Uzbekistan for a bet, swimming a river and walking along the railway line to a place called Teruez where they'd struck the road north. They had got as far as Samarkhand and, by some kind of miracle, back again without causing an international incident.

"That kind of prank. Wild stories," she smiled,

shaking her head. "I was never sure what to believe and what not. But I think it is true that Tom worked at various times out of embassies all the way from Cairo to French Indo-China. I wasn't always supposed to know where he was, but I usually got hints. He loved Indo-China, I think. Saigon was his favorite city."

I put my coffee cup down again. "He told me that Cairo was his favorite city."

She laughed. "Perhaps! But he left Egypt in forty-eight or forty-nine, and he was certainly never assigned there again." Her smile faded. "As a matter of fact I always had the feeling that something happened there which made it difficult for him to return. He never talked about it, but I think he got into trouble with the Department on that tour. I don't know. We were married just afterwards, and I suppose I had other things to think about."

It was all very romantic. But what good was it? I said at a hazard, "What happened to the others?"

"They drifted away a long time ago, even before Tom left the Service. I wondered at the time whether . . ." She faltered.

We sat for a while and looked at the unmoving sea, until I said, "I'd better go and let you rest. I'll come another day, if I may. I'll bring Barnabas next time."

"I should like that. I have no regular visitors now."

"There is one other thing. Do you have any idea whether something unusual happened last March or April? That was when he moved . . ." carelessly I had nearly said "from a hostel." "That was when he moved into the place where he was living." I picked my words. "I got the impression that something unpleasant happened, something he found very upsetting, maybe frightening. I was wondering whether it could have anything to do with his murder?"

The old lady looked at me gravely. "I wonder why you ask me? Does this have anything to do with the will?"

"In a way it does," I said, and told her about the necklace and the letter Tom had left with the solicitor.

There was a care attendant approaching across the grass, and Mrs. Ashe smiled at her and then turned to me again, with the smile wiped from her face. "I see. But it might only have been his age or the effects of his illness."

"Except that he *was* murdered, probably by the person who set fire to his room and attacked me there. I wondered if somebody thought he had something hidden? Possibly something that would identify the murderer? And then there was the man who said that he was your son and told me you were dead. I can't imagine *why* anybody would do that. He must have guessed that I'd soon find out the truth."

"I see," she said again. "I see, but I don't really understand anything. You're sure of all this?"

The attendant arrived, a plump woman with a professional smile. "If you're ready, Mrs. Ashe, I've come to take you back to your room."

"I am ready," Mrs. Ashe said. Her face had grown strained. "Dido, I've written your number into my notebook. I will phone if I remember anything. But don't hope too much that I will be able to help. If anything did happen last March, Tom would never have let me know. Our marriage was based on my willingness *not* to know about most things: he used to say that it was the only way for me to be safe."

"And was he right?" I asked.

She smiled a little. "I always worried about him. I am going to lie down before my luncheon. Will you come again soon?"

I said that I would, and I meant to keep my word.

3

"Then who the devil is Dennis?" Barnabas snapped. As though in response, something under the hood of the Volvo burst into a metallic uproar and the car lost power. I pushed the gear lever into neutral and rolled us into a layby. It was supposed to be a bus stop, but I was prepared to argue the case with anything that came along. In the back seat Phyllis had been roused into a babble of exclamations, but she was drowned out by Ben's disapproval of the noise. He wasn't the only one: I tried the ignition key tentatively and got the result that I deserved.

"Turn it off for goodness' sake!" Barnabas shouted. "Now I understand the true meaning of the phrase, 'driven into the ground.'"

"Are we on fire?" Phyllis asked quietly. "Ssshhhh."

I gathered that the question had been addressed to me rather than my son, and told her that I thought we were safe, merely immobilized. In my heart I knew that Barnabas was right and that not even a big Volvo should be expected to go on forever when the mileometer had already been round the dial at least twice.

"We shall be stuck in this wilderness for hours," Barnabas said grumpily. He'd been cross ever since I returned for our picnic, and I reckoned that Phyllis had been taking charge of Ben too forcibly. Apparently our present situation was the last straw.

I rummaged in the bottom of my shoulder bag, retrieved the phone, and rang my rescue service to inform them that not only was my car making death noises, but I had a young baby and a frail old man with me. The description left Barnabas sulking; but within twenty minutes the desired yellow van had pulled up behind us, and half an hour later a recovery vehicle had loaded the four of us and the Volvo aboard and we were all five being transported home.

"Big end," Barnabas kept muttering. "I would have expected you to notice that the *big end* was going. Now perhaps you'll do as you should have a year ago and get yourself a new car?"

I was feeling gracious. "I shall go out tomorrow morning and buy one," I said, "with air-conditioning. All right?"

It gave me something to think of instead of gnawing on the same old bone, but my mind kept returning to the man who had introduced himself as Tom's son. *Trust nobody . . .*

But when the transporter dropped us off in George Street and vanished with my Volvo in the direction of my service garage, I discovered that good intentions about replacing my absolutely essential mode of transport would have to be put on ice. Because a clipped message on my answering machine in Inspector Lyon's now-familiar tones informed me that a Mr. Simon Cox would be able to see me in the morning at ten o'clock at an address in Westminster to discuss matters of mutual interest. Her tone suggested that she could accept no responsibility for any contact between myself and the monsters of the Civil Service. I was left wondering whether I ought to take an armed bodyguard, or just a policeman?

PART 10

Recording Angel

1

By six minutes past eight o'clock, the sunlight was already slicing through the gaps between the buildings across the street and crashing down onto the pavement. I made the gesture of leaving the sitting-room windows open as wide as I could force them, though I couldn't believe that this would do anything except let in hot air.

My appointment in Westminster was for ten: I had enough time to worry about what I was going to do there and try not to get cold feet. In the bathroom I brushed my teeth and inspected myself in the mirror. The healing cut above my left ear was decently camouflaged by my hair, and the bruising on my face had faded into a tasteful color scheme in which yellow and pale blue predominated. I could now pass for an ordinary victim of domestic violence, and a layer of make-up would probably hide it. Deciding it was too hot for that particular remedy, I patted powder on everywhere and hoped it would survive long enough to get me through the interview. Which I was not anticipating with much pleasure. In the hot light of this morning's dawn I'd woken with the panicky feeling that I didn't know where to begin. Or even *why*. I'd thought, when I put my foot down with Inspector Lyon (not to say stamped it in a temper), that if only I could speak to somebody who knew the real story of Tom Ashe's activities in Egypt I'd miraculously find out about his recent past too: where all that cash had come from, and whether he was likely to have more of it hidden somewhere. His killer's motive.

You're not Nemesis, just the executor of his estate. Suppose they ask you what you think you're doing?

(. . .)

You're enjoying yourself, aren't you!

Yes, all right, I was. In a way. I confessed to my nearly respectable mirrored face and my restless inner voice that I knew I was behaving badly. No doubt Barnabas, if I asked him, could explain just which corner of my faulty personality held the key to my nosy habits. Or my sister Pat. It struck me suddenly that my internal critic always spoke in my sister's tones. I applied lipstick bright enough to draw the eye away from my bruises, grabbed my shoulder bag, and left.

Phyllis had taken Ben out for his walk before it got too hot—she had a passionately old-fashioned belief in the value of gentle motion in the open air for the rearing of infants, teething or otherwise. I left the flat in Mr. Spock's sole charge, double-locked the downstairs door, and let myself into the shop, picking up the morning's post from the floor under the letter slot as I arrived. There were three envelopes containing two foreign catalogues, from which all the best books would already have been ordered, and a check for six pounds. I flung this treasure down on the desk top, found that my answering machine contained no messages at all, decided to walk around two corners to look for a cab in Upper Street, and dived into my deep bottom drawer in search of the Wisby Finch letter. Dealing with officialdom is easier if you have some legal-looking document to back you up.

The box with the necklace was gone.

I scrabbled around the bottom of the drawer as though it might merely have become invisible. Then I got hold of myself. Nobody had broken in—not with my state-of-the-art alarm system primed. When had I seen it last: yesterday? . . . Monday?

There was a pile of my father's catalogue cards on the desk in front of my nose. The top one said DO NOT WORRY I THINK I KNOW WHERE I'VE SEEN THIS KIND OF THING BEFORE.

Oh. Right, then.

Breathing very deliberately, I filed Leonard Stockton's "To Whom It May Concern" in my handbag and then dialled my father's number. His phone rang until I gave up.

2

The taxi deposited me in a tangle of little streets just south of the Houses of Parliament, by a row of Neo-Georgian buildings whose tenants were so unusually modest that even the street numbers on the doors looked shy and retiring. Squinting against the sunlight I identified the entrance I was looking for: a tastefully tiny brass plate was engraved with the words *Foreign Office Annex.* A few hundred yards to my left Big Ben started up. At the second chime I rang the bell, the lock clicked, and I stepped into a small, cream-and-brown lobby. The door clicked again behind me.

In exchange for my name, verified in a register, the burly middle-aged man behind the reception desk buzzed me onwards into a second lobby identical except for its row of upholstered chairs against the wall, a tall electric fan on a stand, and a woman receptionist who could have been his sister. I offered my name again. She picked up a phone and murmured into it. "Mr. Cox will be right down," she growled, "if you'd care to take a seat."

I chose to stand in the breeze from the fan, and it wasn't more than about ninety seconds before the varnished wooden door to the left of the desk clicked open and a tall man emerged majestically. He was distinguished by a glistening bald head, and by being the first man I'd seen in days defying the heat in a pinstriped suit. I duly noted the tightly knotted tie whose tiny repeated pattern had to indicate either a public school education or membership in that kind of gentleman's club which is worth advertising to others in the know.

"Miss Hoare? Simon Cox. Delighted." He pumped my hand briskly and very briefly, and his face showed no delight. "Will you come through?"

I followed his back down a cramped corridor lined with doors which were all shut. Air-conditioning maintained a dank chill. We turned in abruptly at one of the doors, passed through an abandoned outer office, and emerged in a slightly larger room whose windows were obscured by vertical slatted blinds. I tabulated the neat furnishings: a few chairs; a desk adorned by a black telephone, an old-fashioned blotter, and a small framed picture; also a table of moderate size whose polished top held a folder identified by a thick black file number and fastened with pink tape. Apart from the thing that looked like a family photograph there were no signs of any personal habitation.

We settled ourselves at right angles around one corner of the table, like a conference, and tried to size each other up.

"Inspector Lyon," he said abruptly. "Contacted me. Asked if I could offer assistance. Matter of a will?"

I'd decided that was probably the best way to go about my enquiries. "I am," I said in rolling tones, "executor for the estate of Mr. Thomas Ashe, who was murdered recently." I wondered whether his expression would change. It didn't, of course. "There are a great many problems in the situation—apart from the murder itself, of course. I assume that the inspector has told you about that."

He nodded. His eyes didn't leave mine. I couldn't read a thing in them and began to dislike Mr. Cox intensely.

"I've also discussed the matter with his widow. Of course." His eyes still made no comment, and I began to understand how an earthworm feels when it's being considered for dissection. "Mrs. Ashe was as helpful as she could be, but there was a great deal that she didn't know about her husband's life." I took a breath and jumped in. "That's why I asked for this meeting. I need information about Mr. Ashe's career in the Secret Service because there are problems about settling his estate which seem to have something to do with that."

Mr. Cox said, "I am only a record keeper, you know. Many things couldn't be divulged. Still classified. Precisely what do you need?"

Everything, Mr. Cox. What I said was, "Exactly what kind of trouble was Mr. Ashe in when he left Egypt in the late forties?"

He made no move to open the folder. "Unable to say. There is no official record. Or it might be filed elsewhere. You think there was trouble?"

I gave him the easiest explanation. "Mrs. Ashe. She thought so." The clipped sentence style was beginning to affect me. I decided to exaggerate a little. "She told me that something had happened in Egypt which made it impossible for him ever to go back there. It may have been something to do with the others, I think—he was working with two other men at the time, people he'd known at Bletchley during the war."

Looking increasingly gloomy, he untied the fraying pink tape. The folder held an assortment of forms, papers, and notes, mostly on cheap yellowed paper with blurred purplish typing on it. "Late forties? Yes . . . I see a note about travel documents. Cyprus to London, January forty-nine. He stopped in Paris *en route*. Arrived here at the end of the month. Bit of a fuss—the stopover was unauthorized. Note from him here. Says he'd requested leave. No record." He looked at me and shrugged lightly. "Blotted his copy book."

I thought hard. "Was he brought home because of

something that happened in Cairo? Or was it just the end of his tour of duty there?"

Cox hesitated. "It *might* have been a recall. Abrupt, perhaps. Can't be sure. I see that he had a name for being erratic."

I'd been thinking about Mrs. Ashe's story. She had said that Tom had ceased to work for them for a while, that he had been living in England when they were married. Had he got into trouble about his stopover? Perhaps it was something more serious. I remembered the story of the unofficial trip into Central Asia. If that was really unofficial, it suggested an undisciplined, rebellious young man who liked to go his own way. *Erratic.* Not a characteristic that would endear him to such an employer, presumably.

"Did he ever have an official assignment inside the Soviet Union?" I asked on impulse. "He told me he'd once been to Samarkhand."

"Then perhaps he did." I waited expectantly until he added, "That could still be classified."

I tried another tack. "Where was his next assignment after Egypt?"

That caused another hesitation. "Can't be sure. Possibly a break in service. He worked in this country for a few months in fifty-four, and in the Far East in fifty-five."

"For MI6."

I hadn't made it sound like a question, and when he let it pass I assumed I was right. He was riffling through the final papers, pausing to look at a page which might have been a carbon copy of a letter. It took him a few minutes to reach the last item, and I could see him consider a sheet of paper which looked decidedly newer than the rest. "Took retirement in seventy-six," he said.

"Wasn't that rather early? He was only in his fifties then."

Cox laughed dryly. "Common practice. Like the Forces. They don't normally continue beyond fifty, fifty-five at most. Not like us, beavering along to a pension at sixty-five. No."

I wondered how to put the next question. "Was he . . . Do you get the impression that his career was normal from 1954 onwards?"

"Normal?"

Well, perhaps it was an unusual way to describe Secret Service work. "I just mean normal for that kind of work."

"No record of any official reprimands."

I would have given my eye teeth for fifteen minutes alone with the folder, but short of springing on Cox and hitting him over the head with my chair I couldn't see how.

"Are these the only records?" I asked.

My voice sounded plaintive, which is probably why I seemed to catch a glint of amusement. "No. Almost certainly not. Everything presently available, though."

"Could you find anything else if you searched?"

He looked at me blankly. "If I could, I wouldn't be able to divulge it."

"But it's old—twenty years and more."

"Other records," he said roundly, "might be available in some years' time. Or not. We are very cautious about this kind of thing."

"But what possible harm . . . ?"

"You can never tell," he said.

I took a deep breath. "Who could authorize you to tell me more?"

"Prime Minister," he barked in a voice like a door slamming. "Anything else I can help with?"

I struggled to keep my temper and avoid saying something we might both regret. The interview was turning out even worse than I'd expected. "Yes! As a matter of fact, I'd like to know one other thing. Tom Ashe had two close friends in the Service. Mrs. Ashe knew them: Sammy Butler and Peter Mellor. I need to know where they are now."

I'd anticipated either a blank look or another regretful assurance of ignorance and was unprepared when he nodded. "Special Branch also asked. It happens that I have already supplied the information. Samuel Butler, also known as "Ginger," died of a heart attack at North Middlesex Hospital in June of last year. Mr. Mellor resigned from the Service very much against advice in 1958. He was not granted a severance award and we lost sight of him. Traced to a monastery in Normandy. Apparently a Benedictine monk for many years."

I stared and sat up straight. I'd go a lot further than the north of France to be able to talk to a man who had worked with Ashe in the old days. It was a blow that Butler was dead, but Mellor would do nicely. Presumably he could fill in the blanks that Emma Ashe hadn't been allowed to know about and which I needed to understand before I could judge whether my own job was finished.

"Can you tell me the name of the monastery?"

Cox sighed. "Inspector Lyon has the details. But."

"What?"

"Can't hurt to tell you. Enquired of the abbot and the gendarmerie, I believe. He left three months ago. On leave, but didn't return. Unsure of his present circumstances." I gaped at him. He said, "Better talk to the inspector?"

"I better had," I agreed. New Scotland Yard wasn't far away. I considered marching in and threatening to smash windows until eventually somebody gave in and told me something useful.

"Sorry," he said abruptly. "I know—disappointing. Get in touch if you have any other specific questions. Might be able to find an answer."

But not bloody likely, I finished his sentence silently. Then I thought of one other possibility. "Is there somebody else I could talk to? Somebody who knew Tom Ashe in the forties. Maybe somebody in his department that he reported to?"

The question seemed to take him aback. His pale hands faltered on the file for a moment, and I thought he was going to refuse to comment. If I could push him . . .

Inspiration struck. "His case officer?" I added demurely. It's not for nothing that I read spy thrillers.

"Dead."

He had spoken flatly, and he'd known the answer without even opening the file. Some instinct in me flickered. "When did he die?"

"Seventy-six."

"The year Ashe retired?"

"Indeed."

"How did he die?"

"Shot."

"Murdered?"

He hesitated for too long before he replied. "The inquest verdict was suicide."

"You don't think so?"

"I have no opinion." This time the answer was unhesitating. "I am just a record keeper."

We walked back between the offices to the door of the inner reception area and stopped there.

"You've been very helpful," I said. I meant it sarcastically.

He shook his head and did not smile. "One thing. If among his effects you come across any documents that look as though they might be relevant to his work . . . to us here. I'd appreciate if you'd let us have them. Interests of national security."

"It isn't likely," I said. "There was a fire. If the police didn't find anything when they were clearing up, then I'm sure there's nothing to find. But if I see a big manuscript marked Top Secret, I'll try to make sure that it winds up with you." After I've read it.

He shook my hand. "About Egypt."

My ears pricked up. "Yes?"

"Nothing in the record here, but the Egyptians were asking about Ashe for years after he left Cairo. Did we know where he was, what he was doing? That kind of thing. Of course our people denied all knowledge."

I could feel my jaw drop. Not for the first time. *The Egyptians?* "Egyptian police?" I asked wildly.

"Equivalent of our Scotland Yard, I believe."

"But nobody told them where he was?"

Cox permitted himself a flicker of emotion. "Of course not!"

I said, "Of course not," and saw myself out, wondering just how Tom Ashe had really got possession of my bead necklace.

It was a relief, in a way, to be out in the carbon monoxide of Victoria Street and the real world. I used a pedestrian crossing and hailed a taxi. Shutting myself into its air-conditioned comfort, I leaned back in the leather seat and set about wondering just what minute proportion of the truth in the manila folder I had been given. It was my guess that the only way I could force myself into that file, not to mention the other more interesting and more top secret files that Cox had almost admitted to, would be to seduce the Prime Minister. A project which seemed impractical at the very least. Somehow getting Diane Lyon to reveal what she knew looked almost as unlikely, but that was a road I might have to try if I was going to get any further.

3

When I fell out of the taxi in front of the shop, I found the door locked and the Closed sign in position. Assuming that Barnabas was still off wandering around London with the necklace, I rummaged for the key and let myself in. The whiff of hot air and dust flew up into my face and I stood for a moment. I was having one of those moments of strange satisfaction.

Some people have to earn a living by waitressing or servicing cars or fixing roofs. I get to hang around with interesting books and lots of different customers and colleagues, some of whom are pretty interesting too. Though not many of them as interesting as Tom Ashe, fortunately.

Maybe I should learn to mind my own lucky business.

I pulled myself together when the phone started to ring in the back room, flipping the Closed sign to Open in case a customer just happened past, and caught the receiver as the answering machine began to click into action.

"Dido Hoare speaking."

"Good—you're back." It was my father's voice, humming with excitement.

I said, "I am, and where did you go? Is something wrong with Ben?"

"No, certainly not. Not that I've heard. Phyllis has him, and I'm sure . . . "

"So am I," I said hastily. "Where are you?"

"I'll explain, but—briefly—the people at the British Museum phoned. As I should have guessed, your funny little scrap of paper is actually papyrus, not paper in the correct sense."

Papyrus meant Bible to me. "Is it *that* old?"

"They can't put a precise date on it, but they will make further investigations. They asked me if I'd agree to their sending it to Cairo, and I had to say that I thought that it shouldn't leave the country, as it might be evidence in a legal case. I put it that way—there is no sense in shouting murder and getting everybody upset."

"What is the writing?"

"They were cagey about that, but it seems to be some kind of philosophical text. I suspect that they need a second opinion before they'll commit them-

selves. What I did agree to was their sending pho-
tographs of the piece to a Cairo museum. Ahh—yes."
I could hear the rustle of paper. "That's the Coptic
Museum, Cairo."

"We won't hear anything about it for months," I
said grumpily. "Did you really have to go all the way
over to Bloomsbury just to be told that?"

"No, no, I had my reasons. Incidentally, they
asked me to sign a release form. Saying that I agreed
to contacting the Egyptians about it."

It sounded even more peculiar.

"Also I took the opportunity to drop in at the
School of Oriental and African Studies. A Dr. Sharp
is working on our scraps."

"Has he found anything?"

"Nothing specific," Barnabas admitted slowly.
"Not yet. They really are torn up too thoroughly,
though no doubt with time he could do something
with them. However, he has identified the source as
two or possibly three newspapers from the early winter of forty-eight, at least one of them published in
Cairo. Some of the material is in English, and he
can't be sure about the source although it is of the
same period."

"What about content?" I asked with fading hopes,
thinking, *It must be something about the box after all* . . .

"Hard to say. Mostly political, largely about the
Palestine situation. About which they had nothing
good to say, of course. Also domestic news: trouble
on the railway, various minor crimes, rising anti-
British feeling, a murder in Alexandria, political
unrest . . . all life is there, as they say, but mostly in
scraps too small for Dr. Sharp to get anywhere with

them. I've left them there—he says he'll have another look when he can find the time. He asked if I knew what he ought to be looking for, and I must admit that I wish I did. It seems rather an imposition—he is busy correcting the proofs of a book."

I sat down heavily in the desk chair and stared at the blank computer screen. I'd been counting on getting more than this miserable detail from the day's enquiries.

"Dido?"

"Yes?"

"Your necklace."

Feeling foolish, I realized I'd forgotten it.

"I took it . . ."

"I noticed," I said sourly. "You might have warned me."

He brushed it aside. "That was my real reason for going over to Bloomsbury today. It suddenly struck me that I'd seen it, or something very much like it, before. I wanted to check. It's astounding!"

I counted to five. "What is?"

"It isn't a necklace, it's a headdress. There are two on display in the British Museum which are almost identical. I thought I remembered something. It would appear . . ." He hesitated dramatically. I refused to rise. "It would appear," he repeated huffily, "that your piece is one of the court ladies' headdresses recovered in Sir Leonard Woolley's excavations of the tombs of Ur in Mesopotamia, in the late twenties! They date from about 2000 B.C. Restrung, obviously . . . Well?"

"I'm speechless. Why . . . how does that come into the picture?"

"Small valuable objects are always going missing from archaeological digs. Impossible to keep the local workers from pocketing things. Given Tom Ashe's history, I presume he picked it up for a song from some shady dealer. He obviously had all kinds of opportunities to do that sort of thing after the war. If he was in the habit of smuggling the occasional artifact back into Europe, that could well explain his slightly surprising wealth. It may not be the only thing that you come across. I was thinking of your empty storage locker: you might have a long and complicated search for other illicit valuables."

I might. Tom Ashe's extraordinary bank balance in the face of his modest monthly pension income was starting to make sense. My heart sank slowly into the general region of my toes, and I began to wonder whether somewhere in Ashe's burnt den there had been a little note addressed to me that would have solved this whole problem. Obviously he hadn't named me executor just so that I'd pass the contents of a bank account to his wife. Anybody could do that much, including Wisby Finch. There must have been something very illegal going on which a solicitor wouldn't touch. Why hadn't the bloody man written me a proper letter instead of that mad thing Leonard Stockton had handed over?

Barnabas's voice interrupted the onset of a really bad mood. "Well, what about you? Any luck with your visit to the Foreign Office?"

"Mr. Cox wasn't forthcoming. He said he was, 'Just a record keeper,' and he certainly seemed interested in keeping them. I've never met anybody so unhelpfully polite. He answered a few questions, and I did find out a bit more about Ashe's old chums, though that turned out to be useless." I told him about Sammy's death and Peter's retirement from public life decades ago, and about the death of the suicidal or murdered case officer, so interestingly followed by Tom Ashe's retirement from service.

"But you do know that Ashe was in Egypt when the newspapers were published, and that something happened which interested the Egyptian police and annoyed our people. Ashe must have gone into business for himself." Barnabas was silent for a moment. "It all sounds a rather unhappy life for Ashe and his friends. I wonder whether he turned double agent?"

I considered the sum of our hard information without enthusiasm. Yes, something odd had happened. "But even if they still know the truth, they aren't going to tell me. And unless I know that it has a bearing on Ashe's estate, I don't see how I can make a fuss about it."

There was another silence. In the end he said, "You might talk to that police person about what you learned. She seems fairly sensible and practical."

"She's Special Branch," I retorted. "If she knows anything, she isn't going to tell me either."

"We'd better think about how to handle this, but there's no harm trying her. Also the solicitor. And by the way, have you heard about the car?"

"Heard what?" I could hear my voice getting shrill.

"Ah. Your garage phoned while I was returning your Mesopotamian artifact. In a nutshell, they might be able to repair the car for you but they don't want to. They mentioned a list of other things that need to be renewed. They suggested a four-figure sum. I told them I'd get you to ring them, but that I thought you would be throwing it away."

My tiring day had not, in fact, included shopping. I said, "I can't just go out and buy a new car. Not just like that . . . "

"Of course you can!" Barnabas shouted into my ear. "Don't tell me that every penny you got last year has been put into new stock, because I know it's not true! You have quite enough cash to buy a new car, to say nothing of finding a new flat big enough for a woman with a child, and if I've told you once I've said it a dozen times . . . "

"All right!" I shrieked. "Barnabas, OK, all right, you're quite right about it. I will! I'll do it all this afternoon. Leave me alone!"

He had the grace to laugh. "As a matter of fact . . . "

"What?"

"Talking about money. That headdress thing is quite a satisfactory bribe?"

"Bribe?" I repeated slowly.

"Yes, bribe. Don't be slow, my dear. It must be worth a fair sum. There is money in all this, and I don't mean the petty cash in the bank account. We merely haven't been able to find it yet. But Tom Ashe certainly bribed you to ensure that it is found and passed on where his will says—to his wife. I would have thought *that* was clear enough!"

It was. What bothered me, though, was that these great sums of money hadn't even peeked at me around a corner so far; and I most certainly hadn't the slightest idea where to look for them. I was still so absorbed in this new problem that I literally tripped over the man who was crouching in the doorway of my flat mumbling under his breath and trying to wriggle a key into the lock of the box which held my electricity meters.

I apologized in the tone of voice that is intended to demand an explanation.

"Meter reader," he groaned, limping out of my way mumbling that *some bugger excuse my French* had gummed up the lock, and it was the absolute bloody *end* what these effing people got up to. I was so much in agreement that I astonished him with a dazzling smile as I let myself in.

It was the absolute bloody end indeed. How do you go looking for something whose very existence you can only guess at because nobody will tell you the truth?

PART 11

Redhead

1

The nine o'clock news bulletin was having problems, for once, finding anything more dire to report than the record-breaking continuation of the longest heatwave since records (or maybe the country) began. There were dozens of things crying out to be done, and I was waking up slowly in the armchair under an open window in the sitting room, putting off the evil hour.

Ben drowsed on my lap. Mr. Spock, likewise comatose, slitted his eyes at us from what had recently become his favorite seat on the mantelpiece—I suspect he had decided it was safely above the reach of the baby, whose goodwill my cat still didn't entirely trust. Time will tell, cat.

Across the road, my new car glittered wonderfully. Sixteen hours on, I was still filled with a shamefaced astonishment that this thing actually belonged to me: that I had left the flat yesterday afternoon, descended on the dealer who had sold me the dead Volvo five years ago and serviced it for me ever since, and returned with this. I'd intended, of course, to replace my cherished old car very sensibly with a newer version of the same. But the Citroën had been in the window of the showroom. An estate car of course, almost new, with mean, speedy, Parisian lines. The sun had been shining on its deep, deep blue paint. Just seeing it made me feel glamorous. Suddenly I'd become an impulse shopper. One hour, three phone calls, and a visit to the bank, and I'd driven her recklessly back to George Street.

With the air-conditioning full on.

Who could tell what new peaks of extravagance I mightn't be capable of reaching? Thus begun, perhaps I could venture out again to buy a flat with four rooms, or even five, so that my growing male progeny wouldn't need to share bedroom space with his aging mother?

Before I'd argued myself into departing with a shopping bag full of used fifty-pound notes the phone rang.

Barnabas's voice said, "Good morning, how is Ben? I was expecting you to have gone for a drive in the new car, if you can call that monstrosity a car. That car is a slut. I've been asking myself: do you by any chance intend to run away to Hollywood?"

"That's just what I'm planning, when the rush-hour traffic starts to move again and Ernie has got here and I've spoken to Leonard Stockton to find out when our ads are appearing and opened the mail and incidentally wrapped a couple of books that I ought to have posted days ago . . ."

"Stop—I was only joking."

". . . I was just watching it."

"It's still outside, then? Hasn't vanished during the night in a puff of smoke?"

My father knows me well.

The second phone call was from my sister Pat, threatening to arrive from St. Albans on a shopping expedition. I told her she would be mad to venture into central London with her asthma and our pollution, and offered an alternative of driving out myself, in the new wonder-wagon, as soon as I had half a day to spare.

The third call came just as I replaced the receiver.

"Dido? Paul."

I leaned back in the chair, noting the thump of my heart with a certain annoyance.

"Hi! How is everything?"

"Everything might be better," he said. "This is a business call. I'm over at Horsell Road. There's been another fire, and they did the job properly this time. Special Branch has been told, and they've asked us to find out whether you'd be willing to come along and have a look at the place. If you're free, I'll come and pick you up."

"A look *inside?* Is it safe?"

"I don't suppose they'd suggest it otherwise. But of course you don't . . ."

"I will," I said hastily. "Of course." I've never been able to convince myself that curiosity killed the cat. "I can be ready in five minutes, but I'm on my own so I'll have to bring Ben."

Paul sounded resigned. "I guess we can cope."

It was probably lucky that he was delayed by a more than usually impassable traffic jam at Highbury Corner, because it gave me time not only to fret about finding a clean shirt but, having received an apologetic second phone call, to dip myself in and out of a tepid bath. Afterwards I distracted myself by trying to picture Inspector Lyon changing a nappy before rushing off in a police car to inspect the scene of the crime.

No.

I brushed my hair, examined my face in the bathroom mirror again, and decided that the bruises really were nearly invisible now, and was strolling back to the sitting room when the doorbell rang at last. Paul had the distracted air of a man who has just spent twenty minutes sounding a futile police siren in a heavy traffic jam. He leaned over, deposited a warm but somehow businesslike kiss on my mouth, and received the baby seat with a practiced hand—a parent of five years' experience himself.

"Why does she want me?" I wondered, following him down the stairs to the street. It was a question I had spent the last half-hour debating, but I couldn't imagine an answer. I was actually wondering whether it had more to do with my conversation with Simon Cox than with Horsell Road.

"I do not know how Lyon's mind works," he gritted. "Look, I'll put you and Ben into the back seat. We'll try a detour over east. I expect they're all waiting for us." He had left his car in the middle of the road, its blue light flashing, and I noted that a small crowd was waiting around, presumably to spectate my arrest.

Luckily I also noted Ernie Weekes round the corner, stop, and break into a run. I'd forgotten that he was due. I pulled back out of the car and waved.

"You all right?" he shouted.

I made calming gestures with my hands. "I have to go off for half an hour. Would you believe that somebody broke into Horsell Road and set fire to Tom Ashe's room again? I'm going to have a look."

I trotted Ernie over to the shop, unlocked the door, and switched off the security system.

"You *really* all right?" he growled suspiciously from behind me as soon as we were out of earshot. Ernie regards all policemen with suspicion. He makes no exceptions. "You wan' me to come with you?"

"I am *really* all right." I assured him. "I'll have a look and try to find out what's going on. Frankly, I can't imagine why anybody would bother, seeing the mess the place was in. Leave the answering machine on. I'll be back soon. Can you get on with things?"

Ernie assured me that he still had a couple of hours' work to get the catalogue ready for the printer, and that he would keep a good eye on the shop. Paul was in the driver's seat with the motor running. I returned and settled demurely beside the baby seat.

"All right," I said, winding down the window to try to get some air and winding it up again as we overtook a diesel-belching lorry. "What's going on? Why is Islington back in the picture? I thought that Special Branch had told you to go away."

"They forgot to make it public," he grunted, "so when one of the neighbors noticed the damage they rang us. We went over to keep an eye on it. The DI asked me to contact you. She says that since you and she were among the last people to see the place, you might be able to help her decide whether anything's been interfered with. Why they think it's necessary I don't know. It was probably just local kids."

I doubted that. I wondered whether Special Branch knew more about Ashe's money-making activities than they'd been letting on. If so, they wouldn't believe in casual vandals any more than I did.

At the bend by the workshops, two police cars, a fire services car, and an unmarked white van were blocking the narrow road. A uniformed policeman stood in front of the blockage directing traffic eastward into a side street, and a second one was keeping the local children from ducking under the police tape that had been stretched across the front of the workshops. I couldn't see the little girl who had told me where Tom Ashe lived, but Mr. Shah was hovering outside the door of his shop. Paul braked behind the van and we joined the party.

The basement area of number 23 was a mass of bodies. Two men in white coats with what looked like black suitcases were smoking—appropriate for the scene of a fire, perhaps. A man in the uniform of the fire service was staring uneasily into space while a young woman hung about with photographic equipment seemed to be expostulating with Sergeant Pickles. Inspector Lyon was perched at the top of the steps supervising an unfamiliar plainclothes man, with an equally unfamiliar uniformed policeman, who were getting their hands dirty wrestling with the slab of wood which had formerly secured the area doorway and was now sagging drunkenly from one corner. If I wasn't mistaken, Lyon was tapping her toe. I was flattered that her expression brightened when she saw me.

"Sorry," Paul growled over my head. "Traffic."

I said, "What happened?"

"Come down, Miss Hoare. Don't worry—it's safe."

I hesitated. "I've got the baby with me. He's in the car. Somebody will have to keep an eye on him, I'm afraid."

She said, "Oh," and her eye fixed on Paul, who hesitated significantly, said, "Sure" in a polite voice, and retreated. I went down.

Somebody strong had prised up a bottom corner of the wooden barrier, bending the nails that had fastened it to the doorframe. Beyond the wreckage, the inner door sagged. The interior, for as far as I could see it, was darkened with soot. There was a smell as though somebody had parked a car inside.

I said, "Children couldn't have bashed that in, surely?"

The Inspector rubbed her cheek distractedly. "No, somebody used a lot of force."

"When?"

"Sometime last night. It must be quite dark down there, and apparently nobody noticed them, or him. The caretaker next door rang the local police at about seven o'clock this morning."

"What do you want me to do?"

"Our people have been inside and tell me it's safe." She indicated the men with the suitcases. "I'm just going in for a look before they get to work. I'd like you to come with me, if you would. Just to look around. I think that somebody is searching for something."

"Again," I mumbled.

She smiled grimly. "No—still. I know that you were actually here before the first fire, but it struck me that you might be able to help me decide what the intruder was up to. I'm ready to try anything."

"You still don't have any idea who killed Tom Ashe?"

She looked at me squarely. "No more than you do. We're assuming it was the man Ashe was drinking with that day. I'm also assuming that whoever keeps coming back here is probably the same person, and that he's looking for something. But it's all just guess-work, and I can't get any further. Will you follow me in? DC Moore will come with us. Take one of the torches—the electricity's off."

Somebody pressed the handle of a heavy torch into my hand, and I squeezed through the barrier and followed the others into the darkness. We swept the front room with our beams. The place stank of fire and the walls and ceiling were smoke-blackened, but this space looked otherwise undisturbed.

The three of us made our way over a floor that was soft and gritty underfoot towards the inner door. In the passageway the smell became abruptly sharper. I coughed. We gathered at the entrance to what had been Tom Ashe's lair, beside the pile of lino that Ernie and I had left there. That door too was ajar, its paint blistered. The constable led the way and I found myself crowding after him, as though something unpleasant had been left in the corridor behind us.

The stench was intolerable, both organic and pen-etratingly metallic, and the smoke seemed to have lingered in the air here, catching the throat. Most of the room was blackened and charred, but the damage was worst at the far side. The flames had destroyed the cot and bedding and spread along the wall, catching the edges of Tom's collection of newspapers and cardboard boxes without destroying them. The rest of the furniture was recognizable.

Lyon joined my coughing. "Sorry about this," she wheezed. "Whoever did it poured petrol onto the bed and set light to it. That's what the fumes are. Let's not linger."

"What do you want me to do?"

"Just tell me if you see anything that seems different from the last time you were down here—I mean something not accounted for by fire, obviously. Don't look at the burning: look for something out of place."

I thought this was a pretty hopeless idea. I edged watchfully to my right, sliding over a layer of greasy ashes which I recognized as burnt kapok. Apart from tidying some of Tom's smaller belongings into convenient piles, Ernie and I had mostly left things the way we'd found them. I shone the beam of the big torch on where the bed had been, and the hiding place for the U-STOR receipt, but it wasn't possible to see whether anybody else had been busy there. I made a half-circle turn. This was impossible.

Or almost.

Lyon said quietly, "What is it?"

"The cupboard. I went through the pockets of the clothes in it myself, but I didn't pull the cupboard away from the wall like that, and I certainly didn't leave things in a heap on the floor. Of course the firemen might have done it."

"We'll make sure." She coughed again and at the same time stopped. Moore and I both crowded over her. She had noticed a blackened matchbox lying almost invisibly on the sooty floor.

I said, "That wasn't here," without even having to think about it. Tom hadn't been a smoker, and you don't need matches for an electric hotplate.

"I'll send people in to sift through this mess. I should have put everyone in here after the first fire— my mistake. We're so damned short of forensic help nowadays. Constable, keep in touch. Let me know right away if they come up with anything."

I said, "I don't think . . ."

"Don't think what?"

"There wasn't anything hidden here. Ernie and I looked for anything odd, or personal—even a scrap of writing. We were here for a long time, we even tore up the lino—you saw that. It's how we found the receipt." But I could see in her face the official rejection of any idea that an amateur could have done an adequate search. Perhaps she was right, but it annoyed me. "If that's it," I snapped, "I'm off. We're just finishing the copy for our autumn catalogue, and I have some prices to check."

She thanked me in a quiet, absorbed voice that said she was already thinking about other things, and I pushed my way out between the men in the white coats.

Paul drove back silently, apparently uninterested. Certainly not willing to ask questions. As for me, I was trying to work out what it meant that somebody had not only set fire to Tom's room but returned, broken in again, and finally destroyed everything. Why the

hell had he bothered? Alternatively, if Barnabas was
right that there was a lot of money somewhere, how
did an arsonist fit in? Though I knew damned well
that there hadn't been money in Horsell Road. Not in
that grimy basement. Around some other corner, in
some other storage locker, perhaps.

I suddenly knew that Barnabas had been right,
though: because the man who had called himself
Dennis Ashe had been asking about the thing in a
roundabout kind of way. I understood that now. All his
talk about souvenirs of his father ... The only thing
that I didn't know was whether the ginger man had
also been the dark attacker moving in the corner of
my eye, and the arsonist, and Tom's murderer: but I
was prepared to take bets that he was. Then what was
he after? Not, I decided regretfully, my Mesopotamian beads: they were just my little bribe, not, obviously not, the biggest prize. Which must be quite
something, wherever it was.

2

Paul dropped us in front of the shop. He'd been tac-
iturn and I put it down to the heat and resentment at
being used as a kind of errand boy by Special Branch.
It was hard not to sympathize, but I hoped that he
would pull himself together. I was likely to need him.
I watched his departing car until somebody pulled
out from across the road and blocked my view.

Ernie burst out of the shop in a whirlwind of suppressed energy, grabbing Ben's seat and urging us
both inside.

I stared at him and asked, "What's up?" while he was still saying, "You all right?"

This continuing anxiety about me was so striking that I went on staring. One of my local customers, Mrs. Acker—a silent woman who's been coming in for the occasional good read for three years now— was the only other person in the shop. Ernie hustled us past her with a proprietorial grin and slammed the office door behind us.

"Ernie, you shouldn't . . ."

He dismissed my objection in an urgent hiss. "Oh, *she's* OK, an' I'll hear a bell if anybody else comes in. You gotta *lissen!* It's the plod. They been watching us. Guy turned up in a dodgy old green Vauxhall just after you and your friend left, an' he been sitting there ever since. Di'n't you see him just now? Took off after the other one as soon as he left."

I said firmly, "You're dreaming. Why would they do that? It must have been someone waiting for a passenger. You know how hard it is to find a parking meter around here."

Reproach and triumph mingled on my bodyguard's face. "No way! The guy was sat there in the hot sun for nearly two hours. He musta been melting."

I said with appropriate emphasis, "It was *not* the police. I was *with* the police, looking at Tom Ashe's room. Why would the police leave somebody here when they knew perfectly well where I was and what I was doing? Anyway, if you mean the car that left just now, then they must have been interested in Inspector Grant, not me, from the way they took off after his car . . ."

I heard what I was saying, and stopped. Wait a minute, Dido. Let's think this one out.

"You didn't recognize the driver?"

Ernie shook his head. I wondered for a second whether he has hesitated slightly.

"What did he do while he was waiting?"

"Pretended to be reading the *papers*, but he was always looking this way."

"Did you watch him?"

"After I seen he was looking for you I sorta hung about in front, like I was waiting for customers, an' I kept an eye on him in case he tried something. First I thought maybe he was checking the place out, right? So I locked the door. But he just kept sitting an' that lady turned up, so I unlocked, but I still watched him."

"And he was here all the time I was away?"

Ernie assured me smugly that the watcher couldn't have moved a finger without him noticing.

"Are you *sure* you didn't recognize him?"

Ernie shrugged.

"What did he look like?"

"Couldn't see all that much, with him in the shadows. He was pretty old."

"As old as Barnabas?"

Ernie shook his head again. "Not *that* old. Average old. Say maybe fifty? Red hair . . ."

I said, *"What?"* in a tone of voice that surprised us both.

"Well . . . sort of grayish red," Ernie added hesitantly.

Ben obliged by waking up with an exploratory wail at that moment, which gave me a chance to think as I was picking him up for a hug. Somehow the news that "Dennis Ashe" had returned didn't please me.

So he'd hung around the shop and then driven off after Paul Grant. Why? To find out who this man was who'd been chauffeuring Ben and me around in an unmarked car? Paul had been on his way back to the station, and if Dennis followed him that far he was going to get a nasty shock. In which case, he might decide to come back. I did the obvious thing, which was to ring the number of Paul's mobile and fail to get an answer.

I needed to get Ben out of harm's way.

"Ernie?"

He looked at me with eyes that glittered with excitement.

"I think I know him. It sounds like somebody who came in a couple of days ago. I think he bought a book from you." Ernie's expression changed. "Was that him? He came back later and told me he's Tom Ashe's son. But he was lying."

"You don't worry about him," Ernie said, springing right to the point. "You're OK with me here."

"I believe you," I said. "But I think he may be dangerous."

Ernie looked at me. "He the murderer?"

I didn't want to be dramatic. "He could be. Look, I'm going to take Ben upstairs. If the car comes back, I want you to ring the upstairs phone and warn me. Close up as soon as Mrs. Acker leaves, and don't unlock the door for anybody. There aren't many customers anyway, and if somebody really wants something he'll just have to come back. Have you finished with the catalogue? I'll send it off to the printers in a taxi so that you can stay here."

"You haven't done the prices past page forty-seven," he reminded me accusingly.

I could see the material on the computer screen. It was ten minutes' work if I didn't hang about, and I was in no mood to dither. I passed Ben over without a word and listened with half an ear to the two of them while I supplied some rather approximate values to the last twenty items. Then I retrieved the baby.

"Go on," I said. "I'll leave this inside door open so you can keep an eye on the street while you're printing out. I'll watch from upstairs as well. Don't forget to warn me if you see the car. A Vauxhall, you said?"

But despite my repeated furtive visits to the sitting-room windows, and a good deal of traffic up and down George Street, the watcher remained invisible. If he had been there, and if it had been Dennis, and if, if . . . Perhaps following Paul back to the police station had frightened him off. Oh, I hoped so, because the memory of the lying, sweating, red-headed man was frightening. Next time he came visiting I wanted advance warning and preferably a policeman lurking in the next room.

The afternoon wore on. I tried to find Paul again. The switchboard said that he wasn't at the station, and apparently his mobile was switched off. Then I phoned Scotland Yard and was allowed to leave a message for Inspector Lyon. As they say, there's never a policeman around when you need one.

At three-thirty Ernie phoned with the news that the printout was complete and the copy looked good. I was going to trust his judgment because I felt about as much interest in proofreading as in scrubbing the flat. I gave instructions about taxis and vigilance, and supervised the departure of our work from my window above the street. Then there was nothing for me to do but worry. And wait for the watcher to return.

When the phone rang at about four o'clock, I lunged for the receiver.

"It's there now." It was Ernie's whisper.

I made myself speak normally. "Hold on. Across the road again?"

"This side. I almost di'n't see it. Left. He's got his engine running."

I put the receiver down and edged against the left-hand window, keeping behind the curtain. The second car along had a dusty green roof, and I reckoned that was the one Ernie meant. From this angle I could see nothing except a pair of hands on the steering wheel. He was so close that I could smell the exhaust. I debated going down and finding out about this. What harm could anybody do to me out in the street in broad daylight?

"Ernie? Are you there?"

"Yeah."

"Listen, I'm coming down. I can't see his face from up here. You're positive it's the same man as this morning?"

"Same car," Ernie said.

I couldn't let myself think or start to be frightened. Ben wasn't stirring. At the last moment, because of him, I stopped to double-lock my front door. It took a moment too long. As I turned on the pavement my eye caught the empty space at the kerb and the green car turning at the end of the road.

Ernie fell out of the shop door just as I was cursing

ginger-haired men and green Vauxhalls. It struck me
that he was grinning.

"He saw you coming. When you stopped, he took
off. So that tells us, hunh?"

I sighed. "Yes, but I wish it told us more, damn it!
Ernie, I have to find out who that man really is."

That was when I realized that my confederate was
looking cocky. He put one of Barnabas's index cards
into my hand; it held a car registration number. At
which point I heard the telephone in the flat begin to
ring.

The first call was from Diane Lyon.

I said, "I've had a visitor," and told her about
Dennis Ashe. Her silence stretched out so far that I
began to think I was hearing ghostly conversations
on the line. After what seemed like about five minutes she said, "I wonder whether you need protec-
tion?"

I'd been wondering that myself. I explained about
Ernie. She seemed unimpressed. "Anyway, he's gone
for the moment," I said. "The thing is, I'd like to
know who he is. Mrs. Ashe didn't have any idea. I
think he's the . . . " At the last moment, caution made
me stop.

The inspector admitted that she too would be
interested in knowing more. Her voice, when I gave
her Ernie's number, betrayed just a hint of maternal
approval: at last the children had done something
right.

"Hang on, I'm in my office—I'll run it through
the computer," she said.

I was expecting a delay but there was almost none,
and when she spoke again her tone had changed.

"I've got it. Well . . . the car is registered to a Dennis Butler of Lyndhurst, Hampshire."

I tried twice before I could speak, *"Butler?"*

"It means something to you."

I knew it meant something to her, too, no matter how tight-lipped she was trying to be. "Mrs. Ashe told me that her husband had two close friends. One of them was Sammy Butler. And I've just remembered he was nicknamed 'Ginger.' But your Mr. Cox told me he died a year ago."

"He did." Her voice was under control again. "Would you think that he had a son called Dennis?"

I said that I would think that. "And this man has red hair too. Reddish."

"I believe that it runs in families," she said dryly. "If you'll excuse me, I'm going to put out a call for that car. I'd really like to speak to Mr. Butler. In fact I'm going to bring him in for questioning in case he was the man who was drinking with Tom Ashe the day he died. We'll find somebody who saw them."

My heart was somewhere in my stomach. "He's the murderer?"

"One step at a time. Are you going to be there for the rest of the day?"

I told her that I wasn't sure, and gave her the number of my mobile again.

She sounded dissatisfied but all she said was, "You might try to be careful until we get him. He's obviously taking an interest in you. Does he have any reason to harm you? Something you haven't told me about?"

"I don't think so."

She accepted that after a moment's pause. "I'll get

Islington to send a car down your street every half-hour. You keep your eyes open and don't wander around alone after dark."

. . . *and avoid men carrying hypodermics*, I added mentally. Such good advice that when Paul Grant rang ten minutes later I broke all my resolutions and invited him to stay for dinner, where I told him everything. He seemed to feel that in the circumstances the least he could do was spend the night. As a result of which I stopped listening for the sound of cars drawing up in the street outside the flat and slept comforted.

PART 12

Nag Hammadi

1

I leaned against the wall at the foot of my stairs listening to the silence inside the house and the sound of Paul's car pulling away. Ben was sleeping again. Mr. Spock had departed through the kitchen window to the George Street roofs and yards. The air was so heavy that it blanketed sound and movement. I couldn't go on like this.

Envelopes had been piling up for days on a corner of my packing table. I went in and sorted them idly into four piles: bills, checks, catalogues, The Rest. I'd opened most of it before it struck me that I was only going through the motions, couldn't remember what I'd been looking at, and wasn't even remotely interested. Tom Ashe and all the crazy jigsaw pieces of his past danced in a cloud of questions. I picked out the junk mail and tossed it into the wastepaper basket while I was thinking about Ashe's charred hiding place and his dark little lost secrets.

The Thing. Whatever—let's call it X. The intruder was wrong: Tom's grasp on reality might have been uncertain, but he had been sharp enough to know that X would be safer in the locker at U-STOR, or better still in a vault somewhere, than at Horsell Road. Horsell Road had been for keeping *himself* secret, though it had failed. As for X. Ashe had been rich enough and frightened enough to put it out of the reach of dark shadows with petrol cans and matches.

I dug out the bank statements, found the address of Ashe's branch, and got the number from the phone book. An assistant manager to whom I introduced myself as Tom Ashe's executor going about her lawful business consulted ledgers and finally informed me that Mr. Ashe had not left any property with them. All right. But my paranoid friend had certainly left his treasure somewhere like that. *Trust nobody.*

I kicked myself. He hadn't been paranoid. How many murders had there been? Tom. Sammy Butler? Tom's case officer twenty years ago? I turned to replace the receiver and watched the green Vauxhall roll slowly in front of my window. Pure terror took me into the corner behind the desk. By the time I could force myself to look outside again neither yesterday's nor any other green car was in sight.

I made up my mind. No doubt Ernie would have printed out something more professional-looking with the computer, but I just took a spare card and a thick black marker and wrote *This Shop Closed for Holidays. Reopening September 1.* That sounded like a good date. I consulted the calendar on the wall. A Friday. Maybe by then they would have arrested him. Maybe the heatwave would be over. Maybe a few customers would be drifting back from holiday. Maybe my life could go on. In the meantime I was going to remove myself from the places where anybody could find me whenever he chose to come looking.

When I'd put an appropriate message on the answering machine, checked the bolts on the door into the yard, taped the card to the glass of the door, and set the alarm system, I locked up and fled like a thief.

Ben was stirring, talking to himself and occasionally bashing the mobile that dangled from his cot rails. I stepped out of my sandals, went to put on a Mahler CD in the living room, smoothed the bottom sheet, and lay down on my bed with a notepad and a pen. Time to think things out instead of running around like a headless chicken.

The music had finished when I woke up, and the phone must have been ringing for a while. As I flung myself to my feet I noticed that the paper was still blank and the ballpoint had leaked onto the sheet.

"Leonard Stockton here," the telephone told me. "I have some news. I don't know whether you noticed that our ads were in the papers yesterday, but I've already had one reply. A Mrs. Hellenides says that Mr. Ashe left her lodging house in March owing two weeks' rent. Do you wish me to deal with it?"

I said, "If it's all right, I think I'd like to talk to her."

The address that Mrs. Hellenides had given Wisby Finch belonged to an early Victorian four-story terraced house just north of Euston Station which had seen better days—a lot of them. Its peeling brown door frame was decorated with a dozen doorbells. If numbers were to be believed, the house must be full of converted broom cupboards. The name "Hellenides" was carefully printed on the card by the

bottom bell, so I rang that one. There was no warning before the door swung silently open in front of a
stocky, gray-haired man who looked at me with an
expression of cautious unfriendliness.

I said, "I'm looking for Mrs. Hellenides. I'm here
from Wisby Finch, solicitors. She contacted us."

The door slammed in my face. I was thinking of
ringing again when it reopened, this time revealing
an even more stocky woman wearing dull black
under a faded lilac coverall. Mr. Hellenides was hovering in the background, presumably as support.

I repeated my story.

"You bring the money?" she interrupted.

"I am empowered to pay what Mr. Ashe owed,
provided you have evidence of your claim."

She seemed to be thinking about it. "You want to
come in?"

I didn't. Apart from other considerations, I'd left
Ben in the car on the meter just behind me because I
didn't think that Mrs. Hellenides was likely to accept
a solicitor accompanied by a baby: working mothers
usually have to manage things better than that. I consulted my wristwatch. "I have only a couple of minutes, and it shouldn't be necessary. Unless Mr. Ashe
left anything when he went away? If he did, then I'll
have to either take it with me or arrange for it to be
transported to our office."

Mrs. Hellenides snorted. "Him? He pack everything and take it with him. No notice, fifty pound a
week for two weeks he is owing for his flatlet."

I could imagine the "flatlet"—a cramped room
with a bed, table, chair, wardrobe, ancient gas fire,
and cooking ring. You might get some privacy, but no

comfort, for fifty pounds a week—not in this central area.

"Fifty pounds a week," I said craftily. "Yes—but what about the deposit? I understand that you've kept that."

Mr. and Mrs. Hellenides exchanged a look that said my guess was accurate and turned on me the wounded stare of honest folk who were being mugged. I said wearily, "Well, I'm authorized to pay what he owed you, but we haven't found any rent book or receipts, so we have no proof that he ever actually lived here." I thought I detected an unpleasant darkening of Mr. Hellenide's expression. "The law makes it *very clear* that you must prove this is a legitimate debt. Otherwise, if I gave you the money they could make me pay it back. Are you sure that there isn't anything here belonging to Mr. Ashe? If you can show me anything that did belong to him, that's the evidence I need."

Mr. Hellenides was already shaking his head with the bitter expression of a man who had expected to be cheated, when Mrs. Hellenides said, "The card!" and burst into Greek. She turned back to me. "He take everything, but a postcard come after he leaves."

Mr. Hellenides, in the background, was already scrabbling through a bundle of envelopes, mostly junk mail, piled on the floor under a hall table. Presumably letters addressed to former tenants were tossed here until somebody got around to claiming them or throwing them away. It took him a few minutes, scattering envelopes across the faded runner, before he raised himself with a picture postcard in one hand. He thrust it at me hopefully and retreated.

The picture on the back was of Mont St. Michel. I turned it over quickly. It was addressed to Mr. Thomas Ashe, and posted in central London on March 30th. The message space was blank.

"All right?" Mr. Hellenides asked.

"All right," I said, thinking regretfully of what wonderful and illuminating messages might have been written in those square inches of unused space. "I mean yes, I'll take this for our records. And I will give you . . . " I felt in my shoulder bag. "I can give you one hundred pounds in cash. In view of the inconvenience you've had, I can agree to your keeping the deposit as well."

I realized that a genuine solicitor would have wanted a receipt, but I am not a genuine solicitor, and I had the feeling that the omission wouldn't bother them. In fact they remained silent and narrowly watchful as I wished them good morning and swept down the stairs with the postcard in my bag.

It didn't seem worth a hundred pounds. But they probably did have a right to the money. I had read annoyance and indignation in them, and of course they'd hoped I wouldn't remember the deposit; but that seemed only human.

There were fifteen minutes left on the meter. Ben greeted me with a gurgle, so I used up the first five talking to him; the next ten must have passed unnoticed while I stared at a picture of Mont St. Michel at high tide and examined the neat, blue-ink address on the other side.

You hear of messages hidden in microdots, and the absurd thought came to me that I should examine the writing under the magnifying glass. Well, all right, but there was no hurry because I couldn't really believe that what I held in my hand was a secret message in invisible ink. It was more like . . . a signal. A prearranged sign. The idea came to me that Tom Ashe would have understood it at once.

2

The mobile in my bag rang as I was driving past the station. I found it by touch, pulled it out, flipped the switch without taking my eyes off the heavy traffic around me, and yelled, "Hello?"

"Dido? Where on earth are you, and why does the machine say you're away on holiday?" It was Barnabas. His tone suggested that something was seriously wrong, but I had to drop the phone into my lap and use both hands avoiding a suicidal motorcyclist. When I picked it up I realized that he hadn't noticed my temporary absence.

I broke in: "Listen, Barnabas, I'm not really on holiday. We're at Euston, heading home. I just don't want to hang around in the shop waiting for murders to happen. Anyway, this business of Tom Ashe is going to take up a lot of my time for the next few weeks. Look, just tell me what's wrong: why are you phoning?" Barnabas worries too much about me as it is, and there were things about green Vauxhalls and redheaded men that I would try to keep to myself if only by changing the subject.

"Stop!" he roared. "Or rather, turn around, you're going the wrong way. Didn't you hear me? I need you here at once!"

"Where? Barnabas, I have Ben with me . . ."

"Never mind that, we aren't in the Reading Room."

I took a deep breath. "I missed that bit. Where are you?"

"The British Museum. In the office of the Head of the Manuscripts Division. You must come at once and talk to these people. You may have to call the solicitor—one of the gentlemen is inclined to be excitable: I believe he wishes to extradite me in order to throw me into an Egyptian prison."

I could hear an anguished objection in the background without actually catching the words; but I recognized my father's tone and relaxed. Barnabas's joke.

"All right," I said. "I'll bring Ben. It might be half an hour—I'm not far away, but you know what parking is like down there."

"Wait," Barnabas commanded, and I could hear another unintelligible background conversation. During it I managed to edge across the lanes of traffic and make a right turn into the back streets of north Bloomsbury. Then he was back. "I've told them that you will need to park on the forecourt. They will send instructions to the gate to let you in."

I was impressed. To park on the British Museum forecourt you have to be a senior employee, I think, or maybe the Queen. "Don't forget it's the new car," I said. "Tell them it's a dark blue Citroën estate."

"How could I forget that car?" Barnabas snorted and hung up.

The journey took longer than I had reckoned, through narrow back streets heavily used and heavily parked on. At the Museum gates, the guards saw me coming and stood aside; I swept in like a film star at a première, scattering a gaggle of tourists.

Just inside a uniformed security man flagged me down.

I said, "I'm expected by the Head of Manuscripts."

It was unnecessary; he had been sent to direct me into the one empty parking space. My guide then took the handles of the baby seat without comment and swept us through the main doors, scattering the crowds as we made a sharp turn into the quieter areas of the manuscript collection and headed briskly for a door marked Staff Only.

The curator of manuscripts lived in an office of moderate size surrounded by mysterious golden oak cabinets which I assumed were full of precious documents. At the table in the center Barnabas, his briefcase, and a teacup were taking up a good deal of the space; he was in the company of an anxious-looking forty-year-old who was presumably the "Dr. Mackintosh" of the name plate on the door, and two dark men in expensive dark suits—the Egyptians whom Barnabas accused of planning his arrest? At first glance they struck me as even unhappier than the director, and I felt sure that Barnabas had been at his most obnoxious. By now they would all be aware that he was an eminent scholar, Emeritus Professor of English of the University of Oxford, and utterly respectable. He can be rather a bully sometimes.

All four of them rose to their feet on my arrival, and there was a flurry of looking for baby space. Ben wound up occupying the director's desk, which freed me for a round of introductions and handshaking—

Dr. Mackintosh, Professor Mustafa Madkour of the Coptic Museum, Cairo, and Dr. Samie, who turned out to be an Egyptian cultural attaché. The latter two were nearly identical men in their late thirties, suavely polite in well-cut gray silk suits. Luckily Professor Madkour cultivated a narrow beard, which made it easier to distinguish one from the other. They vied to offer me a chair, an ashtray, a cup of tea. We exchanged platitudes, but it was not just *my* attention that was obviously elsewhere.

In the absolute center of the table, resting upon a sheet of white card, was Tom Ashe's little scrap of papyrus.

I accepted the tea, added milk, and indicated that I was all attention.

Professor Madkour was going to take the lead. He had arrived by plane from Cairo that day, but the earliness of his flight hadn't taken the edge off his excitement. "Miss Hoare, I suppose that you have heard of the Coptic Museum? Of course if you have been in Cairo at some time, you almost certainly will have visited us. I have a brochure."

He slid a colored tourist leaflet across the table to me. I showed willing by positioning it beside my teacup as a reference source, if research became necessary.

"Miss Hoare, the scrap of papyrus which Professor Hoare has brought here for identification has been torn from a missing manuscript which is the property of my government. It is from a collection of early manuscripts, codices, displayed in the museum."

Why wasn't I surprised? I said, "Are you saying

that Mr. Thomas Ashe, who gave me that scrap, stole it from the museum?"

Professor Madkour leaned forward. "No, not that. He took possession of it many years ago, and maybe before the hoard of which this is a part came to the attention of the authorities."

"So you aren't claiming that he stole it? My father may have told you that I am the executor of Mr. Ashe's will. I might want to have a solicitor here before we go any further."

Professor Madkour and Dr. Samie exchanged a look which interested me.

Dr. Samie said, "No, not exactly that either. Although the embassy has been making enquiries and representations to your government for over four decades about the whereabouts of Mr. Ashe. We were very anxious to interview him." He, like the professor, spoke with the best of English accents, the kind which told the world that they were the products of English public schools and an Oxbridge education. As Barnabas would have said, it is odd how the British Imperial influence hangs on . . .

Though what my father in fact said at this minute was, "Perhaps you should start at the beginning and tell us the entire story? We know that Mr. Ashe was in Egypt after the war. Perhaps your story begins there?"

Professor Madkour nodded, looking from Barnabas to me and back again.

3

"Of course," said the professor, "you have heard of the Dead Sea Scrolls. What I am talking about is similar, we would say even more exciting in some ways, but not so famous.

"I am speaking about the Gnostic Gospels of Nag Hammadi.

"They were discovered near a village in the Jabal-al-Tarif by a local man, a peasant farmer. Thirteen leather-bound books of papyrus, and some additional leaves. Some were burnt, some given to the local priest for safekeeping, and one sent to the authorities in Cairo to be identified by the people then at the museum as lost versions of Gnostic gospels."

Barnabas appeared to know what Gnostic gospels were. I didn't, and asked. Professor Madkour looked annoyed but gamely set about the further explanation.

Scholars had known for several centuries of the existence in Egypt of suppressed manuscript translations of even more ancient Christian gospels dating originally from A.D. 50 or 100. They were at least as old as the New Testament gospels but recorded a different view of the history and theology of the early church. They belonged, in short, to the Gnostic tradition of early Christianity—a mystical tradition influenced by far eastern religions, which had defied the Christian orthodoxy established by St. Paul and his followers.

By the fourth century the Gnostics were lost, scattered, pronounced heretics. To possess their writings was dangerous, and somebody in Upper Egypt had buried this collection in pottery jars for safekeeping during some time of persecution.

Fragments had been reaching Europe ever since the eighteenth century. There was a long, tiresome account of legal barriers and colonial manoeuvrings. What it came down to was that, faced with the samples sent to them by various interested parties, the people at the Museum had realized exactly what had been found and set about retrieving it. The government purchased one book and confiscated ten others, but the collection was incomplete.

"Such situations," said Madkour, "are never so tidy. There were other papyruses, and from 1947 these were hidden from the authorities to avoid confiscation. The man who had made the original discovery found more material and tried to sell it in Cairo. An antiquities dealer bought whatever he could. An Italian collector had other things which the government did not obtain until 1952. A Belgian dealer smuggled some material from Cairo to the United States, where our representatives managed to prevent a sale; but it was then taken to Europe where the gentleman died before he could be jailed, and his widow sold the material to a foundation in Switzerland. You see, it was an international problem. There were many problems."

Barnabas was growing restive. "You paint," he interrupted, "a fascinating picture. However, you haven't offered any evidence about this particular scrap or any illegality in Mr. Ashe's actions."

"It is not just this one scrap," Dr. Samie intervened angrily. "But even if it were, it is the property of the Egyptian government, which nationalized all such materials in 1952."

"I did hear that," Barnabas said. I was alerted by the mildness of his tone. "I repeat: what are we talking about? Where did it come from? How did it get to Tom Ashe? Or don't you know?"

Madkour intervened. "We do know," he said. "I will now tell you the end of the story, so far."

Cairo was bombed in 1948, and at that time a small antiques shop was destroyed. The widow of the dealer then sold a codex containing one complete gospel and part of another to a British tourist. She had written out a proper record of the transaction in a ledger, giving the purchaser as a Mr. Ash staying at the Kings Hotel. Despite her misspelling, the authorities had taken steps to approach Mr. Thomas Ashe, but when they questioned him he claimed that he had sold on the manuscript to a certain Italian dealer in antiquities. By the time that they had traced the supposed purchaser and received a vigorous denial from him, Ashe was on the point of boarding a ship to Cyprus. A rapid search of his luggage in Customs had revealed nothing, and as he was travelling on a British passport the authorities felt unable to take the matter any further. In any case, they were unsure whether the Italian could be trusted to tell the truth. There had been delays, investigations, recriminations.

"In the end," Professor Madkour finished rather grimly, "our people were convinced that the Italian was innocent, at any rate of that particular transaction, because we offered to give him some consideration regarding other irregularities in exchange for the manuscript. But he was unable to provide this. We realized that Mr. Ashe had somehow arranged for the Codex to be smuggled out of Egypt. But when

we made enquiries in London it seemed that the
police here were not able to help us. They informed
the Embassy that to the best of their knowledge Mr.
Ashe had not returned to this country. We have made
other enquiries over the years but without success."

"You're talking about a codex," I said. "A whole
document—or several pieces? What makes you think
this scrap has anything to do with it?"

"It is not a matter of 'thinking'," the professor
said. He sounded offended. "I have looked at this
piece very carefully. Even you might have noticed
that, although three sides of the piece are aged naturally, the fourth side has recently been folded and
torn from a larger sheet."

Even me? "As a matter of fact," I told him, "I did
notice that."

My voice may have expressed something. He said,
"I beg your pardon. The other thing is that I have
been able to identify the three incomplete lines on
the scrap. They are undoubtedly a passage from the
document known as the *Secret Book of Peter.* We possess another version of that document, probably
slightly later. There is no doubt about this: it is a very
famous text of great interest because it contradicts a
number of central Christian doctrines such as the vir-
gin birth and the resurrection of the body. The whole
document is of the greatest concern to scholars."

"Indeed," said Barnabas gently. A kind of shutter
had come down across his face. I recognized the
symptom and would have given quite a lot to have a
private word with him before he spoke again.

I said brightly, "I presume that you want to be
allowed to take this scrap back to Cairo?"

"Certainly," said the professor. "There can be no argument that this is a part of my country's heritage, and belonged to materials which were nationalized forty years ago."

"There could be such an argument," I said. "As executor for Mr. Thomas Ashe it is my duty in accordance with the laws of this country to protect the interest of his heirs. Apart from that, I suppose that the authorities here might refuse the export of historical material without a license." I hadn't any such certainty, but I was standing after all inside the British Museum, which houses those Elgin Marbles that we have been steadfastly refusing for decades to return to the Greeks. I looked at the two officials. "In other words, I have no intention of permitting you to remove this piece. Though I'm perfectly happy for it to remain here in the manuscript collection for the time being, where I am sure that Dr. Mackenzie will be able to keep it safe."

The babble of voices had the effect of rousing Ben to a hearty protest. He drowned everyone else. I went to pick him up, and faced the Egyptians with him in my arms doing my best to look like a Madonna with Child. I ignored the amused glint in my father's eye—the one person to remain calm in all the uproar.

After a moment, I shouted, "I'm going to have to change the baby. May I use your washroom, Dr. Mackenzie?"

I ignored Barnabas, who turned his back on the room to look out the window.

In the end we drove from the library unscathed. I'd given them the address of Wisby Finch, informed them loftily that further negotiations should be carried out through Leonard Stockton, and agreed in a civilized manner that I would let them know if any more fragments surfaced. Then I'd added the *coup de grâce:* the fire that had destroyed Mr. Ashe's living quarters and, so far as the police could discover, everything he owned.

The Hoare family left an anguished silence behind them.

Ensconced in the rear seat of the new car, peering alternately at his grandson and the non-standard blue leather upholstery around him, Barnabas said, "That's it, of course. That's the money I smelled."

"It does sound valuable. And it belongs to Mrs. Ashe. That's what he wanted me to deal with. All his insane jabber about going south from Cairo—the lot. I imagine that if we look at a map of Egypt, the towns that he named are on the route to Nag Hammadi. Do you want to take my bet?"

"I'm not a fool," Barnabas said, "and don't get above yourself." His words made me aware that there was some kind of atmosphere in the car.

"What's wrong?"

"You were being ridiculous, you know. Childish. You embarrassed those people terribly, waving the baby at them. And his wet nappy. They are Arab gentlemen. Scholars. They aren't used to these things."

"Then they should be," I said. "I am not going to be bullied like that, not even by you. Besides, I'm sure I saw you laughing."

I thought he mumbled something about women having no moral sense—something like that, but I chose to ignore him. "But Barnabas . . ."

"Well?"

A delivery van cut across from the right-hand lane, and I lost the track of my thinking for a second while I dealt with the problem.

"The rest of it. I mean, obviously Ashe tore off a loose corner as bait and fed it to me to make me look for the rest of the Codex."

"You don't believe it was destroyed?"

I said, having started to think it out, "Of course not. It wasn't there. If it had been in the fire, we would have found something. There would have been the remains of the binding at least. Don't you know how hard it is to burn a whole book? Destroy it completely, I mean? I tried, a few years ago, with some damaged volumes of old sermons. They caught along the edges and smelled like a rubbish tip, but they wouldn't really burn."

"Are you sure it isn't in the room still?"

I considered that. "She said—Inspector Lyon— that she was going to have her people go through the room with a fine-tooth comb. If there was anything there, she'll have found it by now."

I didn't wait for Barnabas to suggest it, but pulled over on a yellow line and found my mobile. The lady in question was in her office. The search had been completed, the forensic report was with her. There had been books. I'd seen them myself. The fire had not reached them, though they had been damaged by chemicals and smoke. The contents of the room, apart from furniture, had been bundled into sacks and were sitting in the incident room. I was welcome to come down and have a look.

"I'll go," Barnabas said. "Let me out, this door is locked."

I undid the central locking. "Are you all right? You aren't too tired? You're taking your aspirin?" Barnabas was on a maintenance dose of half an aspirin a day since his heart attack nearly two years ago. That, or simple stubbornness, appeared to be keeping him in excellent condition.

From the pavement he looked down at me. "I am certainly not too tired for this. Tell the woman I'm on my way. I have taken my aspirin. For goodness' sake get out of here before I spank you. Before that traffic warden arrives to give you a ticket."

I pulled away from the kerb and the ticket to rejoin the stream of eastbound traffic before I remembered the second thing I'd been going to tell him, the point that I had not felt it necessary to make to the Egyptians.

According to Mrs. Ashe, Tom wasn't alone. The three musketeers had all been in Cairo together: Tom and Sammy Butler and Peter Mellor. There'd been no mention of the others; presumably the Egyptian authorities hadn't known about them. But I couldn't believe that Butler and Mellor hadn't known all about Tom's acquisition and helped him to get it out of the country. I remembered the story about the silver. Those young men had all been working for themselves as well as their country. The Egyptians had stopped Ashe and searched his bags, but what about the others'? And Sammy Butler's son obviously knew about the Codex. Had to. That was the only explanation for his behavior.

And I hadn't asked anybody its value, but I didn't have to. I'm a dealer in antiquities myself. Such a thing, with its age and provenance, was very valuable indeed, and if the contents were as historically and theologically interesting as the Egyptians had suggested, then it wouldn't be an exaggeration to call it priceless.

So Dennis Butler was looking for the Codex, and I reckoned that he had threatened Tom; and Ashe had hidden the thing and written his will and my letter. He'd given me the Mesopotamian beads, more of the loot he'd brought back to England. Maybe the beads and the little fortune in his bank account were the only things left—apart from the Codex which was the most valuable, most dangerous thing of all? I was going to work on the assumption that Sammy Butler had told his son about the Codex, and Dennis had said something about it at his father's funeral, as a result of which Ashe had left Brighton. Dennis had finally located Tom again, presumably last spring, and demanded his father's share. His inheritance. I reckoned that Tom had been uncooperative and things had got out of hand, since it certainly wasn't in Butler's interest to kill him.

In George Street I drove slowly past two parking spaces and circled round the block before I finally stopped the car. If the Vauxhall had been in sight I would have called for help, but there was no sign of it, and a police car rolled quietly past me as I was manoeuvring the baby seat out of the car. The Inspector had kept her word.

The light on my answering machine was flashing. A colleague wanted to know whether I was interested in seeing a Pepys when I returned from my holiday; Barnabas's outdated message informed me that he was going to the British Museum and would contact me later in the morning; and Pat wanted to make an arrangement for the three of us to go up to St. Albans for the day. The fourth caller spoke in a soft voice which I didn't recognize for a moment.

"Hello, is that Dido Hoare?" Silence. I could hear the uncertainty. "This is Emma Ashe. Oh dear, I don't like these machines. I wanted to tell you that I hope I haven't done the wrong thing. Peter Mellor came to visit me this morning. Tom's friend. Do you remember, I told you about him? He is on a short visit to this country. It was so good to see him again after all these years. He was upset to hear about Tom." I waited through a long pause, thinking she was about to ring off. When she spoke again, her voice seemed strained. "Also, I don't want to alarm you, but you must know . . . Peter was very upset when I told him about your visitor. You know . . . He said that it must be Dennis Butler, Sammy's son. He said that he is a dangerous, wicked man. He wants to see you, to warn you about him. I gave him your address. I hope you don't mind."

Mind? I was buzzing with delight, because she had just solved my problem. If Peter Mellor turned up, the last of the comrades still alive, he could give me some answers that weren't just guesses. I poured myself a glass of chardonnay from the bottle in the door of the fridge. I would have opened a bottle of champagne if I'd had it, because it seemed that the end of a nasty business had just come into sight.

PART 13

The Final Piece

1

Waking ... heart pounding, muscles tensed, body flexed to run ...

The bedroom was dark. There must have been a noise. Now it was quiet again.

Breathe quietly. Lie still. Listen. Perhaps it had belonged to a dream I'd already forgotten.

Then I sat bolt upright, startled by a high-pitched voice screaming up and down the scale. The illuminated numerals on my bedside clock told me it was just after three. I swung my feet to the floor and was pulling Ben out of his cot before I'd thought about it, wrapping him in his blanket, carrying him out protesting into the passage.

The darkness beyond the door of the sitting room was torn by flashes of intense red light. That was when I really woke up. The light, like the screaming, was coming from the security alarm on the front of the building. Still holding Ben in one arm, I leaned out the window to check the front of the building. Except for the alarm itself everything was dark and still. I reached for the phone.

But I was already hearing a police siren. A light sprang on in the window across the street and somebody shouted.

I leaned out cautiously again. Of course it was possible that the system had failed and I was going to spend the next twenty-four hours apologizing to the neighbors, but I didn't think so. I gave Ben a little jiggle that stopped his roars and carried him back into the bedroom. It seemed safe to put some clothes on before the police arrived. I laid the baby in the middle of the bed while I dug out a T-shirt and jeans, and when I looked again he was sleeping with his fist in his mouth. I moved him into his carry cot and felt under the edge of the bed for my sandals.

The back! It was as though I could only start thinking after my panicky body was organized. I cursed my stupidity and trotted over to the open window. The security grilles prevented me from leaning out; but I pressed my face against them and inhaled. There had been a lot of fire in my life recently, and I was expecting smoke now. Nothing. Light from a high window in the pub over on the main road shone peacefully into my yard, where nothing stirred.

The siren had arrived. I grabbed my keys and shot downstairs to find a patrol car blocking the road, blue lights flashing, and two uniformed officers peering through the door of the shop. One of them turned.

"Constable Harris. You the key holder, madam? If you'll open up, we'll take a look."

"Is there a way out at the back?" the second one asked.

I explained about the walled yard as I was unlocking the door and standing aside. Peering around their solid frames, I could find no sign of an intruder. I followed at a modest distance and edged along the side wall to switch off the alarm: no point waking the last sleeper in the neighborhood, if there was still such a person.

In the startling silence one of them called, "Madam? Can you come here a minute?"

He was in the back room. I said *Shit!* in anticipation, remembered to flick the light switch and joined them, blinking. I was ready for the catastrophe and felt confused when at first I couldn't see it.

They were at the back door. I stared past them to the distorted metal bolts. The screws that held them to the door had been twisted and pulled with great strength, and the leading edge of the door itself had splintered. I shivered.

"Somebody's taken a crowbar to this," one of the men said. "Better have a look." And my memory went back to the moment of waking. I'd heard the splintering noise in my sleep.

It took them a while to force the bent metal, and by the time that they'd opened the door in a little shower of splinters, it was obvious that the yard was going to be empty. Had been long empty.

The paved yard behind my shop runs the width of the property and extends fifteen foot back from the outer wall of the office. It is surrounded on three sides by the original ten-foot-high brick walls. Apart from the rubbish bin, the place was empty.

"How the devil did he get in?" one of my rescue party muttered.

"Must have walked along the top of the wall from the next street," the other suggested. "It's not far to drop down."

"And got a boost up from that bin when the alarm went off. Shame that was here or we might have got him."

That was the point at which I began to consider that they *hadn't* got him. Which left a potential robber, or worse, on the loose. It could be a coincidence that somebody had decided to break into my shop just now, but I didn't think so.

One of the men added, "What's that?" and delved into the shadow by the bin. "Is it yours?" The beam of his torch had picked out the kind of red can that people use for carrying a spare gallon of petrol in their cars.

No, it wasn't mine. My voice said, "I think you'd better contact the station and tell them about this. They may want to call Scotland Yard." I sounded calm.

Constable Harris, already pulling his radio out of a breast pocket, threw me a knowing nod. "We have instructions, Miss Hoare. My partner will try to get this door closed again while I'm calling in. You'd probably better get a sheet of ply screwed on over the door frame as soon as we're finished here. We can give you the number of an emergency boarding service. You might want to have a metal-sheathed door put on later—they'll stand up to anything bar a hydraulic jack."

Or barring a petrol bomb chucked in through a window. That thought didn't quite leave me during the comings and goings that followed, culminating in the arrival of Sergeant Pickles in a police car. And a temper.

His fault for leaving instructions to contact him in case of trouble in George Street—not mine.

We sat at my kitchen table an hour later drinking tea and staring at one another over Mr. Spock's head. They had removed the red can for examination, as well as the crowbar that they'd found in the gutter one street to the north. Whoever had visited me must have been well away before the patrol car had arrived.

"Why here?" Pickles said. "Why you?"

"It's crazy. There's no reason," I yawned. So much for the excitement. I could feel my eyelids closing and poured out two more cups of slightly stewed tea. My own eyes felt bloodshot; his were.

"Unless somebody thinks Ashe left something in your shop."

"Dennis Butler?"

"Yes. It's the same as at Horsell Road, or would have been if the alarm system hadn't gone off. He must have been looking for something, and he was going to set fire to the place to cover his tracks."

I put my mug down a little more vigorously than I'd intended, and Mr. Spock fled. "Why would he set a fire? If *I'd* just burgled somebody I'd try to get my loot away, I wouldn't stop to light matches."

Pickles looked at me with the strained attention of somebody who was trying not to yawn, but all he said in response to my certainty was, "It's a mistake to believe you can out-guess a criminal. Put it another way: Dennis Butler isn't an experienced burglar." He hesitated, and I had the impression that he decided not to say something else. "There's nothing on his record except one speeding ticket and a few parking fines."

"But he's a murderer. We know that."

He waved a hand impatiently. "We suspect it. Even if it's true, his actions tonight could be a consequence of whatever caused him to kill, not the other way around . . . am I making myself clear?"

I was much too sleepy to be sure, but I thought not. I said I understood in order to encourage him: he was being much more forthcoming than his boss.

"His breaking in here seems out of character. I don't care to guess what was in his mind when he brought the petrol can with him."

I tried another tack. "But why does he think I have anything in my shop that concerns him? He's been around here a couple of times in business hours, once when I was out, and he obviously couldn't find anything then."

He wanted to know when that had been, and I tried to count up on my fingers, then made a guess.

"And he's been back since?"

"He first came to persuade me he was Tom Ashe's son. He may have thought that I wouldn't find out he was lying. I suppose he told me Mrs. Ashe was dead to keep me from getting to her for as long as possible. But he couldn't really have believed that I was going to hand over Tom Ashe's estate to him just like that? And there's *nothing* in my shop." I stopped as soon as I'd said it. This couldn't only be about the old bead necklace, surely? There hadn't been anything to suggest it was so very valuable, and even less to suggest that Dennis Butler knew about it. I certainly hadn't mentioned it. But it might be best to put it somewhere else.

The Sergeant said abruptly, "I want you to let us send somebody in later today to look. I saw the sign on your door—at least we won't be disturbing any customers."

"It will disturb me," I said, "if my valuable stock is damaged."

"It won't be." He looked at me. "One man. Sergeant Hewlett. He works for the Art and Antiquities Division and he knows how to handle valuables. He knows what a codex is."

I stared at him. "You know about that?"

"Tom Ashe's Nag Hammadi Codex? Ashe's department has known about that business for years. We think that they made some trouble about it at one time, but dropped it. They never mentioned it to us—I suppose they thought it wasn't important after so long—but Cairo contacted us recently and Scotland Yard agreed to help if possible. The Inspector spoke to Dr. Samie and advised him to meet you and your father through the British Museum contact and explain the situation."

I considered that. "Inspector Lyon didn't mention that to me. Is it," I asked carefully, "Scotland Yard's opinion that the Codex is the property of the Egyptian government?"

He in turn considered the question. "Miss Hoare, we don't know. I think we'd expect to see that decided in a court of law. A claim of this kind by a foreign government can be a legal minefield."

"If Tom Ashe bought it in good faith . . ."

". . . then the question is whether he bought it from somebody who had a legal title, and it doesn't sound to me that he thought so." He looked away. "Do you know where it is?"

"No. No, really."

"Well, it can't have been in Horsell Road by the time you and the Inspector looked. She got people in there immediately afterwards, and they are ninety-nine per cent sure that it wasn't. Presumably you've worked out that it must have been in his storage locker for a while, but there's no reason to believe Ashe ever took it to the room. I was wondering whether the intruder had removed it before he fired the place, but tonight makes it pretty clear he didn't, or he wouldn't still be hanging around."

"So Dennis Butler doesn't have it either."

"The old man must have found another hiding place. It would be to your advantage if we can locate it."

I could see his point. "I can tell you that Ashe didn't leave it with either Wisby Finch or his bank."

He smiled bleakly. "No."

"You don't think that Mrs. Ashe has it?"

He shook his head. "There's certainly no sign of anything where she's living."

I looked at him.

"We got a search warrant. And yes, we cleared it with the nursing home, but as a matter of fact I managed to have a look through her things without her even realizing that I'd been there. Considering her age and her state of health, it seemed better that way."

"I think it was immoral," I said, sounding priggish.

"We were acting in her best interests. I'm sorry, but her doctor said it was better not to worry her."

We exchanged a long look and came, I think, to the simultaneous realization that this was not a matter on which we were going to agree. I wondered whether I was starting to like him, but I was also left wondering why so many officials think that they have a special insight into other people's best interests. I said, "If your careful man wants to come around mid-morning, when I've had a chance to get some sleep, I won't make you get a search warrant. But I am going to stick to him like glue." I gave way to my impulse. "In Tom Ashe's interests. In the interest of the heirs, actually."

"Your privilege," he said sharply. "They'll have finished downstairs by now. I think I heard the van leaving, so your back door will be secure again. You'd better reset the security system, though I don't imagine you'll be disturbed again. He must have got a shock when that thing went off!"

I was past caring, but I managed to rouse myself long enough to go downstairs, check my blockaded rear door and set the alarm. As I was locking up, exhaustion settled over me like a cloud. I'm not sure just how I managed to get back up the stairs. I certainly didn't bother to undress.

2

It was one of Phyllis's days. The sound of her key in the lock roused me, and I managed to lift a tousled head from the pillow when she appeared in the bedroom doorway. Her look at my face seemed not to reassure her.

"Dido? Are you sick? It's nine-thirty."

I closed my eyes again and pushed myself blindly into a sitting position. When I'd stopped feeling dizzy I squinted at her. "Somebody tried to break in. Middle of the night. Is Ben all right?"

She rushed to the cot, but I could already hear his contented greeting, so I collapsed again. "I could do with another hour."

"Well, why not? You don't have any appointments?"

I did. I was sure I did. *Damn!* "The police. Ten o'clock."

Phyllis said, "Suppose I make a pot of tea? What happened: did they take much?"

I said, "No," and, "Tell you as soon as I can speak," and headed for the bathroom where I managed to turn on the taps. A bath sounded like a good idea— provided I managed not to drown myself.

Sergeant Hewlett gave me precious extra minutes by being delayed, but he was at the door by ten past. I descended the stairs with the careful movements of an invalid to greet a rather ordinary middle-aged man with thinning hair and a pudgy face. He looked more like a butcher than an expert in art and antiquities.

In accordance with my threat to Sergeant Pickles I followed him around the shop and watched him suspiciously. He was the silent type. He looked wordlessly along and beneath every shelf and into, under, and even at the back of every drawer. It seemed pointless to argue that there was no way Tom Ashe could have reached most of these places without somebody noticing. He poked his fingers into the drain of my little sink, unscrewed the trap, investigated the space under the packing table, poked into my carton of padded envelopes, and searched for loose floorboards. At the end of two hours, having found a good deal of dust, he asked to borrow my phone and I listened to him make a negative report to somebody. Then he bought an anonymous Victorian novel in three volumes, which I had vaguely been thinking of pricing a little higher. He remarked that he collected Victorian novels in two to four volumes and asked me to send him my autumn catalogue. Then he departed as quietly as he had arrived.

Phyllis had taken Ben out for their morning walk and so there was no reason for me to move. The air in the shop was thick with recently disturbed dust. With the back door screwed shut there wasn't much I could do about it. I most wanted to go back to bed, but the sight of the same old pile of partly opened mail on the desk, with the morning's new letters thrown on top, bothered my conscience. So far, the day had been a dead loss, and I should try to salvage something from it. When the phone rang, therefore, I let the answering machine pick it up; but it broadcast Barnabas's voice saying plaintively, "Dido, where are you? You aren't answering the mobile. Are you . . . " I had to intervene.

"I'm here."

"Ah, at last! You haven't forgotten that you were going to pick me up at twelve-thirty for lunch?"

As a matter of fact I had. I described the attempted break-in and my disturbed night's rest, not to mention Sergeant Hewlett's attentions. Barnabas heard me out in grim silence.

"I was just going through the mail," I said finally, "but I'll leave it. Shall we go up to the open-air restaurant in Highgate Woods?"

"If you think you can leave the shop empty," Barnabas said. He sounded angry. "Thank goodness you had that alarm system installed last year!"

I agreed dutifully.

"And there's nothing there?"

"Of course not! I just hope that Dennis Butler has the sense to realize that even if there was something once, the police would have found it by now. Barnabas, those beads—I have them upstairs . . ."

"We'll put them in my bank today, in an envelope with your name on it. But in case he isn't very intelligent, you'd better get out. You're supposed to have gone on holiday, remember? Go! You don't want to be on your own with him hanging around to set fire to you. Where's Ben?"

I told him that Phyllis had him until five o'clock.

"Then come along at once."

But now that he had accepted my careless offer to follow the original scheme, I was having second thoughts. What if Butler *was* still hanging around in the street? There had been no sign of the green Vauxhall today, but that didn't mean much; and the idea of a petrol bomb smashing through the window of the shop in my absence and destroying my home and livelihood suddenly seemed all too horribly possible. Should I have the big window boarded up? No—not if I was going to stay in business.

"Barnabas . . ."

"What is it now?"

"I'm going to be delayed. I don't like to leave the place empty."

"I'll come over," he said grimly.

But that wasn't the idea either. "Wait . . . I'm going to phone Ernie and see if he can come in and stay until I get back. He can keep an eye on everything. I'm sure he won't mind, he needs the money to pay his course fees next month. I'll tell him that I'll pay for a taxi."

Barnabas agreed grudgingly and I found Ernie's number and negotiated with his mother, who seemed only too happy to have the chance to get him out of bed and on his way to a job. Out of bed! I whimpered with envy and hung on until the sleeping beauty came to the phone. He was so pleased at the offer of some action that I took heart and suggested he might sleep in the shop for the time being. Ernie thought that was a great idea! He left me with such a sense of relief that it was almost embarrassing. I could borrow a mattress from somewhere. Damn it, I'd buy him an antique four-poster if necessary! He could act as night watchman and day bodyguard until something was resolved, I said; he said he'd clear it with his mother. I wondered fleetingly whether he would tell his mother just what kind of work I was giving him and whether she was likely to approve, and crossed my fingers.

Feeling almost cheerful I sorted out the checks and wrote a deposit slip, paid two bills by phoning my bank, answered a letter, and slid a book and invoice into a padded envelope ready for posting. It was only twenty minutes before the bell rang and I ran to let

Ernie in. I actually had my hand on the lock before I glanced through the glass.

A stranger stood there, a thin old man in an ancient, well-pressed brown cotton suit: weatherbeaten, balding, with a hooked nose and prominent cheek bones. Dark, almost black, eyes stared at me through wire-rimmed spectacles. He smiled slowly. I opened the door, and we looked at each other with deep interest.

"Miss Dido Hoare? Mrs. Ashe said I might find you here."

"Mr. Peter Mellor?" I said. "Please come in. I desperately need to talk to you."

3

We shook hands—he looked frail, but his skin was rough with physical labor and there was a surprising strength in his grip. He refused my suggestion that we go upstairs, refused a cup of coffee; in the end we sat across the desk from each other, and he said simply, "So Tom is dead. Emma has told me that you are looking after things. It's very kind of you." His voice was soft, the accent old-fashioned. There was something about the clipped formality of his speech that reminded me of wartime radio announcers, or the romantic leads in old black-and-white British films.

I said, much less elegantly, "She told me you'd been to see her and I was hoping that you'd come. I seem to be in trouble." He was looking at the barricaded door, so I added, "You know Sammy Butler's son?"

He focused on me. "Dennis? Oh yes, I met him last year. I came over to his father's funeral, you know."

"That was why you came back to England—for the funeral?"

"Yes, although I think now that I've probably come home for good. Yes, I came for the funeral. We were very close years ago, but I'd lost contact. Emma must have told you that story."

I agreed that she had—or as much as she knew. "There's something she didn't know about," I said quickly, "not for certain. What happened in Egypt?"

A crease appeared suddenly between his eyebrows. "You mean in 1948? Yes, of course you mean that. Miss Hoare, can I ask you one thing? How did you know Tom? What is your connection?"

That simple question stopped me. On one level the answer was easy. I told him how Tom had come into the shop and talked about Dido, Virgil's queen. Then I told him about my father.

"My God," he said. Perhaps it sounded more like a prayer than usual? "Barnabas Hoare . . . I knew him slightly. And he's still alive?"

I said that he was; and Mellor laughed thinly, "The sins of the fathers." Even at the time, the comment seemed obscure. "Well. So Tom wrote a will and made you his executor, and you are acting for him. Were you fond of him?"

I looked at him helplessly. "No, I don't think I liked him very much. But he was an old man and in trouble, and . . ."

He was laughing at me, but all that he said was, "You are his guardian angel."

"I don't know about that. I can't really explain, but he seemed to need something from me. My father thinks I'm crazy. Especially now."

He looked at me, puzzled. I noticed his eyes were so dark that it was almost impossible to see the division between the pupils and the cornea. Eventually he murmured, "I understand duty very well, though I don't know that I can judge your motives."

"Dennis Butler killed Tom. He was looking for something that Tom had gotten in Egypt. Last night he came here looking for it." I indicated the door. "He tried to break in. He was going to burn my place down, the way he burnt out the room where Tom was staying. If you want the truth, I'm frightened. I have a young baby here."

I thought he was confused. "A baby? I thought . . . You call yourself 'Miss Hoare.'" He hesitated again. "I know I am very old-fashioned."

I reminded myself that this old person had been a monk for thirty years or so, and so I said ambiguously, "Ben's father died before he was born. Ben is six months old, and he's one reason why I can't let this go on. I won't have him in danger. Special Branch are looking for Dennis Butler now, but the address he gave me doesn't exist. Do you know where he lives?"

"No." The word burst out abruptly, and he slapped his bony knee as though the question had angered him. "I wish I did. Though he is the son of an old comrade, nevertheless he is a greedy man. Dangerous. I'm afraid you're right to fear him."

We stared at each other. The eyes behind the glasses glared at me.

"Do you know about the thing he's looking for?"

"Of course. You mean the codex, the *Secret Gospel of Peter*." He spat the words.

"Yes . . . Were you in Cairo when Tom Ashe got it?"

Mellor whispered, "He bought it for a few pounds from a dealer's widow. You understand, Cairo was being bombed, she wanted to get to her family in the country. Tom got it for a song."

I wondered how much more of the story he knew. "I heard that the authorities tried to take it from him."

"Of course. But you see they didn't know about Sammy. Tom gave it to Sammy to smuggle out to Cyprus. When they met in Limassol, Sammy handed it over as planned; but he told Tom that he wanted half the profits of any sale, seeing the risk he'd taken. I think he got a dusty answer. Or else Tom reneged on an agreement."

"Weren't you involved?"

"No, they both knew my feelings. They travelled to Cyprus without warning me. When I got there, they'd both gone on to the Continent."

"I don't understand."

"Don't you?" His voice grew harsh. "That document is black heresy. Do you understand what that means? They both knew that the thing disgusted me."

I thought I did understand. "You believe it's wicked?"

"I *know* it is!" There was such heat in his voice that I suddenly understood that he really could not possibly have joined in that smuggling operation, however profitable it might have looked. The sincerity of his beliefs shone out of his face.

"And Dennis?" But I already knew the answer.

"Dennis grew up believing that Tom Ashe cheated his father, and that by rights he should share in a great deal of money. It could be sold for a great deal of money, you know: more than someone like myself can even imagine. Can't you understand how evil that thing is? Or are you a modern young lady who doesn't believe evil really exists? It corrupted everything. The friendship between Tom and Sammy continued, but it was never again trusting as before. And Dennis, since his father's death, has come to feel that the thing was his personal legacy. I tell you, it corrupts. I'm afraid he will do whatever is necessary to get it."

Including murder: it all sounded as bad as I had been imagining. I whimpered, "He's been watching the shop. He has an old green Vauxhall—I've seen him parked outside here."

"A green Vauxhall? Outside here? Then you *are* in danger. Please, you mustn't trust him an inch. The police . . . ?"

"They're looking for him."

He was on his feet. "I'll pray for your safety."

I remembered that there were other questions that had seemed important, but at the moment I was too anxious to recall them. I tried to keep him there for a moment longer by asking, "You're a monk? Mrs. Ashe told me you've been in a monastery in Normandy for a long time."

I thought the question surprised him. "A postulant only. I was a teacher in a boys' school for a long time, and now I help on the farm. I was not called to more than that, but I serve Our Lord as I may."

I followed him towards the front of the shop.

"Will I see you again?"

"I am staying at a church hostel. Yes, I will come back if you wish, but your story has upset me. I had thought ... I need to go away now and pray and think."

He had reached the door. Ernie was just arriving. Mellor and Ernie stared at one another and then the old man edged past abruptly and was gone.

Ernie looked impressed.

"You're here," I said. "Good. I'm leaving right away, because Barnabas is ..."

"Who was that guy?" he interrupted.

I laughed, "An old friend of Tom Ashe."

Ernie mimed mopping his brow. He said, "Jeez, he looks like Death in the Terry Pratchett books."

"Maybe," I said, "but he looked more like a god-send to me. I have the feeling that he's going to be able to help us find Ashe's murderer. Look, Ernie, Barnabas is waiting for me. Will you stay here until I get back? And if that man in the green Vauxhall comes here, whatever you do don't let him in! I've left a telephone number under the phone. If you ring it you'll reach a man called Sergeant Pickles. Special Branch wants to arrest, so they'll send somebody around the moment you contact them. Ernie, he's the killer: be careful."

Ernie grinned—a little too confidently, I thought. "No problem. I can deal with it. You can count on me."

4

Lunch was all right. We ate at a garden table under an umbrella and the shade of a hedge, with north London mothers and children all around us. And I did not tell Barnabas about the arrival of Peter Mellor, nor yet what he had said about Dennis Butler.

For two years after his heart attack I'd been terrified that Barnabas would die on me. I'd got into the habit of keeping immediate dangers to myself. Of acting gingerly at all times. But I was uneasy eating falafel and salad, drinking lemonade. I had the sense of vultures circling overhead.

"All right," Barnabas grumbled eventually, "shall we go? And while we're finding the car, perhaps you'd like to tell me what's going on?"

"They have very good Dutch-chocolate ice cream," I said. "Or peach?"

My father glared.

By the time we'd returned to the car, he had extracted the whole story of the night's attack and Mellor's warning and was glaring silently and even more savagely.

"There was no harm done!" I insisted guiltily. "The alarm frightened him off and he won't get another chance."

Barnabas whirled me round to face him. "What does he want from you and what makes you think he's given up? He could come back. He could attack you in the street. Or Ben!"

I'd had hours to think just that, and I surrendered before he asked. "I'm willing to run. We're supposed to be on holiday: so we'll go, but you have to come with us. We'll leave right away and let Leonard Stockton look after the legal problems, and Ernie if he's willing can keep an eye on the shop. The police too. They did get there a few minutes after the alarm went off last night."

Barnabas stared at me. "Good. I'm glad you're taking this seriously at last."

"I'm just tired. Tired of it all, and tired. We'll leave in the morning," I said, "because I need some sleep and I'll have to pack and phone a few people. I should at least cancel my stand at the book fair. I'll come and pick you up at about ten."

He would be ready, and by the time I'd dropped him outside the house on Crouch Hill we knew that we were going to drive up to the Scottish borders and find rooms in a little hotel somewhere and forget about Tom Ashe.

At mid-afternoon, the street was full of parked cars so I drove past the front of the shop and turned right at the bottom of the road. It was several hours before the parking regulations lapsed, and I'd noticed the traffic wardens giving out tickets in Upper Street.

I turned right again into a road running parallel to mine, a narrow street of converted houses with a couple of little workshops that have been closed ever since I arrived in the area five years ago. Cars were parked along the left-hand side, mostly illegally, but there was space at the end of the residents' section there. I backed the Citroën in, slid out, and locked the door.

I might have turned either right or left in order to walk home, but I thought I'd pick up a newspaper and so I walked towards the shops. The Vauxhall was parked just in front of a big van, and I had got almost close enough to touch it before I noticed it and the figure leaning on the steering wheel. Butler was facing away and appeared not to have seen me yet. I took a step backwards. I wanted to run, but I couldn't make myself turn my back on him. Anyway, he would certainly notice a sudden flight. I glued my eyes to his back and fumbled for the mobile phone in my bag.

The street was deserted. I stepped towards the nearest shop, but it was past closing time—no help there. I thought of turning around and walking quietly away, and yet I was afraid he might follow me into the half-deserted back street with its row of empty buildings. When I glanced out of the corner of my eye he seemed to be dozing, or maybe just so sure of himself that he could wait.

I was still edging backwards when, down at the corner, two women carrying shopping bags came into sight.

Now!

I stepped warily towards the ambush. The ginger man still didn't move. I was already dialling the digits of Inspector Lyon's personal number and hearing her phone start to ring, and when I got to the side of the car I couldn't stop myself looking. Butler was staring straight ahead of him as though he hadn't recognized me. The women were close now, and their presence gave me the courage to stare, wondering why he was refusing to admit that I was there.

The passenger door was closed but not locked, and when Butler slumped away from me I snatched at the handle and tugged it open. His face turned towards me as he sank down. His eyes were open, but there was nobody inside them any more. Then he slowly rolled forward, and one of the passing women let out a little, breathless squeal, and at the same time Lyon's tinny, distant voice was saying, "Hello? Hello, who is that?" in my ear, but I was sitting down carefully on the kerb with my head between my knees and couldn't answer her yet.

PART 14

Sanctuary

1

They were crowding round my chair—Sergeant Pickles, who had left his people blocking off the side road and setting up traffic diversions; Paul Grant, notified by the constable in the patrol car who had found three women having hysterics on the pavement by the Vauxhall; Ernie, bursting with protectiveness and curiosity; and Barnabas, whom Ernie had phoned when they brought me back to the shop to pull myself together. Ernie had made a cup of tea which was milky, strong, and horribly sweet, but perhaps I *was* in shock, at that. Then Barnabas had arrived by taxi carrying half a bottle of his Irish whiskey, in whose restorative properties he believed absolutely. This mixture of tea and whiskey had stopped my shaking.

I looked at them all. "I'm sorry. I've never found a corpse before." Although in fact I wasn't sorry, just tired—really tired now.

There was a chorus of consolations, Barnabas patting my right shoulder and Paul my left. I felt slightly silly.

"He is dead?" Barnabas was asking everybody.

I knew that he was. The strangest thing had been seeing the absence: the physical thing under my hand from which the human being had entirely vanished.

"It wasn't natural?"

There was a silence as though everybody was waiting for someone else to say it. "It might have been," Pickles observed without expression.

I knew that it wasn't, and knew perfectly clearly why I was so sure. "It was the same as Ashe, wasn't it—the same person killed them both."

It was Barnabas who said the obvious thing: "Only Peter Mellor is left."

"And he was here." And through their exclamations, I told them what had been sitting on top of everything else like a big rock. "I've been bothered all day by one thing he said. He told me that he'd met Dennis Butler at his father's funeral. He made it sound as though that was the first and last time. And yet the way he spoke about Dennis and his feelings, his ideas . . . he must have been talking to him since. More than once, I'm sure. And I told him that Dennis was watching me. I told him he was driving a green Vauxhall . . ."

Barnabas said fiercely, "It wasn't your fault," and I said, "Don't be silly, I know that really," and Sergeant Pickles was insisting, "Tell me everything that happened."

I did what I could.

Halfway through retelling, and suddenly conscious that Barnabas was in the chair occupied by Peter Mellor a few hours before, I looked up to discover a second wave of arrivals: the two men in white coats who had been at the Horsell Road fire, followed by Inspector Lyon, whose car had just pulled up. Ernie let them all in and escorted them fiercely between the bookcases.

"An injection," the first one said, "and then he was strangled with something like a thin nylon line. Either could have killed him. No signs of a struggle, so it must have been unexpected. He could have known his assailant."

"Two prominent sets of fingerprints inside the car," the second one said. "One of them matches the body."

"Barbiturate?" Lyon asked the first.

"Might be. I'll get the body out of here and do the tests."

There was a memory, an image in my mind of Peter Mellor sitting by my desk angry and sympathetic, wanting to destroy the world's evil. "He was sitting there where Barnabas is, a few hours ago," I interrupted.

Paul looked at me. "Could he have touched anything here?"

I didn't know. I told him it was possible, that the old man had been close to the desk. Lyon looked at us both for a long moment, shrugged, and made way for the forensics man, who opened his case.

"I'll see if I can find anything," he said. "If I can get a match with the second set from the car . . . I'll need to set up some lights."

The Inspector looked at Barnabas. "Could we go upstairs and continue this?"

I pulled myself together and replied, "We could." I looked meaningfully at Ernie. "Will you stay and keep an eye on things? Phone upstairs when they've finished, and I'll come down and lock up. Then you'd better go and get something to eat and we'll sort out your sleeping arrangements. If you're still willing to move in."

Ernie flashed an ecstatic grin which said that he wouldn't miss all this for the world, and the rest of us got out of the way and processed towards the stairs to the flat, Barnabas carrying his bottle. Perhaps it was the two stiff measures he'd already given me, but I was starting to feel in control again. A third one would just about get me sorted.

In the sitting room with the windows open and the little portable fan stirring the air, we gathered for further consultation. Lyon produced her notebook and pen and said, "Go from the beginning—I'll just take notes for my own use," and I told her about Mellor's anger at Dennis and the Codex. I described the outburst, the disgust.

"I think I understand," Barnabas was saying in a tone of deep interest. "It's not that he wants the thing and it's not even that he is merely angry, as presumably this Butler man was, at Tom Ashe's greed. Mellor is a religious man who hates the document in itself. He said that it corrupts all. Isn't it odd?—You think that kind of theological passion died out of Christianity, at least, a couple of centuries ago: yet he feels just as the Orthodox Church did back in the fourth century. If he is thinking of the Codex as a satanic document, that explains the petrol can and the fires, of course. He doesn't *want* it, he'd probably only touch it with the most extreme reluctance—he wants to *destroy* it."

I thought of Professor Madkour's description of the *Secret Gospel*, and of Mellor's reaction, and I knew that Barnabas was right. He's good at this kind of thing. "Perhaps he feels that it's partly his fault the thing ever left Egypt. I don't think I've ever met a religious fanatic before. I thought he was sympathetic, but really he's insane. Ernie thought Mellor looked like Death. Isn't that funny?" I caught myself wanting to giggle again, so I administered another dose of the whiskey.

The front door banged, I squeaked, and Phyllis appeared carrying Ben over her shoulder and encumbered by his bag, saying, "What on earth has happened *now*, Dido? They wouldn't let me into the shop. I had to leave the push-chair at the bottom of the stairs."

"There's been a murder. The man who was watching us." I took Ben from her; we did some clinging to one another and, by way of comfort, he punched me sharply on the nose.

Barnabas had turned to the Inspector. "If he was in a monastery for thirty years, they must have some idea of the situation. His thinking. You must have spoken to them?"

She nodded. "This morning. He wasn't exactly a monk: they called him a postulant—some kind of lower grade, presumably. They were being tactful, but I think somebody had decided he wasn't very stable. He lived and worked with them for a long time, though. He was known for his extreme piety. I don't quite know what they meant, but it sounded as though they disapprove of extreme piety."

Barnabas was saying, "They must know where he is?"

"They've lost track of him. He told them a story about a dying brother, an old quarrel or something, and they gave him leave to come back to England— for a reconciliation, they thought, and to see his brother through his last days. But that was months ago. They arranged for him to stay at a place in Ealing, but he hasn't been there for a while. *They* didn't report him missing—they assumed he'd gone back to France. And if Mellor had a brother, it's not in the records."

"Sammy Butler died last summer," I said, "and Tom Ashe was at the funeral. Mellor met Dennis Butler then, and of course he must have spoken to Ashe. Tom was frightened into leaving Brighton because of one or both of them. Both, probably. He must have seen their meeting as a threat to him. He must have known what Mellor would do."

I saw them staring at me. Didn't they understand? "Ashe realized that Mellor was still just as serious about the Codex as he had been fifty years ago. He must have decided it would be safer to vanish. Mrs. Ashe told me that he ran away. He brought the Codex to London with him. He was hiding it from Mellor and Butler now *as well as* the Egyptian authorities. It was all terribly dangerous, but he'd been guarding it for decades and it was much too valuable for him to consider giving up. I don't suppose it would even have occurred to him that the best thing to do was hand it back to the Egyptians. He put it into storage where he thought nobody would find it."

I could see Barnabas raise an eyebrow at this *naïveté*.

"And then last spring Mellor found him. He'd spent months looking. Or maybe Dennis Butler had found him and told Mellor. I'll show you . . . " At first I couldn't remember what I'd done with the cards, but after a moment I found them both in plain sight on the sideboard in the mess of oddments I'd been meaning to put away or throw out. I located the religious card first and handed it to the Inspector. *Repent for the Kingdom is at Hand.* Lyon looked at it without comment.

The postcard was near it, among a pile of odds and ends from my shoulder bag.

"A French card," she said, "but with an English postmark. I see. That address—it's where Ashe was living at the time?"

"He left there just before this arrived," I explained. "He may have been approached by Dennis Butler; or else he saw Mellor or had other warnings like these. He ran away again. He must have been nervous about the Codex, so he went and got it back. He may have decided he wanted to keep it in his sight."

Somebody was muttering, "A bunch of nutters."

"I wonder why there's no message?"

Barnabas craned over the Inspector's shoulder. He hadn't seen the postcard before. "No message?" he echoed her. "Of course there's a message! It's exactly the same as on the other card, the one that arrived via the solicitor. This says, 'I know your address, as you see, and I'm in England—I'll be seeing you.' Or words to that effect." He threw the Inspector the kind of look that he normally keeps for me when he thinks I'm being unnecessarily thick. "Mellor and Butler were collaborating to keep track of him, though each of them had his own reasons."

"But Ashe himself must have kept in touch with Dennis Butler," I added slowly. "Why would he do that? When he was ill, he actually phoned him from the hospital. I can't imagine what he was thinking of."

Barnabas looked intent. "Well, Tom Ashe turned up at the funeral of a very old friend and found two people, the dead man's son and another very old friend, reaching some kind of understanding which could only be inimical to him. What would *you* do?"

I was moderately certain that I would turn and run, assuming that the two in question were Dennis and Mellor.

Barnabas sighed deeply. I've known for about twenty-five years that his main purpose in life is to teach people like me to think logically, but I wasn't in the mood for a public tutorial just now. My father looked at my face, cleared his throat, and said, "No, consider the situation. There on the one hand is a man who is a trained operative, a madman who has held a serious grudge against him for years. There on the other is a—well, think of Butler. What was he?"

Pickles' voice came into the silence: "Actually, a police sergeant from the Hampshire Constabulary. He took early retirement last autumn."

My mind shot back to my very first impression of Dennis, and I had to suppress a fit of giggling. It was just nerves.

Barnabas said, "Well, there you are: greedy, complicit, thuggish—Ashe must have thought he could handle an amateur like that. So although of course he couldn't trust him, he did the obvious thing."

"Which was?" Lyon inserted sharply. I could hear her controlling her impatience.

Barnabas looked at her. "Well of course he wasn't so silly as to take young Butler into his confidence, to let him know where he was actually living for instance, but he must have played him along, offered him hope, tugged his chain . . . He would have been invaluable as a line of communication with Mellor. Disinformation, you see: the old spy trick. Through Butler he would hope to have news of Mellor and to feed false information back to him. Perhaps even persuade him that the Codex had been disposed of a long time ago . . . So all that you have to do now is find Mellor," he added airily. "He'll be in some Church hostel, as he told Dido. He couldn't have any money to speak of—I believe that monks don't have private bank accounts."

Diane Lyon closed her eyes briefly and said that as a matter of fact they had been putting all their resources on that matter for two days past, and it couldn't possibly take much longer.

"He'll move again," I interrupted her. "He must realize that I'd put two and two together the moment I knew Dennis Butler was dead. He'll be hiding."

The Scotland Yard people looked at me. Paul was looking at the carpet, or something.

"But he'll still come back here." I couldn't stop talking now. I listened to my voice growing shriller. "He's been to see Mrs. Ashe and make sure that she doesn't know anything. That leaves me—Tom Ashe's executor. That's why he tried to break in here. He feels sure I've got it."

Diane Lyon said with a surprising force, "If you have any idea where it is you'd better tell us now."

At which point I realized that they still thought I might be lying, and Barnabas glared indignantly and said that there was no need to take that line while simultaneously Paul barked, "Dido, for Godsake the man is dangerous," and I said, "You'd all better go," loudly enough to be heard over the noise.

It seemed to surprise them.

I elaborated loudly, "I'm fed up. Phyllis, could you take Ben home with you for the night, please? I can't risk having him here. Take the carry cot. Make sure you have enough formula for him. Barnabas will go with you on his way home." I looked at Paul. "I'd like you to drive them, please, and make sure they're safe. Barnabas, I'll keep my mobile beside me and there's no way he can get in here with my security system: he's only a crazy old man, and Ernie will be downstairs if he tries; and in the morning I'll be ready to leave just the way we planned. Please don't say anything, because I'm thirty-three years old and I know what I'm doing." I looked at the Inspector. "Ben and my father and I are leaving on holiday in the morning. I'd go tonight if I could, but I have to tie things up and get a few hours' sleep. If you catch him, you have the number of my mobile. When you can tell me it's safe then we'll think about coming back. In the meantime I'm going to get Ernie sorted out downstairs, and then I'm going to lock myself in and have a bath and go to bed."

In the silence that followed, Lyon finally said, "Right, then, we'll talk again before you leave London."

And by a kind of miracle, everybody went away before I told her that I never wanted to see either

her or Peter Mellor again, or even think about
them.

2

The doorbell woke me. I heard it ring, looked at the
clock, looked at the crib before I remembered with a
pang that I was alone, and decided that the post office
was attempting to make an early parcel delivery and
that I couldn't care less. On the third and increasingly
lengthy peal my nerve snapped. As it tends to. I tottered to the sitting room and leaned out the window.
What faced me was not one of their big red vans but
a smaller, white-and-blue vehicle with the logo of the
electricity board on the side.

I resisted the temptation to lean out and scream, *Go
away!* There was just a possibility that I was on fire or
about to be cut off . . . no, I remembered paying an
estimated bill quite recently. I shouted, "Wait a second!", staggered downstairs and opened the door to
what looked like a twelve-year-old boy carrying a
toolbox.

He flashed an identity card and muttered,
"Yrmetersbroken."

"I'm sorry?"

"Th'readr c'n'topen't."

I recalled the occasion when I'd found the meter
reader struggling outside my door and managed to
translate the mysterious sounds. I looked at the boy.
Then I pointed dramatically to the meter box, highly
visible on the wall mere inches from his ankles, and
said, "Go ahead. *I* don't know what's wrong with it,"

and slammed the door. As I ascended the stairs, feeling old (though not as old as Dennis Butler, whose staring eyes came back to float ahead of me in the shadows), I could hear his toolbox hit the ground.

Mr. Spock, ready as ever for nourishment, urged me into the kitchen. I hesitated momentarily, but the image of my ginger cat patrolling the corridor outside my bedroom door and calling for attention made me accept that sleep was finished. Besides, I was feeling all right. Yes, as a matter of fact almost human again. I put on the kettle, opened a tin of cat food, made a mental note to remind Ernie that he would have to feed Spock for the duration, ground some coffee beans, and set about the day.

The doorbell rang again. I poured water onto the grounds and descended for the second time. The boy from the electricity company crouched at my feet.

"Soopglue," he announced. His voice rose above its earlier inaudibility and vibrated with indignation. "Hadda changealock."

Was he accusing me of gluing the keyhole in a wild attempt to evade my electricity bills?

I said, "Dear me. It must have been some child."

"Zit yours?" He thrust something at me and achieved unusual verbal clarity. "That was inna box. Y'shouldn put things inna box."

It was one of my fancy plastic carrier bags with the sketch of the shop on it ... the top folded over and taped down ... and I could feel a hard slab inside. I nodded, fell back into the shadows of the stairwell, and slammed the door. Then I put the chain up.

The plastic had been stuck down with turn over turn of tape. I scrabbled at it, got a finger under a fold, and ripped the bag away. Inside was a burlap bundle sewn tightly with coarse black thread. I stumbled into the kitchen, fumbled blindly in the drawer for the scissors, and edged the tip of one blade through the coarse cloth. The fabric was old enough to split easily when I pushed it along the weave.

The thing inside was leather: dark, hardened, doubled over twice to form a book-like cover with a rounded spine and a flap along one edge. Thin leather ties sewn both vertically and horizontally to the cover were knotted together. The leather was dry. It took me long minutes to persuade the strips to loosen, and two of them crumbled before I was able to open the cover, leaving me feeling guilty about damaging something so old . . .

It wasn't an ordinary book, of course, but a pocketed folder wrapped around a block of brown sheets of that strange, rough, flaking stuff that I had discovered is papyrus, still just held together by the remains of coarse stitching. The dust of old centuries lay in the texture of the material. In the dim light of the kitchen I barely made out the Greek letters marching dimly in uneven lines along both sides of the golden-brown pages. I scarcely dared to turn the flaking sheets to find the one which lacked the rectangle from its lower outside corner.

In my mind's eye now I saw Tom Ashe falling ill, coming for help as he had decided to do months ago when he recognized my surname, finding the flat empty, and at the last minute forcing the cover of the metal box beside my door with the screwdriver he always carried because he had something valuable to defend, pushing his parcel inside and gluing up the lock so that nobody would open it until he returned. In his fever he had forgotten, or perhaps Butler had followed him too close and pushed him too hard for him to try to retrieve it. So the *Secret Gospel* had simply waited for somebody to come and take it from the box on my doorstep.

My phone was ringing. I expected to hear Peter Mellor's voice, as though he knew telepathically that I'd found the Codex. But it was Sergeant Pickles.

"We think we've found him. We're outside a hostel near the Fulham Road. A man is staying here who answers the description, but he's given the name of "Fitzgerald." Will you help? You're the only person we can locate who knows Mellor personally. We need somebody to identify him—we need to be sure."

As they'd said yesterday, they'd been inquiring of every religious organization in southwest London, Roman Catholic or otherwise; and this morning they'd turned up somebody who sounded right. He had gone out early, but the housekeeper at the hostel expected him back soon. "If it's Mellor, we want to arrest him as he returns. We don't want to risk any more violence. But the Inspector is afraid it might turn out to be some harmless old Irish priest with a weak heart. Will you come?"

I didn't hesitate. "We're leaving London in about two hours, and I still have a dozen things to do." *And I never want to lay eyes on him again.*

He said impatiently, "Look, he's out there somewhere and we don't know where, and we'd rather have you with us just at this moment. Don't you understand?"

Well, yes: I did when he put it like that. But there

was the new complication: I had to put the Codex somewhere before I could pick up Ben and Barnabas, and the only thing I'd thought of so far was to get it to Wisby Finch when they opened and ask Leonard Stockton to put it in their safe. On the other hand if Mellor was nearby I didn't want to be here waiting for him.

I said slowly, "I'll get dressed. I'll come."

I had trouble, at first, finding suitable clothing that wasn't packed; but this wasn't the time to be fussy. I pulled what I'd worn yesterday out of the top of the laundry basket and dressed in the bedroom, with the Codex sitting on the pillow where I could watch it. Eight-fifteen. I hid myself behind the sitting-room curtain to look out at the street. It was starting to be busy with cars and pedestrians, but there was no sign of the man I was afraid to see.

I got my shoulder bag, tipped everything out, and replaced it with a big paperback taped into one of my plastic carriers. If he found me I'd throw my bag at him and run. Then I wrapped the Codex in a clean pillowcase and slid it into the waistband of my jeans, sucking in my stomach to make room for it and letting the T-shirt flop loosely over the bulge. Looking down I thought I'd get away with it, though the arrangement didn't flatter my waistline and I wasn't sure how long I could go on not breathing. Instead of my sandals, I put on an old pair of trainers. Shoes for running away in. Then I tucked my wallet into a back pocket, hooked my keys over a finger, grabbed the bag and my mobile phone, and set the alarm.

In the street I hesitated, but I'd moved the car just across the road last night, and I saw no reason to wake Ernie up. I looked through the rear windows to make sure it was still empty, and activated the central locking even before I turned the key in the ignition. Halfway to King's Cross, it felt safe enough for me to stop watching my surroundings quite so hard; I phoned my father and Phyllis and told them both that I was going to be a little late getting away. I didn't have the nerve to tell either of them why.

3

The address that Sergeant Pickles had given me was in a street of five-story Georgian houses just off the Cromwell Road. I found it with the guidance of the street maps in my glove compartment, and turned into a side street just short of my goal. It was full of people walking to and from the tube station at the end. Safety in numbers, I hoped. Or, alternatively, cover for an old man stalking me. There was an empty meter waiting, perhaps my reward for cooperating with the Law. I stuffed coins haphazardly into the slot and then, armored by the parcel digging into my abdomen and by my determination that I would see Peter Mellor before he saw me, I trudged stiffly across the next junction. Pickles had told me where to look for the cars. They would be inconspicuous, but I was pretty sure that two men sitting in a black Rover were up to no good. Although drivers in central London are not shy of waiting on single yellow lines, there was something about their concentration that drew my attention. I relaxed a little.

A little further on, a dark red Ford was also inhabited and I recognized Inspector Lyon's profile, checked behind me for Mellor's dark figure, and made a dash for safety. The rear door opened and a hand beckoned. I slid into an empty seat beside Diane Lyon—the Codex dug agonizingly into my thighs.

"Good morning." She didn't turn her head. Sergeant Pickles and DC Moore nodded at me more warmly from the front seat. "I hope you're feeling better today? He's supposed to have gone out to attend Mass, and he isn't back yet."

"Do you think that something's wrong? That he's noticed you?"

"We hope not. Would you like some coffee? There's a thermos."

The street was a busy one, with vehicles parked along both sides giving any pedestrian plenty of cover. Lyon, Pickles, and I exchanged a little polite conversation between the front and back seats about how cloudy it was today, and how we wondered whether the weather was going to change at last. I don't suppose that they cared any more than I did.

When the radio finally crackled we were sitting in silence. A man's voice said, "Do you think we should move up to keep an eye on the next cross street? A car's just pulled out there."

Sergeant Pickles said, "Don't get out of our line of sight."

The radio crackled at him, and in a moment the Rover I'd noticed before moved away to the end of the street and pulled in again on the corner. I watched the sun fade behind a haze and said, "I can't stay here forever."

"Give us half an hour more. If he doesn't turn up by then we'll have another think."

I filled in time with my mobile, phoning Phyllis for reassurance. Then Barnabas rang me and simultaneously Lyon straightened up and hissed a warning. A gray-haired man in a brown robe was slowly climbing the hostel steps.

I said quickly, "No. It's all right, Mellor is taller. And I don't think he'd be wearing robes. He was wearing an old-fashioned linen suit when he came to the shop."

"What's that?" Barnabas was asking plaintively into my ear.

"Police," I said. "Pay no attention. They think they've found him, but he's not at home. We're staked out in South Kensington waiting for him to turn up."

"What!" In the silence, I could almost hear my father grudgingly decide to postpone saying any number of things to me. It took him some time. Eventually he growled, "I thought we were leaving this morning. Remember the Borders? The Island of Lewis? Or do I mean Timbuctoo? I'm packed and waiting for you."

I commented he was being pathetic and promised not to be much longer. There was something else, but I didn't think that I was prepared to let Special Branch hear it. Or, for that matter, that I dared to tell Barnabas that I was going to have the Codex tucked uncomfortably into the waistband of my jeans for the foreseeable future. In the end I said I wanted to call in on Wisby Finch before we left. That committed me to silence. I wondered whether Lyon would send me to the Tower when she found out the truth.

At eleven she muttered, "Something's wrong. We'd better have another word with the housekeeper. Miss Hoare, will you stay for a minute while the driver goes across? Mellor might recognize the rest of us, but I don't imagine he's ever seen the constable."

We watched Moore saunter across the road and ring the bell. After a moment it was answered by a middle-aged woman. Their conversation was lengthy, and accompanied by head-shaking and shrugs. The constable returned, shook his head silently, and resettled himself behind the wheel.

"We'd better think of something," the Inspector sighed. "I'll give it an hour, and then we'll leave the other car here. Sergeant, will you fix up a changeover? Miss Hoare, I'm sorry."

I shrugged. But she hadn't finished. "You wouldn't stay in town for another day, would you, just in case?"

I scowled at them all and rehearsed the argument. "My father is an old man with a weak heart, and the baby is six months old—well, seven. You're the ones who've been saying we're all in danger. Sorry, the answer is no. If you arrest somebody, you can send a Polaroid over to the monastery for identification."

"Then will you ring us when you're settled, in case something has happened by then?"

That much I agreed to. I would have suggested it myself when I thought of it, because in the back of my mind I'd been remembering that I hadn't had a holiday for four years, not a real one rather than a buying trip or a book fair, and that this was a good time of year to be away for a fortnight or two. But it was also a long time to be out of touch. A reassuring phone call would give us the signal that it was safe to come back when we wanted to: when the weather finally broke. The gray haze over the sun seemed to have made it hotter than ever this morning.

I wished them luck before I left. They'd need it. London is a big city.

The time on the meter had expired, and a kindly passing warden had glued a huge police notice to my lovely new side window which said that the car had been approved for clamping. I flung myself behind the steering wheel and made a getaway, tires squealing. Inspector Lyon could square the Traffic people: I wasn't prepared to let them spoil our escape from London.

The cars were solid along the Brompton Road. We edged in three creeping lanes past the front of the Victoria and Albert Museum towards the next junction. I watched the lights there turn red and crept forward in second gear.

It was because the traffic was moving so slowly that I had the time to notice the dome to my left, and the white face of the church beneath the dome: Brompton Oratory behind its wrought iron railings; and in the porch just opening the door as the lights changed and the traffic picked up speed, the old man in a brown suit with his back turned to me.

I missed the first turning, but twisted the wheel violently at the last moment and steered into the narrow road just beyond it, car horns blaring behind me. Wondering what to do, I edged the Citroën towards a little square, found space on the yellow lines where I wouldn't actually be blocking the road, hopped out and locked up. Then I trotted back.

No guarantees, of course. But this must be the closest Catholic church to the hostel. Must be. And Mellor—or at least Fitzgerald if he was not the same man—had been going to church. It struck me suddenly that it was also on the route to my home. Or from it. I was running again.

PART 15

It Was Raining

1

I pushed through the first pair of doors and stopped in a small entrance lobby. A woman entered behind me. I edged out of her way and peered in through the glass of the inner doors.

It was my first visit to a building I'd often driven past, and it wasn't as big as I'd imagined. Rows of wooden benches stretched up the nave towards the altar. A scattering of worshippers, maybe ten or a dozen, sat or knelt between the rows. Someone else passed me, hurrying inside. I didn't bother to look. The notice beside the door promised a twelve-thirty Mass. I checked my watch: just under twenty minutes.

The old man wasn't visible from the lobby, but I'd seen him heading in, and he wouldn't have left already. The likelihood was that he intended to stay to hear Mass. I pulled myself together and concentrated on the scattered figures, searching for a sight of that balding head, the tanned, intelligent face, the old suit . . .

There might be another exit? No—because everybody was entering through my door, so providing

Mellor was inside he must pass me eventually to leave. Even so, I couldn't do this on my own. I switched on my mobile phone and found that I'd forgotten Lyon's number. For a second I panicked, but of course the answer was to get Scotland Yard to patch me through to the car. That was only half a mile away. I pressed myself into a corner where I'd be at least partly invisible to the worshippers inside, dialled, and cajoled a switchboard operator to put me through to Special Branch, where I found it was about as likely that they were going to let me speak to either Lyon or the Sergeant as to the Queen. It was a case of a resistible force called Dido Hoare reaching an immovable official object.

Two more women drifted past me, throwing disapproving looks at this person who was attending to earthly affairs where the spiritual should have been her only concern. I thought hard and bullied the voice in my ear into agreeing he would contact the car himself and tell the Inspector that I was at the Brompton Oratory with the man they were looking for. And unarmed except for a mobile phone. I switched off hoping, but I knew that if they failed to get the message through I could be standing here at the entrance until Judgment Day. Or until Peter Mellor turned and saw me. I was so desperate that I almost dialled 999, but I could imagine trying to persuade a police dispatcher to agree to raiding Brompton Oratory. I could almost see Mellor's sneer as I was carried off in a straitjacket.

If he was still there. I couldn't count on his remaining for the whole service. That meant I was anchored to the area immediately around the door, which made locating him difficult. I repressed a hopeful picture of Lyon bursting in to rescue me. Until and unless she did, I silently promised the absent Barnabas and Ben that I'd stay well back and watch, just watch.

Unless . . .

I dialled the number of the shop. *Answer it, Ernie. Answer it . . .* My answering machine clicked on, but if Ernie was within earshot he would hear my voice broadcast through it. I turned my back on the interior of the church so that I could speak more loudly.

"Ernie, this is Dido. *Pick up the phone, quick.* I need help!" I spoke as clearly as I could, but after a while the machine switched itself off. I gritted my teeth, waited thirty seconds, and redialled.

"ERNIE! Pick up the receiver, Ernie, qui—"

His voice was saying, "Dido?" uncertainly.

I half-shouted at him before I got control. "Ernie, listen: I've found Mellor, but I'm alone. I don't think he knows I'm here, but I can't get on to the police, so I need you, quick. Get a taxi. Have you got any money?" He mumbled something. "If not, don't worry, I'll pay when you get here. Tell the driver that you have to get to Brompton Oratory inside half an hour. If we can just keep him here until the police arrive, we may all get out of this pickle!"

I was expecting incomprehension, or maybe an argument, but what I got back was calmly reassuring. "Brompton Oratory? You got it. You keep outa sight an don't worry." And the line went dead. As I switched off, I found myself feeling almost hopeful. Anyway, I'd done everything I could think of, and maybe Lyon would get my message. Maybe she'd ring. After all, I was in a church and maybe there'd be a miracle.

I let myself quietly in through the second pair of doors.

The stifling sweetness of the incense hit me. And the waxy smoke from the candles banked in the side chapels. It must have been a couple of years since I'd been to a friend's wedding in a Roman Catholic church, and I'd almost forgotten the smell. I set my back against a marble pillar by the door and looked doggedly up the benches. A figure on its knees about twelve rows ahead of me on the right might be the person I was looking for, but his back was hunched, his head deeply bowed. I edged to the right.

A voice spoke suddenly through a loudspeaker above my head: not a divine warning, just a prayer echoing among the mosaic figures of saints in the barrel-vaulted ceiling. I slid towards the chapel and took cover in the entrance, half-hidden from that bowed figure by another column, ignoring the woman who knelt nearby at the altar rail. It was no good: I needed a different sight-line to his face, so I crept up the little side passage into the middle chapel and found myself in front of Mary Magdalene, who knelt in her dark oil painting above her altar, behind a barricade of tall candlesticks and a cross. Just a bit further . . .

He sat upright now, looking straight ahead. I froze. He looked frozen too, as unmoving as one of the saints on the ceiling. He was wearing the same suit as when he had visited me, and this time I could see the poverty of his clothing. The jacket looked too large for him, like a hand-me-down, or maybe age had shrunk him since he had bought it. There was a little blue zippered holdall on the floor at his feet. His face was quiet; he was staring straight ahead of him, and his expression struck me. I don't think he was seeing the Oratory or the people around us.

And the question was what was I going to do now.

I edged backwards into the chapel in case he turned. Nothing I dared do but stay out of sight and wait.

A long time later there came a stirring among the seats as people moved to kneel between the rows, and afterwards silence pressed the high ceiling like an invisible hand. Time stopped. I forced myself to drift steadily leftwards. It felt like fighting against gravity to move closer to the exit again; but I had no idea how much longer this silence would last, or whether the service would finish immediately afterwards. What would I do when he got up to leave?

The silence froze solid.

Then the amplified voice burst from the loud-speakers: "The Mass is ended. Hallelujah! Hallelujah!" People suddenly unfolded themselves, standing. Murmurs. Footsteps clattered on the wooden floor. I ducked frantically into the side passage, and when I looked again he had gone. Yet he hadn't passed me.

The family group reached the door and started through it, and Ernie erupted among them. He stopped just inside and I reached him in a second; his face broke into a grin of relief.

"All right?"

He had spoken in his normal voice, but after that heavy silence it was a shout.

"Ernie, I've lost him! He was sitting up there by the middle arch, and then suddenly he was gone. He can't have got out, but . . ."

Abruptly Ernie was planning. "You stay here," he ordered and he was running up the other side of the nave, staring into the faces that stared back, dodging into the side chapels . . . I watched his quick search with a gasp of relief and I set my back to the wall. One part of me just wanted to hide under a bench and whimper. The other part needed to get this over with.

Now there were only stragglers left: the woman still kneeling in the side chapel, another one to my left, and an old couple on a bench ahead of me. No old man. Had he seen me somehow? He would have to break cover if he was going to get away.

Then suddenly I knew how I could stop his escape. I breathed in hard, pulled the Codex out of its hiding place and unwrapped it, tossing my old pillowcase onto a bench. Then I held the book in front of me like an offering: the old gospel, bait for the murderer. I held it higher.

Ernie came into sight across the nave, trying the handle of a door in the short passage between two of the chapels and finding it locked. Then he turned back towards the exit, and I was rushing forward into the middle of the church. I knew Mellor hadn't left yet. From the shelter of some pillar or niche, he would be staring at the Codex. I held it up.

A priest in a black cassock had appeared with a clipboard which he waved fiercely at a bank of candles in the chapel opposite me, extinguishing them with a gust. A woman, perhaps a tourist, moving towards the altar tried to pass him, and I heard him say to her, "You'll have to go. We're closing." And the thought came to me that Peter Mellor, murderer, had somehow transformed himself into Brother Peter, that he had found some way of slipping out through the vestry or some other door he knew about, some exit the priests used. *Where?* I hurried along the altar rail holding the Codex in front of me, still with half an eye on the main doors, wondering whether he would materialize there and escape after all in front of my very eyes.

The Oratory was empty now except for myself and the priest and the sightseer moving slowly towards the exit. Where the devil was Ernie? I almost ran back down the nave. The priest had turned towards me, and I stopped at the last minute and looked back helplessly. Pillars, arches, altars, high up under the clerestory the chiselled inscription DILEXI DECOREM DOMUS TUAE ET LOCUM HABITATIONES GLORIAE TUAE . . .

Ernie was in the end chapel standing in front of the altar, quite close to me, and facing half away towards an arched door that was barred by wrought-iron gates. He stood still—a protector, a threat . . . I saw Mellor. He was on the floor with his back against the gates, his legs spread out in front of him, and his little bag on his lap. They were watching one another like cat and mouse, but which was the hunter and which was the prey? I stepped towards them. At the movement, the old man turned his head. He looked at what I held. His expression did not change. I pushed past the priest. As I joined Ernie, the old man turned his head away and a white tube fell from his hand and rolled across the wooden floor. At the last minute, he turned back. I thought he looked at the Codex again, because a shadow crossed his face; but his eyes were focused on something else that I couldn't see.

The voice behind me said, "I'm asking you to leave now . . ."

I turned and said to the priest, "This man needs an ambulance."

He passed me and knelt by the old man. Mellor did not move. When the priest straightened up, I didn't realize what was happening until he bowed his head and crossed himself, and then I knew that he was giving the last rites as the double doors banged and Inspector Lyon with Sergeant Pickles and DC Moore came running in like the U.S. Cavalry arriving among the corpses on the field of a battle which has ended.

2

I'd positioned the Codex squarely in the center of my desk, whose surface Barnabas had unceremoniously cleared. It looked like nothing much, but my father was standing over it like a Head Librarian over a Gutenberg Bible. Or a High Priest. Both of which images were appropriate.

The others pressed forward. Ernie stood at my father's elbow with a face on which awe struggled with disappointment. Phyllis, returning Ben to his errant mother, had been unable to bring herself to leave until she had seen what would happen; she perched on the rolling step-up, jiggling the push-chair whenever she thought Ben was bored. Leonard Stockton sat in the visitor's chair. He was obviously enjoying himself.

Even Paul was there. It happened that he had dropped by apparently to tell me he'd heard that Peter Mellor had been dead on arrival at hospital, although I already knew I'd watched him die. I'd seen the expression on his face when he had killed himself with the little hypodermic he had been carrying in his bag.

His choice. I understood that. I was grateful he had made it.

Professor Madkour and Dr. Safie, contacted through the Embassy, had arrived a moment before in a limousine. The two of them stood side by side between the table and the door, giving the curious but probably accurate impression that they intended to prevent the Codex from leaving the building without them.

As for me, I had just spoken privately to Emma Ashe on the upstairs phone, so I had the advantage.

Dr. Safie said, "It is the property of my government."

Leonard Stockton replied smoothly, "I am sure you know that the point is debatable. The manuscript was purchased legitimately, for a sum of money, from its *pro tem* owner. You don't deny that?"

Dr. Safie looked sulky. Professor Madkour was listening.

"And its purchaser removed it from Egypt at a time before the Egyptian Government made any possession order."

"Confiscated the materials," Barnabas translated.

"My government . . . " Dr. Safie began.

It was his colleague who interrupted him. He was looking straight at my father, not at Stockton. "The Codex belongs with the others. As a scholarly source, and a part of a study resource—not just as our national treasure. You must see that." It was academic speaking to academic.

My father nodded. "As a matter of fact, I do."

Leonard Stockton sighed gently.

Professor Madkour said, "I have come for the Codex and would like to take it back with me. If you would accept a reward for its return to the Coptic Museum, I am prepared . . ."

"The manuscript," my father said stiffly, "is not my property, nor my daughter's. However, Dido has a duty to protect the interests of the deceased owner's heir. When the will is proved, this Codex will become the property of an old lady who may not have long to live. It is important to my daughter . . . " I opened my mouth, being under the impression that I am capable of speaking for myself, but Barnabas seemed to be doing so well that it was a shame to interrupt ". . . that Mrs. Ashe should live comfortably and pleasantly through her last days." His manner was so courtly that I could have sworn the two Egyptian officials sketched hasty bows in his direction.

But Professor Madkour stuck to his point. "I am prepared to offer on behalf of the government of Egypt a reward of twenty-five thousand pounds for the safe return of the document."

"That's not very much," I said.

Dr. Safie remarked tartly that Egypt was a poor country, so I walked to the door of the office and stared the length of the shop at the ambassadorial limousine waiting outside my door. The uniformed driver appeared to be dozing at the wheel. When I felt I'd made my point, I turned around again.

Leonard Stockton looked at me and then at the Egyptians. "I will put it to our client for her consideration. In the meantime, the book will be kept safely. After the will has been proved, Mrs. Ashe will be able to consider the matter. Perhaps she will feel able to accept your offer. Alternatively, of course, she could place it with a private collector. Miss Hoare tells me that the Americans would be very interested. As an antiquarian book dealer, Miss Hoare is well able to judge markets and values of course."

We agreed on sixty thousand pounds. Also I sold Dr. Safie my fine copy of the first limited trade edition of T. E. Lawrence's *Seven Pillars of Wisdom*, the one with the colored plate, for nine hundred and fifty pounds. It appeared he had noticed it in the cabinet on his way in. The impoverished Egyptian official paid cash and, as I saw, retained enough fifty-pound notes afterwards to pay for a taxi not just back to the Embassy in case the limousine broke down, but probably all the way to Cairo. Nevertheless I wrapped the book very carefully and placed it in one of my pretty carrier bags, and persuaded Barnabas to write out the receipt in the copperplate handwriting of which he was capable sometimes on special occasions.

3

I delivered the beaded headdress to Sotheby's before we finally left London. The auction catalogue, when it appeared in October, called it *The Property of a Lady*, as is the convention; the auctioneers had it on their books as belonging to a Miss C. Ashe of Vancouver, Canada.

It wasn't my style. And I didn't want a souvenir. It felt as though I'd been walking among other people's ghosts for the past three weeks, and some things are better forgotten if possible.

Tom Ashe was cremated in Hove on the tenth of September. The mourners were Emma Ashe, Barnabas, Leonard Stockton, Ben, and me. It was raining, just the way it's supposed to at funerals.